Black Feathers

L.G. Hale

authorHOUSE®

AuthorHouse™
1663 Liberty Drive
Bloomington, IN 47403
www.authorhouse.com
Phone: 1-800-839-8640

First published by AuthorHouse 12/22/2011

ISBN: 978-1-4670-0756-6 (sc)
ISBN: 978-1-4670-0757-3 (e)

For my family

1

The television blared out the news as I finished my cup of tea on the sofa, heavy-duty boots resting on the glass coffee table. Lucille hated it when I did that, but I argued it was my flat, I'd bought the table, so I could rest my feet on it if I wanted to. Just because she had legally been my guardian since I was thirteen didn't mean that she was still allowed to tell me what to do at twenty-one.

'The Amputees have staged another attack, this time on the home of a vampire politician. They set it alight during the day. The fire brigade were called out but could not quench the flames, as it seemed an Amputee witch had helped set the blaze' the television said. Everything on the news sounded like that these days. 'The Amputees', what a name, a brand for a whole generation, the generation whose childhood had been cut from them with the revelation that the monster under the bed was real. I was an Amputee, I'd been four at the time, but I didn't have to resort to futile displays of public violence to get my revenge. Hell, I lived with a vamp, and I loved the supes. The difference was, I got government permission to kill the bad ones for a living.

I turned off the television, finished my tea, and headed out to work.

It was a dark night. To be honest, I'd be surprised if it was a light night, that's just wrong. But it was particularly dark tonight, what with the new moon, and the clouds obscuring most of the stars. Dirty streetlights were all that lit up the grimy pavements, and the city alleys smelt dreadful.

Hard-as-nails mercenary that I was, I could put up with a little city stench. I carefully peered round the corner of the alley to see if I could spot my target for tonight: one Dylan Forbes, werewolf, wanted by the Lord of Thurudīn Castle. Thurudīn was in No Man's Land, the territory of the supernaturals, which had been enchanted for millennia to avoid detection by humans. In No Man's Land, the King and his Lords were the law, and it looked like good ole Dylan had broken the rules.

I needn't have bothered with the caution. There was a figure slumped against the wall with a needle in his arm, apparently passed out under the glare of a streetlamp. His shaggy, dirty blond hair fell over his face, but I'd seen the pictures, read the descriptions; it was him alright.

Sighing a little at the un-eventfulness of the catch, I holstered my gun and walked over to check his pulse. He was alive. Good for me, probably bad for him seeing as the Lord of Thurudīn wanted him for 'interrogation'. What did I care, the Lords pay well. But still, it made work tediously boring when a snatch and grab was as easy as this. My name only ever gets into the papers when I get a kill job; the tabloids would laugh to see the great Raven hauling an unconscious werewolf to her car.

Thurudīn's Lord wanted him delivered by nightfall tomorrow, but seeing how quick and easy the job had been I had time to take him over tonight and deliver early. Happy customers. Easy money.

Fatigue is to be expected in my line of work, and so are numerous phone calls, but damn do I hate it when they coincide.

My mobile phone went off seconds after my alarm. I tend to flail pointlessly in the general direction of my bedside table whenever I hear a loud irritating noise that wakes me up, and I managed to knock my mobile on the floor. It blissfully fell silent, only to be followed momentarily by my house phone. It was one of the biggest mistakes of my life, letting Hammer have my home phone number. I knew it was him without having to check caller ID, because whenever I was face down in a nice comfy pillow and my phone woke me up, it was Hammer.

"Hey boss," I grumbled into the receiver.

"Raven," he said. His deep, thick-as-molasses voice was so very familiar. "HQ, fifteen minutes."

"Twenty," I bargained.

"Done." He hung up. Hammer was ever concise and to the point.

HQ, known affectionately by the mercenaries as The Concrete Palace, was a fifteen-minute walk away through the streets of Edge. I don't remember what the town had been called before the Great Revelation, but it was Edge now, as we were the closest city to No Man's Land. HQ, and my flat, were in Northern Edge, the rough bit, nearest the supes' playground. Though there'd been debate about it, I was only human, and so though I may be Hammer's favourite mercenary, able to bag the bad guys and kill the most terrible beasties, I was not able to shower, sort out my hip-length hair, dress, and do my make-up in five minutes. So the Harley it was.

I parked in the 'employee' garage, set up in The Concrete Palace. I stared up at the block of concrete as I parked my bike and wondered vaguely who'd be inside. There were seventeen of us, so you never knew who'd be around; it's not like mercenaries stick to a roster. We were The Hammerhead Sharks, sanctioned by the government to deal with the *'threats posed by the malignant supernaturals in society'*, put in Edge to warn the supes what would happen if things got out of hand, and to make Joe Blogs feel safe. That of course meant we got away with murder, legal murder.

There were a handful of Sharks littered about the place when I got in. The Scarlet Belle, or just Scarlett, or Belle, was five seven of pale skin, black hair and kick-ass leather. Shamrock was… well he was being his usual mental self. I could make him out despite the fact that he appeared to be running manic circles around Cannibal, who was laughing, because of his bright orange hair; not ginger, full on orange. It was natural and he loved it. Shamrock was the epitome of the demented Irishman. Cannibal was a dark pillar of muscle in the centre of the carrot-orange whirlwind. He was seven foot four, because he was an exiled drow. The drows are the 'dark' elves, and hate their high elf cousins. Even after five years he wouldn't tell me what he'd done to be exiled, but I was hoping it wasn't anything to do with his mercenary name. He had the grey-black skin, white hair, and red eyes of the drows.

I walked past Sham and Cannibal, and smiled when I saw all five foot one of Torturella in the firing range. She and I had gone to school together, and it had been hard to not call her Jade when we started up. She hated her merc name, but it's always the least favourite nicknames that stick.

A few more of the mercs were with her, testing out a new batch of weapons Hammer had ordered in. The firing range was massive, because of how many of us there were, and just how much weaponry we had. To get to Hammer's office, I had to walk behind everyone along the back of the room, through a corridor-like space a few metres wide. The sound as I walked through was tumultuous, but it was background noise to me after all these years. I saw Pierce, Ace, and Coal with Jade. Ace was shorter only than Hammer and Cannibal, and he was with three of the four shortest mercs, making him look a little bit like a father with his children. Of course, you'd have to be a terrible dad to give your kids guns. The sight made me smile as I eventually neared the far end of the room.

Hammer's office itself was really a place to show off our new weapons. The concrete walls were pitted and pockmarked, sometimes in interesting patterns that made you think twice about what weapons we had here. His office had an antechamber, with what I called a drug dealer sofa from watching too much of *The Wire*, as it was dilapidated and stained. There was a metal weapons table by the sofa with cabinets in it for storage and several weapons on the top in pieces. Predator was sitting on the sofa. He was six foot even, had dark skin and long, dark brown dreadlocks. He also happened to have three deep gauges across his face in silvery scar lines from a weretiger attack. I'd called him Predator when we first met because of the dreads and it stayed. He was carefully studying the mechanisms of the weaponry. We customised a lot of stuff; we had to know how it worked. He didn't look up when I came in, but I wasn't offended. That was just how Predator was. If he was working, that was all he was doing; people, food, and other such insignificant things wouldn't distract him.

The room in which Hammer actually sat was screened off from the antechamber by windows set in peeling frames that had once had bright blue paint on them. There was a doorway and a window frame above it, but no door or window. Shamrock had been too enthusiastic with his flamethrower, and Hammer saw no point in wasting money on mundane things; he'd much rather buy another flamethrower.

Sitting in this empty frame was the man himself. He was six foot eight, had skin so dark it had purplish highlights, and shoulders so wide it was a wonder he could fit through doors.

"Reporting for duty," I said sarcastically.

"We may be friends but I'm still your boss, Raven." He lowered his head to conceal a smile under the pretence of looking at some paperwork. The light shone off at a peculiar angle from his head due to an indented scar. His mercenary name came from that scar, the result of a fight in which he was smashed in the head with a hammer. I had never seen someone with such a dent in their skull before I met Hammer, or since for that matter. I'd long had a theory that he was descended from giants, with a skull that thick and being that tall.

"So what am I in for this time?" I asked, sitting in the chair opposite him.

"You make this place sound like prison."

I just shrugged, and smiled.

"I take it you're getting the werewolf today to deliver him to Thurudīn?" he said, as he shuffled through some papers that I assumed to be a new job.

"Did it yesterday, he's in their cells for them to do with what they will."

"Oh, so you can get this new job done today rather than tomorrow." He smiled at me sweetly and looked up, his eyes a startling brightness in his face.

"Damn it." I leant back and put my feet on his desk, right in the way. "I'm listening."

He shoved my feet off. "Raven, behave." He was still smiling, like he didn't really mean it. "The job is for one of your friends." As soon as he said it, the smile lessened, until it disappeared altogether. Not a good sign.

"Why do I get the feeling you mean that sarcastically?" I said, not really wanting to know who the job was for.

"Because it's Vittorio."

There was a pause then almost a full minute of extreme profanities ensued. When I had calmed down, Hammer recommenced as if nothing had happened. He was used to my temper tantrums by now.

"It appears Cirque Mort have lost their Master Vampire for the show, and also their pet tight-rope-walking wolf. The wolf was apparently in love with Master Malcolm. Malcolm they know is dead. Robin is missing. The job is to find Robin and deliver him back to Vittorio, that is all."

I gave a grunt of frustration. "With Vittorio that's never all. Either I'll have to fork out a ransom when I get there, or it'll take me months to find all the pieces of him."

"He's offering you twenty-seven grand."

"...What?"

"It's a lot of money for an easy job."

"No shit Sherlock. Still, it's Vittorio, and he's a pain in the arse, so tell him to throw in a couple of favours and I'll do it."

Hammer rolled his eyes. "I'll phone at nightfall. 'Til then, look for Robin Tremaine." He threw a few photographs and a document across the table to me, so they slid and spun to face the right way like they do in films. I had a sneaking suspicion Hammer had been practicing. "If Vittorio doesn't agree to the favour debt, which I know he will, then you don't have to hand him over. If he does, you'll have a job done in record time."

"Fair enough." And that was that, meeting over.

I went back home to sleep. In the sunlight, I could see

Lucille's coffin on my floor, the glossy cherry-wood shining, always as if it was just polished. I put candles on it when she was up, but that also annoyed Lucille, so I only did it if she was out now. She's a very tidy person, so it must be hell living with me. Eight years she'd put up with me, an undead and ancient surrogate sister. Vampire in her daytime slumber.

Daytime slumber suited me just fine.

It was two in the afternoon when I next woke up, blissfully not to the sound of an alarm or a phone. I guess two pm was as good a time as any to start work.

The first place I went was The Sunken City. This was the stronghold of No Man's Land, the city of the King of the Vampires of England, and also where the King of the Werewolves lived. The vamp King was, ironically, an Italian, and a man I sought to avoid at all costs after a certain disagreement we'd had five years ago. I still hadn't forgiven him, so I only came by during the day. I hadn't been for over a year, but I'd grown up a bit, and come to realise that going to the supernatural melting pot of the country can save you a lot of time when looking for a missing supe.

As a display of peace between the two species, the King of the Weres worked for the vamp King, and was part of a trio whose name made all supernaturals shiver in fear – The Master's Hand. He was the only day riser in The Hand, and had been a friend before the King caused that terrible mess and I stopped visiting. But of course, by the whim (and spite) of Fate, who should be there to meet me when I arrived but the Werewolf King. I just called him Asher.

"Phoebe!" he said, surprised, as soon as he spotted me. One of the other Weres with him jumped. I forget that Asher is the big bad beastie sometimes. He bounded over like a happy little golden retriever. Nice doggy. "Staying away finally became unbearable? Miss me?" he asked, batting his eyelashes at me like he expected me to be moved to adoration and throw myself on him. No such luck.

"I'm here on business," I said, trying to give him a stern look and failing, because no matter what, Asher always made me smile; one of the reasons I had difficulty imagining him with his loyal subjects.

"Ooh, sorry Raven." He was smirking, and not sorry in the least.

"Shut it, and stop being so in love with yourself."

"I'm not, I'm so in love with you." He gave me big puppy dog eyes. I just glared, but again, the smile sort of ruined it.

"I have some enquiries as to the whereabouts of a werewolf."

"I'm right here darling."

"Asher! For once in your life, shut the hell up and be serious. I'm on a missing person's case."

"Okay babe, all serious now."

"Don't call me babe." I looked at him until he managed to control his face and stop grinning, then continued. "I'm looking for a Robin Tremaine."

And so Asher shut up and listened. It turned out my trip to the Sunken City was fruitless, he had no idea where he was, as it became apparent that Robin was clan-less, and so had no pack leader to report to his King. Asher wasn't completely unhelpful though; he gave me a few hints as to where he might be. I followed those up, and though it took a few more hours of asking around and tracking people, I eventually found Robin Tremaine. He didn't look too healthy. On the plus side, he was all in one piece, so I didn't have to continue looking for him.

It was sundown soon, and Vittorio had to be told.

Cirque Mort was setting up for the following night when I arrived. They were having their circus on the edge of No

Man's Land near a village aptly nicknamed The Dead Zone, a short drive out from Edge. Vittorio had agreed to throw in a debt of two favours along with the handsome £27,000. Favours were a more versatile currency than money. If someone paid me in favours, they were obliged to drop everything and do my bidding at my behest. It was exceedingly useful.

I'd known Vittorio however many years, and he really had not changed a bit. Some vamps had cut their hair to show they were modern people, not stuck with the longer hairstyles of 'ye old-e fashioned-e tymes', but not Vittorio. He didn't give a damn. His hair had a barely detectable wave to it, and was medium brown, medium length, falling over a mid pale face which had a very ordinary nose and mouth and plain brown eyes. He was almost remarkable in his unremarkable appearance. It was the kind of face you easily forget.

I had been told I was the exact opposite. I was the notorious mercenary The Raven, so it was essential no-one recognised me. Fortunately for me, and for reasons unknown, I could produce glamours. It was originally fey magic, the ability to create illusions that make the mind see whatever the one making the glamour tells them to see, but some vamps could do it too. My glamour, however, was a little different. It didn't alter my appearance, but rather made people forget what I looked like once I'd left, and it made any photo or recording of me unintelligible. In its own way, it hid my real appearance from the world. I'd seen numerous drawings speculating what I looked like, and most of them thought I was some icy skinned, dark eyed, black haired, emaciated monster. People came to that assumption from my merc name. The reality was I had hip-length, blonde-brown hair, olive skin, and blue eyes. I was called The Raven because of a tattoo I had of a raven perching on my right shoulder, not from black hair or a propensity to shed feathers.

But the glamour meant that even Vittorio, who I'd known

for a long time, had no idea who I was when I approached him.

"Can I help you madam?" he asked politely in his upper-crust English voice once he was certain I was heading for him.

"Not really, Vittorio. I thought the reason you paid me was for me to help you."

"Ah." He frowned, recognition settling in behind his muddy brown eyes. "I may not be able to remember your appearance, Raven, but I do always remember you're moody and hostile."

"Believe me, this isn't hostile. Do you want to know what happened to Robin or not?" I looked at him and let him see the dislike in my eyes. Honesty made business go more quickly, as we were dying to get out of each other's company. Well, I was. He was already dead.

There was a pause as he put down a string of vampire teeth lights. They were tacky beyond belief and I made a face at them, which he ignored. Reluctantly, he led me away from the general mayhem of setting up the carnival to the shadow of a tent in which we could talk privately.

"Well?"

"Robin is dead. He wrote a note to Malcolm and hung himself in the ruins of a church, saying he would meet him in hell, or words to that effect. Nice and cheerful, isn't it?"

"Indeed, heart-warming. One question though, where the hell am I meant to get a Master Vampire and a tightrope walking werewolf by tomorrow?"

"Beats me. That's not in my job description." His eyes lit up as an idea occurred to him. "Whatever you're thinking, no."

"Am I really that terrible?"

"Yes."

He sighed and rolled his eyes to the ground as if dejected.

"Just hear me out?" he said, going up at the end of his sentence in hope. It was an act. He was King of the Circus Ring; everything was an act.

"You have twenty seconds," I said, frowning.

He began. "You have an old... adversary in town. He's staying at the Sunken City, where I'm sure a woman like you has some leverage to procure a werewolf, and ask the vampire if he will oblige us in our request."

I looked at him long enough for him to squirm just a little. I didn't like his reference to my adversary as 'the vampire'. "The fact that you won't mention the vamp's name disturbs me. Which of the many asshole vampires I've met is it?"

A pause. A guilty glance at my face. A glance away to the floor.

"Sol," he said quietly. He almost looked like he was afraid I'd hit him. I had half a mind to.

To say Sol and I didn't get along was a bit of an understatement. He was the most irritating person I had ever met, in love with himself beyond all rationality, and a general annoyance I could do without.

"What the hell makes you think I would ever want to talk to that prat again?" He wisely stayed mute. "Besides," I continued, "I can't go to the Sunken City at night anyway."

"Why ever not?"

"Next stupid question that is invasive of privacy." I raised an eyebrow at him in disapproval, and hoped it would shut him up. It didn't work.

"I wasn't meaning to pry. I just cannot fathom a reason why you wouldn't go to the Sunken City at night." He was all wide-eyed sincerity as he asked. I knew that he was hamming it up, but I also knew he really wanted to know. Vittorio trades information as a side-line to his stupidly lucrative carnival business. Greedy bastard.

I gave him a look. "The King and I don't get on any more."

He looked right back at me, waiting for me to elaborate, which of course I didn't. "Forget Sol, or find someone else to do the job."

When I got back home, there was someone besides Lucille in my flat. I had known Guillaume, her brother, as long as I had known her. Although he didn't live with me like she did, he kept a spare coffin in my house because he was such a frequent visitor. He actually lived across town in the Vampire District next to his pub/restaurant The Red Fang.

"*Bonjour* Guillaume. *Ça va?*"

"*Oui.*" He paused. "Actually Feebz, I've got a favour to ask. I've got a big private party in at two and—"

"Yes, I'll help out."

"Thanks *cherie.*" He grinned.

"You shouldn't humour him so much or he'll put you to full time work, and you do need to sleep sometime you know Phoebe," said Lucille, coming out of the kitchen with a mug of tea.

"But how could I say no to that face?"

"Very easily, I find."

I rolled my eyes at her, and Guillaume grinned at me.

"When was the last time you ate?" Lucille said, a hand on her hip and a frown on her perfect pale face. Lucille in disapproving mother mode.

I checked the clock above the kitchen door. "Erm... fourteen hours ago," I admitted. Only Lucille could make me feel like a chastised child.

She looked at me with a familiar expression of exasperation. "You'd forget to look after yourself at all without me around."

"Very true."

The work for Guillaume was easy. I waited tables for

13

a bunch of vampires who eyed me up as if expecting me to be the appetiser and got shirty when they realised I wasn't. Guillaume kept them in check. Same old, same old.

Being a merc had its drawbacks, and not just the obvious ones like the short life expectancy. The thing I hated the most about the job was the necessity to be always contactable. My phone went off just as I was taking an empty tray back to the kitchen. My caller ID was telling me it was my favourite person. Lots of people who'd worked with me enough times had my work mobile number. I was regretting that slightly.

"Vittorio, I'm working."

"Not a mercenary job or your phone would be off." That was the only time I was allowed to switch it off. Sometimes I pretended I was doing a job and turned the damn thing off anyway.

"If you're going to beg, pissing me off isn't going to help."

"Oh you and your temper." He exhaled unnecessarily, as if to tell me he was weary of me. The feeling was mutual. "Apologies Raven. I'm appealing for you to take the job to contact Sol. No-one else will or can. Please, I'm putting the imminent future of the circus in your hands."

I sighed. I didn't care about Vittorio, but not everyone in his Circus was as abominable as he was. Some of them I even liked. "Guilt tripping me into taking a job is a sly and shitty form of persuasion."

"Does it work?"

"This time." I hung up.

Unfortunately for me, I wasn't quite out of hearing range of the nearest table. Their better-than-human hearing meant they'd heard both sides of the conversation. Well, crap.

"What do you want with Lord Sol?" one of them asked aggressively. The last thing I needed was a pissy vamp. I mentally rebated myself for using the word pissy. It was an

Americanism. If you were pissed, over here it meant you were flat-out drunk.

"I don't," I said, smiling at the vampire. "Vittorio wants him for something. He just wants me to ask him to pay him a visit."

I turned to leave, but the vamp was in my face and had grabbed my arm. He was quite old to move that fast.

"Are you who I think you are?" he asked, leaning in, his breath having that salty-sweet coppery scent of blood to it.

"I'm whoever you want me to be." I smiled sweetly, but I could tell my eyes were conveying hostility. There's only so much I can disguise when I'm angry. Thank god I'd used a little extra glamour to hide the scars; that would have given the game away completely.

The vampire holding on to me relaxed his grip a little, then looked at the others at the table. He took a deep and unnecessary breath, before turning his attention back to me and squeezing my arm tightly again.

"Are you The Raven?"

"I'm going to have to ask you to leave if you can't behave yourself and treat my waitresses with proper respect." The new voice was Guillaume, who had emerged from behind the bar in a bubble of barely contained anger. He was extremely over-protective.

"It's a simple question which she might as well answer."

"He's right Guillaume, it's fine. No I'm not The Raven. I'm working in The Red Fang waiting tables, does that seem like something some über-rich killer would do? I'm doing this because I need the money. Kindly let go of me, Sir."

His eyes narrowed, then he smiled. He gripped my arm crushingly tight, then dragged his nails across my arm, making little red lines, but not quite cutting the flesh. That was just rude, and crossed a line. The problem with me, well, one of the many problems with me, is I have an appallingly bad temper. He'd been out of order, so I didn't really think the next few moments through. I thrust the heel of my hand into his nose and smiled when I heard the sickening crack.

"Get out."

"You bitch! You have no right to hit a member of—" He broke off mid-sentence as he caught the look I was giving him. I moved in towards his ear and in a very low voice so none of the other vamps heard, and I spoke. "I'm not The Raven, but in this society do you really think I can't defend myself against your kind? Pull any stunt like that again in here and you'll find you have worse bruises than the ones you just gave me. Now. Get. Out."

As I drew back, I saw the fear glittering in his eyes, the uncertainty. You never really knew these days how much people could defend themselves, whether they could make good on their threats, because there were monsters under the bed walking around now, and everyone had to be prepared. Defence classes had skyrocketed since the Great Revelation. It was the new money-maker.

Unfortunately his nose had healed really quickly, so he left with nothing but his pride wounded. His cronies followed him out.

"Are you alright?" Guillaume murmured in my ear when they were out of hearing range.

"Fine. I'll see you back at home. I'm done for the night." He frowned, but said nothing.

"Sure. I'll drop by later."

I gave him a cold smile, empty as a starless night, dumped my waitress apron on the bar, and walked out.

I was furious, and the more I thought about it, the angrier I got. I hated bastards like that vamp who were nosy and pushy and inconsiderate. You didn't touch someone unless you were willing to instigate a fight of physical contact.

You didn't detain someone like that unless you thought you were too powerful for them to try anything. I wasn't sure what made me angrier: that he'd done it in the first place, or that I'd lost my temper. Then again, I was always losing my temper.

Guillaume had taken me in his car, so I walked home. It probably wasn't a good idea seeing as I was in the Vampire District at night, but I never go anywhere unarmed. If anyone tried anything, I had ample weaponry to protect myself.

The night air was cold, but I was heated by my rage. It was warm and familiar and enormous. I was so angry, that when someone rushed at me out of an alley, I roundhouse kicked them in the face rather than just dodging out of the way. There was another of those delightful cracking noises of bones crunching out of shape and pushing into softer, wetter things. The man, for it was a man, had hit his head on the corner of the building and gone down like a lead balloon. Within a few moments, he was slumped in a pile of his own congealing blood.

It was oozing over the pavement, and as I was deciding what to do with the body, I saw something unexpected. The flesh was knitting together over the skull. The hair became again silken smooth and perfect. The moon made it look very silver, but I'd seen that hair in the moonlight before. It was gold, pure gold, with shining silver highlights where the gold paled beyond its hue.

I only knew one person with hair like that, a person who my glamour didn't work on, a person who enjoyed trying to scare me.

"Ah shit."

"Remind me," he said, voice as silken as his hair, "to never rush out at you again."

"Just goes to show that you should cut the theatrics. I've been telling you that for years."

"Well since I just got my skull caved in just for wanting to frighten you a little, I think I may actually start paying attention to that advice."

He stood, and smoothed out his silver suit jacket, and skinny gold tie, adjusted his silver shirt collar and made sure it lined up perfectly with his dark silver waistcoat. The silver trousers were spotted with grime from the pavement, which he brushed onto the floor. His shoes were, regrettably, black. I was almost disappointed at the breach in uniformity.

"What do you want, Sol?" I said, not making any attempt to conceal the fact that I hated his guts. He should know that by now.

"Temper, temper. Aren't you meant to be being nice to me? I thought it was you that wanted something from me."

"You sly bastard. How would you know that?" He chuckled and re-readjusted his tie. "Do you practice that laugh in front of a mirror when you get up?" I asked.

The humour leeched away from his pale gold eyes, and he got that look that was unique to vampires and snakes. Cold. "You're not going in a good direction to get me to help you with anything," he said.

"Makes no difference to me either way, so you can get over it. Do you want to know why I've been seeking you out?"

He waved his hands in front of him as if to say *that's why I'm here.*

"Vittorio, master of Cirque Mort requires your services."

He scowled. I was guessing the reason Vittorio needed me to do this job so much was because he and Sol didn't get along. Just a hunch.

"What kind of services?"

"The kind you'll like. Master Malcolm is dead—"

"You?"

"No, actually. I'm not the only mercenary in the country, and Malcolm wasn't exactly universally loved."

"Don't speak ill of the dead," he said mockingly.

"Why? I speak ill of you all the time." I smiled sweetly, but with an ego like his, any slighting remark pushed all the wrong buttons, and pushed them hard.

I had really pissed him off. In the blink of an eye, he had his perfectly manicured hand on my throat and had pushed me against the wall.

"Go on then Sol. And may all the Hammerhead Sharks descend upon you in bloody vengeance."

He moved his face closer. My heart was pumping, but only a little from fear, mostly from the thrill of it. Yeah, I know there's something wrong with me. The fact of the matter was either of us could die right now. He'd left my arms free and I could get to a weapon and kill him. I knew that. And he knew that he could just tighten his hand and rip my throat out.

"Spilling your blood would be such a waste. If I were to kill you, Raven, I'd suck you dry and enjoy every last drop. I often fantasize about how you would taste." He ran his nose along my neck and inhaled, making a small sound of delight. He was narcissistic and a psycho, always a dangerous combination.

"You don't need my blood. If you do the job for Vittorio, you'll have more than you can drink."

He opened his eyes again and stood back, letting go of my throat. "I'm listening."

I took in a deep, slow, breath. I reckon he'd bruised my neck, but nothing more. "As I was saying, Master Malcolm is dead. He used to be the Circus' vampire. People would pre-book tickets, and pay through the nose, to be allowed into a tent in which Malcolm was sat on a throne. One by one, they'd go past him and he would feed a little from each one. He'd get happily drunk every night and get paid an astronomical amount of money."

"I see. Where, exactly, do I come in?"

"Vittorio wants you to do Malcolm's job."

He laughed, and it wasn't his musical, well-rehearsed one, but cruel and cynical. "Knowing V, he'd probably infect one of the people with a blood transmitted disease to make me ill. I can't be the only vampire he knows."

"You're the one of the highest social standing, and probably the only one with enough grandeur to make it a worthwhile event. He actually thought you'd like it, and it would mean both of you would make a lot of money. People will pay more to have Lord Sol bite them than mere Malcolm."

He stared at me for a minute with a look of musing about him. There was the choice plain to see in his eyes, could he trust me?

"When am I needed?"

"Next week, I think. Vittorio wasn't specific, but it's usually in the last few days of the Circus."

"I'm no use then. He'll have to get someone else."

"You do realise he'll want a reason."

"Tell him I'm dead. I don't care." His voice was harsh and bitter, and something in his face changed. If I didn't know Sol, I'd say it was defeat.

Shocked, I stayed mute for a few moments. Sol hadn't left, so I decided to bite the bullet. "Why can't you do next week, really?"

He glared at me, and with a clenched jaw, spoke. "The King has given me... feeding restrictions." His anger turned to shame, and he had to look away.

My immediate reaction was to laugh in his face and tell him it was his own bloody fault. Luckily, I didn't act on that. Sol didn't do shame, he didn't do humility, and he certainly didn't admit when he'd done something wrong and he was being punished for it.

But he just had.

"Raven?" he asked, a note of uncertainty in his voice. "I could do it, if I applied for, and was granted, permission to have those restrictions lifted… Would you come with me to apply for permission?" He sounded sincere in his request, then he added, "I'll pay you handsomely." What the hell was this? Does years of antagonising each other result in friendship? Nah.

"Could you tell me why you're banned in the first place?"

He shifted uncomfortably onto the other foot. It was a small gesture, but a very human one that, after centuries of death, he didn't make any more. Severe distress is the only reason he could have conveyed such discomfort. I was quite alarmed.

"I killed a girl. She was irritating and I hadn't eaten in a while." That was so Sol. Hell, if I was a vamp I'd kill everyone that annoyed me and turn them into a snack. Realising I would have done the same thing as Sol was not a comforting thought.

There was a brief silence.

"You need permission from the King I'm guessing," I said.

"Indeed."

"Well, as much as I feel for you, it would have to be a hell of a lot of money to get me anywhere near the Court again." I said that more as a gesture to show him I would say no, but of course vampires can be very literal sometimes.

Without hesitation, he said, "£300,000. And that is, of

21

course, to keep everything off record. I can't go through the Sharks with this. This is just you and me."

I don't know whether it was greed, or pity, or shock, but I heard someone say "Agreed." And that someone was me.

Oh the stupid things I do for money.

2

I don't think I had ever been to The Sunken City at night and it not be an all night affair, what with all the politics you have to wade through. In preparation, I took the strongest sleeping pills I owned at 9am, and slept until three in the afternoon.

After two hours of grogginess and moodiness, I got a call from Sol on my work number. I don't know how he got the number, and I'm not sure I wanted to know. He was awake somewhere underground where the sun's effect was less, which he informed me of right away. Kind of him to ensure I didn't have a heart attack thinking he was up during sunlight hours. It would be dark soon, and so he asked to meet at six. He was all humility and meekness. Perhaps I'd been wrong about Sol. Or perhaps he'd had a personality transplant.

I'd spent the last couple of hours drinking tea and nursing one of my arbitrary but painful headaches on the sofa. I got them increasingly often when I took sleeping pills. But now that I had a deadline, I couldn't lounge around; it was time to actually get ready.

At precisely six, I met Sol at a village on the outskirts of No Man's Land. He looked dejected and woeful, and far less chipper than usual. Out of the goodness of my black little heart, I offered to take him into The Sunken City on my bike, and he accepted without so much as a quip about it ruining his suit or an innuendo. We were silent as we sped along the shiny black tongue of tarmac that licked its way in a straight line from the village to the infernal glow of the City.

I'd forgotten what it looked like at night, at its best. Breathtaking is one word I would use to describe it.

As the name might suggest, The Sunken City is all below ground level. There is a city-sized crater, sunk low in the earth, which you can fit twenty storey buildings in and still have a stretch of sky above you before you reach ground level. In this chasm, the Sunken City sat, carved out of the rock, for the crater wasn't there by accident. It had taken hundreds of years to carve this place, to get running water, electricity. It was hell to get building materials down into, and so the buildings themselves were a motley assemblage of natural rock and bricks. It was certainly dramatic. At night, all the city lights glowed, and poured out over the barrenness of No Man's Land, spilling into the darkness. It was red and yellow, fiery, like hell itself had come up to meet you with the lakes of fire burning bright.

It was strangely familiar, coming back here after five years of daytime-only visits. It seemed odd to me that I'd been falling out with royalty since the age of sixteen. One thing our argument did mean was that I didn't have private access anymore. I had to go in with the vampire junkies and the plebeians. Huzzah.

There were hundreds of desperate mortals lined along the main road, dying to see the infamous City and its glittering night-time occupants. Some of the mortals, it seemed, didn't get along. We are British, and we queue, so perhaps some

Italians had pushed in and a fight had broken out. The closer I got, I could see it was a mortal and a Were, a sure combination for a messy end.

Sol, thinking he knew the Were in question and therefore maybe able to calm him down, asked me to stop. When I pulled over, we were fairly near the front of the queue. I was allowed to push in. I was on business.

There was a ripple of unease in the crowd that seemed almost tangible, making the hairs on the back of my neck stand to attention. Backlit by the city glow, three figures emerged, rising over the top of the rough-hewn staircase that sank down into the city on the other side. They were heading towards the fight. People fell silent, and people fell still, as they passed. Their faces became clearer as the intensity of the city light receded, and the moonlight picked out their features. But the moon's milky glow was redundant; everyone knew who these three were.

The Master's Hand.

Two vampires, one werewolf; three of the most ruthless and feared killers in the country. They did the King's dirty work, and they enforced the law. They were, essentially, the biggest, baddest, most supernatural police force, with the fewest morals, in Britain. That made them a formidable foe.

But I knew this trio, all too well.

Jean-Pierre, leader of the Hand, was a centuries old vampire with speed, agility, and an ability to kill like no other. He looked just as I remembered him, wavy brown hair, creamy skin, and emerald green eyes.

Asher, pain in the arse and frequent daylight guardian of the King, as I well knew, was second; the most powerful Werewolf in Britain. He'd grown up under Nero's tender care, so to set an example to all the wolves, who always seemed to be fighting the vamps, he subjected himself to

Nero as his master. I'd have thought that made him a dead man, but it hadn't. He was more respected than ever. Looking at Mr blonde hair and blue eyes, I found it difficult to find him frightening in the way the Were community did.

Carlos was third, silver eyed and icy skinned. He was a winter weather worker of magnificent power, a rare jewel. His hair was silver too, not grey. It shone like metal in the cold glare of the moonlight, and picked up the reds oranges and yellows of the City's infernal glow.

You could smell the fear in the air, taste it, roll it around on your tongue like your favourite boiled sweet. The fight had ceased as soon as the tangible unease had crept its way over. Jean-Pierre looked from the human to the Were, and back again. I blinked, and the sight that greeted me when my eyes re-opened was of two men lying face down on the barren ground with a dark, glittering, liquid spreading out from their heads. I hadn't even seen Jean-Pierre move. The Were was beginning to heal, but the human was lying ominously still.

"Blaze," said Jean-Pierre quietly to another werewolf who was on guard, "get someone to heal him, then ban him and whomever he is with." He pointed at the human, who was definitely not breathing. "We don't tolerate people who start fights with the guards."

His French voice was still beautiful, but it was also terrifying; if you didn't know him. Sol was certainly standing rigid and alert. I allowed myself a small smile. Blaze had been my daylight guardian when Lucille took me into The Sunken City. I'd visited the British Court a lot during that time; it was the main attraction in No Man's Land, and also King Nero's seat of power. It was how I knew The Hand well, and Jean-Pierre's sameness after all these years made me smile wider.

It was just at that moment that Jean-Pierre turned

around. I was still astride my bike, and trying to hide a smile behind the fall of my hair.

After the slightest pause he asked softly of the night, "Can it be?" advancing, arms spread before him in disbelief. Asher and Carlos followed silently behind. Asher was trying not to smile and failing somewhat, Carlos was passive and unreadable as fresh snow.

Everyone was staring at the woman on the bike.

"It has been a very long time, Raven," Jean-Pierre purred in his silken French accent, emerald eyes glittering with evil amusement. His voice was low enough for the gawkers to be unable to hear.

"Why have you returned?" asked Carlos, anything but amused.

If he was going to be cold, so would I. I knew he couldn't help it, but when someone's cold with you *all the time* it's a little difficult to not take it personally; especially when you haven't seen them for five years. "I'm here on business with Lord Sol. We seek an audience with the King."

"Who are you to want an audience with the King?" a random Were I'd never met before demanded. I was guessing he was another guard, but he just screamed teenage angst what with the green Mohican and attitude. It was bad enough being a teenager, I'd hate to have been a Were too, no matter the flavour. You're just as much a Were if you're a wolf or a tiger.

Just as I was turning to answer him, with my best sinister smile in place, Jean-Pierre said, "Why, she's The Raven."

Exclamatory whispers of 'The Raven?!' were spreading like wildfire through the crowd. Just what I needed, *more* publicity.

"I'm only here on business Jean-Pierre, this isn't a social call."

"Oooh, business. We're quaking with fear babe." Asher was grinning like the Cheshire Cat.

"You should be darling."

Sol tensed. How dare I talk back to the Hand? I dared, because they were old friends and used to it. They'd been a part of me growing up. It saddened me a little to think the last time I'd seen Jean-Pierre and Carlos I'd been sixteen. Five achingly long years of killing and solitude had passed since then. I was amazed they even recognised me.

Jean-Pierre chuckled and held out his arm for me. "Please, Raven, this way. Blaze will park your bike in your old spot." I looked over at Blaze and smiled. He got his nickname because his hair was flame red, darker at the roots, and his eyes were bright orange, too light to be amber. He was happy to take my bike to the garage, though I could tell he'd come up through the ranks in the past few years, and so he probably shouldn't be doing work that was beneath him. He always was kind hearted, and he hadn't aged a day. Damn all these semi-immortals. I gave him a firm handshake when I handed over my keys, sensing this was not the time for a hug.

Blaze grinned, and said over his shoulder as he headed to my bike, "I like the improvement in transport you've got going for you." He looked like a small child at Christmas as he sat on the back of my bike and heard the engine purr as she started. He threw me another grin, then zoomed off far too fast on my shiny, shiny Harley.

I was smiling to myself as Jean-Pierre held his arm out to me for me to take. I didn't really do the whole social graces anymore, but he expected it, and I didn't want to upset him the first time I saw him in years, so I took his arm with a, "*Merci beaucoup*, Jean-Pierre." His vaguely sinister but ever so charming smile seemed like a permanent feature as he led me down those rough-hewn stairs.

There were pairs of eyes all the way down the sides of

those gigantic stairs, more often than not attached to faces, but you get some pretty strange… entities in The Sunken City. Each carved step must have been at least twenty metres wide, cut deep into the rock to make for a quicker descent. It was a long way down. Even when we reached the bottom, there seemed to be no thinning of the crowd. People lined the streets and filled the alleys. They skulked in doorways and hid themselves behind protrusions of stone. But this was still the outskirts, the part of the city everyone had access to, but the further in you got, the more exclusive the inhabitants were. There was only a handful of days a year that the plebeians would be allowed right into the heart of the city, to the British Court, and that was usually an event of some sort so the vampires could gain popularity and publicity, allowing mere mortals a glimpse at the glittering exterior of their high society.

We passed from the pedestrianized outskirts into the wider streets where cars are possible, if you're important enough. Apparently I was, as a typical black limo pulled up with dark tinted windows.

"We'll take you to the Court." Jean-Pierre made a gesture in the direction of the car, and a chauffeur got out to open a door for me. I turned to Jean-Pierre.

"Just so you know, I'm not so big on the social graces anymore. I let you take my arm out of courtesy more than thinking it appropriate. Equally, I can open a damn door myself."

"Darls, shut up and get in the car. We need it because you're human slow, and we're impatient." Asher grinned at me angelically.

I was informed, ever so politely, by Jean-Pierre to get over it and get in the car. I think Asher had finally rubbed off on him. For once, I did as I was told. I'd try not to make a habit of it.

We eventually pulled into a courtyard paved with dark stone, uneven slabs that had been corrupted by centuries of shifting earth. The Court was at the deepest part of the city, a black chasm stretching above it, and beyond that the open night air and the stars. The gold dome of the Main Court glinted in the firelight. There were no electric lights outside, just torches embedded in sconces on the walls. They didn't provide enough light for you to really see the guards prowling through the shadows. I often wondered whether guard duty was dull at The British Court, because despite the fact that the most powerful supernaturals were haunting its corridors, they were bound by decorum to be on their best behaviour. Ironic.

When we stopped, Jean-Pierre let me open my own door. Smart man.

As I stepped out, the first thing I saw over the low-lying limousine, was a fountain near the steps to the Court. It was made of turquoise, carved into the likeness of a dragon twisting round upon itself to knot in complicated and graceful patterns and spewing water out of its mouth into a large circular basin. Parts of the dragon were made in gold, and these bits picked up the firelight, and made the watery beast glitter.

I hadn't realised I'd been standing there for some time until Jean-Pierre put his hand on my shoulder.

"It's been such a long time, Jean-Pierre. Sometimes I forget how beautiful this place was."

"Is. It still is."

I just shook my head, and didn't answer. Sol looked at us with confusion written plainly on his face.

"Can I ask how you were persuaded to return," Carlos said, coming to stand near me.

"Sol's paying me three hundred grand," I said absently, eyes still transfixed by the dragon.

30

"Oh shit," said Asher. "If Nero finds out three-hundred large got you back here, he'd kill us for not offering you money sooner. He went a bit mental at me when he realised I'd seen you this week."

The place seemed even less beautiful now we were on the topic of King Nero and his borderline obsession with me. The fountain was just a lump of stone and metal. The columns with their ornate Corinthian capitals were just vanity, the carved obsidian double doors, with the last of the ancient gold leaf just clinging to them, were just doors.

"Let's go," I said softly, turning my head away from the fountain. "I want to get this over and done with."

Stepping through the doors was sensory overload. There was a constant sound of chatter, the smell of the most expensive perfumes to mask the scent of the undead, and too many bejewelled wrists and throats to take in at once. It was more crowded than I remembered, especially as we were just in the entrance hall, at the very edge of The British Court. This was just the tip of one hell of a crowded iceberg.

You'd expect to have to shove to get through such a dense crowd, weave your way between people and pillars of marble that soared to a lofty ceiling, but this was not so. We were with The Hand tonight.

It was an unspoken rule that The Master's Hand were not to be touched, unless you had specific permission. I think it became widely adhered to when Jean-Pierre took off some courtier's head for slapping his backside as he walked past. Can't say I blamed him. The crowd parted like the proverbial Red Sea, and a subdued hush fell upon them. I got some disgusted looks from the up themselves vampire women, and I realised almost immediately why; in their eyes, it was illegal for a woman to wear trousers, never mind to wear them at Court. One particularly snobbish woman turned her back as I walked past, hitting me in the face with the enormous feather sticking out of her hat.

"Hey, back off lady," I growled, ripping the hat from her head and ruining her meticulous hairdo. Her astonished face gave me great satisfaction.

"Behave, *Ms* Beaudelier," Jean-Pierre said, turning to face her and give her a look that was colder than ice. She visibly paled, which doesn't often happen to a vampire.

"I never intended to hit the lady, I-I-I just brushed—"

"Silence. I don't want to hear your excuses. Apologise to our guest and we will be on our way."

"So s-s-sorry madam," she said, eyes a little too wide. I made an I'm-watching-you gesture, smiled sinisterly, and then followed behind The Hand. No-one touched me after that.

We marched through the hall like we were on important business, and straight through doors which were magically opened by servants before Jean-Pierre could walk into them, and into the antechamber to the Main Court. Without so much as pause for breath, those doors too were thrown open with the proclamation 'The Master's Hand, Lord Sol, and Honoured Guest'.

The Main Court is arranged in a very particular fashion. Around the edge, there is a platform several metres in depth, with steps down to the Court floor, which is just an expanse of polished, honey-coloured wood. All around this platform are long banquet tables in darker wood. Behind each table is a thirty-foot flag, the kind that fasten at the top and hang straight down. They hung from ceiling to floor, and bore the crest and colours of each of the Houses of the Court. The families themselves sat around the banquet tables. If one family wished to converse with another, they had to walk all the way round the platform, the long way if their shortest route was past the King, as no-one traversed the Court floor unless they wanted the attention of its occupants. The gold dome I had seen from outside was the roof of the back half of this room. I didn't look up, preferring to keep my eyes on the ground, but I knew what I would see. The circular roof had a bar across the back, from which hung the King's flag. It was black as pitch, with a teal and gold eastern-looking dragon on it, serpent-like, akin to the one outside in the fountain. The ceiling had been painted with the nightmares we tell children to keep them behaving, of goblins, ghouls, the bogeyman, weres and vamps.

I wanted to stay on that little platform just before the steps went down to the Court floor. The Raven, frightened? No. Terrified. Jean-Pierre did not hesitate, did not falter. He just kept on walking and so I had to as well.

We went down the few steps, and onto the glossy floor. Silence fell, and we walked the entire length of the Court towards the thrones at the end with just the echoes of our footfall to keep us company. Well, my footfall anyway. There was a platform raised higher than the one running round the edge, upon which six thrones sat, a cluster of three on the left and three on the right. The left ones were empty, seeing as their occupants were standing in front of me; The Hand. The right ones contained second in command to the King in the Court, a Robert DuBois, and his two flunkies, Juillet Silverfox and Blair, which made up the British Court's Judge, Juror, and Executioner. Higher still, with a spill of teal cloth falling over all those steps, the flag as its backdrop, was the gold and black glorified chair that was the main throne, in which, sat Nero. Thankfully, my intense observation of the grain of the wood floor stopped me from seeing the King with my eyes, but I could feel he was sitting there, like a weight in my mind.

I was grateful for the cover of the three men in front of me.

Jean-Pierre began. "Lords and Ladies of the Court, Master DuBois, and my honourable King, your Hand, your Lord, and your guest come before you." We all made a swift kneeling bow. The Hand stood up first, the Sol, then me, as was proper. It's not a gender thing; it's a social standing thing. I often forgot, but one of those tables around the edge bore Sol's family crest. It had always puzzled me that he was a Lord of this Court, and that his symbol was the sun. I'd often wondered if his clan could daywalk, long ago. I wanted to search the tables for the face of his sister, the second-in-command of his House, seeing as his wife had died. She had the same gold hair as Sol, and looked eerily like a bitch version of Lucille.

There was another table I was dying to look at, the table of the Fifth House, with its navy and red banner, the dark backdrop with the embroidered bleeding heart on it in true scarlet. I'd known the Lord of that house when I used to come to Court. I hadn't seen him in five years, and I missed him.

"And who does my Hand bring before me?" My attention was back on the task at hand. The voice that had just rung out over the Court was Nero's. I'd never forget that sound: those rich tones dancing over the ear like an exquisite ballet. I loathed it. The shiver down my spine told me the opposite, but damn it my head was going to win out over my heart this time. I collected my anger around me, my anger at the King, and didn't feel moved by his voice at all. I felt furious. I had to rein it in so I wouldn't lose my temper. In front of a full Court and directly to the King, it could mean my head. Illegal? No. I was in his territory. The British government had no say here, no jurisdiction.

"Your Hand bring before you Lord Sol and… The Raven,

34

Sire." Jean-Pierre had hesitated, a definite pause. I stared fixedly at the ground, hoping everyone around would think my bowed head a sign of respect and submission, and not realise that I was using my anger to distract me from the fact that I was bricking it.

"Stand aside," Nero said to his Hand. My heart thudded. I didn't want my cover to be taken away from me. I wanted to hide, to run away. Why the hell had I come here anyway? Three hundred large and an attack of conscience? Damn it all to hell.

"Please step forward."

"My King," said Sol, doing as he was bid. I moved closer, fewer dreadful inches separating myself and the King, and said nothing, keeping my head bowed.

I was staring at the spill of teal cloth that hugged the wooden steps, as if the cloth had been liquid, and poured by some giant hand over the wood. My eyes were fixed on that stripe of colour, as if nothing mattered more in the world.

As I stared, there appeared in my vision a pair of feet, clad in old black leather boots. The boots descended, bringing into my sight large turnover tops. I dared move my eyes a little higher, and saw an entirely different kind of leather, black, yes, but patent, shining. Like the cloth on the stairs, it looked like someone had poured the hide over Nero's legs. The fastening was a meticulous and intricate-looking set of black laces that tied together in a criss-cross fashion, set in gold eyelets in a matte leather panel down the centre. The trousers glided over his hips and up to his waist, into which was tucked a teal shirt. It was such a rich colour; it looked like it had been dyed with ground-up precious stones. It was of an old fashion, loose, with billowing sleeves that would have made Mr Darcy proud. The neckline was the most interesting bit. It was wide, and revealed a very pleasant expanse of toned honey-brown chest. The collar was excess material that folded over to give a border of falling fabric that, for want of a better word, was most alike to frills.

By this time, I daren't look any higher; I daren't see that face. I could see his neck, thick and muscled. There was a pulse jumping beneath his skin, a sign that he'd fed and had blood flowing through his veins. I looked down at his feet again, and cursed my curiosity.

"She does seem to be the right age The Raven would be, but your eyes must deceive you Jean-Pierre, as this cannot be she."

"I am certain it is, my Lord."

There was silence. I could tell Nero was looking at me, and I felt his gaze, burning me.

"In that case," he said slowly, "the Court is to be dismissed for the night, and we shall go and talk privately."

That sent all kinds of alarm bells ringing in my head. If I wanted out of everything I had to leave, and pretty sharpish. The Hand hadn't bothered to search me for weapons, because last time I came here at night I wasn't The Raven yet. I was sweet, and lovely, and all those other things that are gone now too. So, I had the option of pulling a weapon and getting the hell out of there, but if I did, and I *didn't* get out of there, it would be my life. It would also mean I'd gone through all of this for nothing. No, my favourite answer to any problem was not going to help now.

Asher and Carlos departed to goodness knows where, and Jean-Pierre led Sol and I out of the Court and through a labyrinth of corridors. We neared the stench of raw meat, and I knew we were in the servants' part of the court, somewhere near the kitchen. It was actually to that very room we arrived. The last of the startled servants were being ushered out by Carlos. Asher was standing with Nero, all professionalism. I didn't like him when he was part of The Hand, I liked him as my friendly neighbourhood uber-werewolf.

"So snooping Court members won't come, I take it," I asked Jean-Pierre as quietly as I could manage, indicating the kitchen. Of course, Nero heard.

"You sound older, wearier, and more cynical. I wasn't aware that was possible, you were fairly cynical five years ago."

"Life's been a bitch to me. I have every reason to be cynical, Nero. Your little part in it didn't help." There, there was my anger. I wish I had better control of it; life would be easier if I did, but alas.

"I think it's better we not discuss that now," said Carlos coldly. I agreed, and his coldness calmed me a little. Carlos had a pacifying effect on people occasionally, not through anything supernatural, but through sheer coldness. Winter weather was perhaps not the best to get. "To business?"

Nero nodded in affirmation. "Why are you here?"

"Because Sol paid me to be." Nero's eyes flickered to the Lord of his Court as if remembering for the first time that Sol existed.

"I see, so the transgressor gave you money and that was all it took. All those years and the simple answer was right in front of me."

I gave a frustrated sigh. "Nero, I am not here to have an emotional battle with you. I'm here on business, which I plan to get done, and then I'm gone. You can consider this a blip on the face of history. I intend to return very shorty to my severe aversion of this place."

Nero looked like he was going to say something, but again Carlos interrupted. "My lord, the night is waxing and you are due to receive your visitor shortly. If you agree, it is perhaps best we attend to the business that has brought Raven here."

Nero had a silent internal battle, before reluctantly saying, "To business. For what has Lord Sol hired you?"

"To make a simple request, that you alleviate his feeding restrictions for next week to enable him to replace Malcolm in Cirque Mort for the Carnival."

"And why should I do this?"

"Because Vittorio needs a vampire to sustain his circus' success, and because I get a nice big paycheck if you do." I smiled sweetly. It doesn't quite work when you're looking at the ground, and not at the person you're talking to.

"Is it always about the money now?"

"Since there is very little I can rely on, I might as well be rich. Money won't let you down."

He studied me for a moment. "Definitely more cynical." He sighed, as if weary. "I'll lift the ban entirely—" enter dramatic pause— "if…"

"If?"

"You come back tomorrow night." My head snapped up, and the only thing my eyes saw were his teal ones, black-rimmed and burning like they were backlit by fire.

"Oh hell no. I've only been back a mere hour and already I'm sick of the Court. And everyone in it."

"I'll pay you."

"It's still a no."

He started shouting. Not good. "So you'll come back here for money if it's from Lord Sol will you?! I don't even remember you liking him!"

I shouted back. Even worse. "I don't! But he had the guts to ask me to come here even after I'd smashed in his skull and insulted him! He discovered this remarkable thing called sincerity with humility along with it. You could never do that, Mr High and Mighty. You're never wrong are you? Not even when you're so wrong you've reached the bottom of the abyss already. You weren't wrong when you tortured a man I love!"

There was a blast of icy cold air, and a cutting voice, "Enough, Raven. You've spoken your piece."

I glared at Carlos, those silver, desolate-as-winter eyes, and dropped my gaze to the ground again, hands in fists at my sides. "I'll come back tomorrow," I said, addressing Nero, "but not because you'll pay me. I'll come back for free, out of the goodness of my heart. Seeing as you don't possess one, you won't comprehend the notion of selflessness, or that it could motivate someone to do something they don't want to." I took a deep breath in, and let it out. "Now, Asher is taking me to my bike, and I am leaving."

3

It was stupid; the entire thing was stupid. I should never have let Vittorio convince me I should contact Sol. I should never have given in to pity and gone with Sol to the Sunken City. I should never I should never I should never.

I was trying to convince myself that one more night visit to the British Court was bearable, but really, I knew it wouldn't end there. There were always strings with Nero. He was like some great egotistical puppet-master, who had attached a thousand strings to each joint and who delighted in making you dance to his tune. Or maybe I was just grumpy today.

Defiance was a personal trait I'd had a hard time ironing out. In fact, I'd been completely unsuccessful, and although my desired act of defiance – not going – was impossible, I had one, somewhat smaller, act of defiance up my sleeve.

If you looked at everyone in the British Court they'd be in all their splendid finery. I was planning on doing the reverse. There was no set dress code, but people just decided to be posh as the situation seemed to require it. It would be like turning up to The Ritz in jeans. Sure, I'd look shabby next to all that opulent décor, but it would irk Nero, and that was the plan. Pissing off the Vampire King of England is not necessarily the most sensible thing to do, but I had an overdose of attitude and a deficit of common sense, so what the hell.

I found exactly what I wanted in my wardrobe: old jeans, the light grey, faded kind; a baggy grey knit jumper that fell to almost mid thigh and had a tendency to fall off one shoulder; and the most utilitarian boots I could find. The jumper was good, because I could hide weaponry under it very easily, and put a vest top on underneath so the holster straps didn't rub.

I got a call from Asher on my home phone. He'd apparently got the number off Hammer, who had to oblige the vampire King of England in his request, of course. The call came a couple of hours before dusk, informing me that the King would like me there at nightfall on the dot, and that I should go to staircase thirteen. The Sunken City had many sets of rough steps down into its depths, and they'd had to number them all in case of emergency. Saying there was a suicide bomber at the top of the stairs really was no use. That might almost be funny if it hadn't actually happened.

When I got there, and shut down the engine of my bike, the night seemed very quiet. It wasn't just that the massive queue of people was a long way off, but there was something peaceful about tonight. Perhaps it was the thin crescent of the moon in the vastness of the sky that made tonight so quiet. The main staircase was, naturally, staircase one, and although you could fit a tank down there if you had a mind to, staircase thirteen might just accommodate a bike if you were willing to risk a few scrapes. I wasn't, but then again, I couldn't think of a reason to need my bike in the city itself.

Asher and Blaze were there to greet me. I gave Blaze an

unexpected hug when he offered me a handshake, and gave him the keys to my bike. He gave me that familiar grin. Asher was less cheery than usual. He looked tired.

"Have you been up since last night?" I asked after Blaze had gone with my bike to the garage.

"Pretty much." He paused and looked at me. "You do know people generally go for formal when going to the Court."

"Exactly."

"Oh Feebz."

"It's Raven now Asher, you of all people here know that."

He looked at me again, and sighed. "I hadn't seen you for over a year until last week, and before that it was even longer. You're older and more tired, hate to tell you but Nero was right."

"You look exactly the same Asher. Perk of being immortal I guess."

We stood at the top of the staircase, shrugged at each other, and walked all the way down. Come into my parlour, said the spider to the fly...

I spent the time pondering how I'd ended up in this situation, and came to the conclusion it was foolishness. I was apprehensive, because I guessed Nero wanted something. I asked Asher, but he closed up like a clam. Either he didn't know or, as was more likely, he couldn't tell me because he was under oath to the King not to; and breaking your word was a heinous crime indeed.

After a long walk, a bit of a trek through secret passageways and an odd underground shuttle, we reached the Court. My casual attire received glares of disdain and disgust. I decided, almost instantaneously, that they could all go to hell. No-one knew what happened to vampires after their final death so who knew, maybe they would.

Asher and I were announced in the Main Court, just like the five of us had been the night before. It was already familiar, and that was a bad thing. The doors swung inwards to reveal the decadently dressed vampire elite. Asher and I crossed the large wooden floor like before and knelt in front of the throne. I was less nervous about seeing Nero now, having seen him yesterday, but more nervous about what he wanted.

Asher stood and announced me. "The Raven, sire." He walked away, and I was left to the scrutiny of the upper echelons of night-time society.

I don't know what I had expected his first words to be, but they weren't the ones I got. "So beautiful," Nero said softly. "So very beautiful." Focus shifted from me, to him; The King had spoken. "That shoulder, striped scarred skin bare for all the world to see." It was a great effort on my part not to pull my top up. He took his time over the words, annunciating each one clearly so they could have their full effect. His gaze was so focused I half expected to spontaneously combust. Okay, no, not really. He seemed to shift his attention to the Court in general, and I let out a breath I hadn't know I was holding. "At least she has the dignity to show her scars, and is not so sly or cowardly to hide them." All my tops with wide neck preferred to fall off the left shoulder, not the one with the Raven tattoo on it, but the one with the triple stripe scar of a Were claw. I normally glamoured away, but I was trying to make a point. Not the point Nero thought I was making though. He turned back to me, and I was irritated; I hate plans that backfire.

"I have a question for you," he said to me. I came out of my over-thinking-things daze enough to answer.

"A job?" I asked, looking up. Mistake number one. In first my fear and then in the heat of my anger, I hadn't taken in his face yesterday. And what a face it was. Full lips, a perfect nose, high cheekbones and all that delicious honey-toned skin washing over it. His eyes were teal, ocean-deep and beautiful. Escaping black curls fell over his face, the rest of his hair tied up with a gold ribbon, a little of it spilling over one shoulder. I'd forgotten quite how breathtaking he was.

"I'd rather you didn't think of it as a job," he said with a small smile curving his lips. I just looked at him. "I'm having a ball, and my question is whether you would honour me by being on my arm that night."

The scheming little bastard. He knew by asking me in front of a full Court I had to accept unless I show grave insult to the King. And so I did. I told him it would be an honour, I accepted graciously, and the whole time I glared daggers at him, willing him to keel over. Regrettably, he didn't. Most people don't look a vampire in the eyes for fear of falling into them and opening their minds to manipulation. I wasn't most people. I stared him in the eyes and watched the triumph wane from them.

He looked away first. We must have these small victories, or else we will go mad. Or is it we must take our pills or else we will go mad?

"Jean-Pierre, please keep Raven company. Take her to my quarters and I will be with you shortly once I have attended to some business."

I started to object but Jean-Pierre appeared in an ebony and ivory blur in front of me.

"As you wish sire." He took me by the arm, and led me out of the Court. We walked for a while before he said, "I see you've lost none of your fire." We were deep in the underbelly of the Court complex, in hushed corridors far from the buzzing crowds.

"Rather gained some more over the past few years."

The leader of the Hand thawed before my eyes, and allowed himself a smile. "I wasn't aware that was possible."

He opened a pair of heavy black doors with a gold dragon stencilled on, and with a sweep of his arm he ushered me in. It was a grand reception room that I barely had time to take in before I was led into a living room. Ironic.

The carpet was thick and gold, the kind you want to walk around barefoot on. There was a black rug with the same dragon on as was on the door, but this time in teal. I was sensing a theme. A black glass coffee table sat low in the middle of the rug on thin silver legs, complimented by a large black leather sofa, with so many gold and teal cushions on it some had spilled onto the floor.

"Make yourself at home," Jean-Pierre said, and without any further ado, he kicked off his boots, threw his jacket on what seemed to be a gold velvet armchair, and collapsed on one of the smaller sofas. He pulled a ribbon out from his pocket, and in one smooth movement tied up his dark brown tresses. It brought his cheekbones into sharp relief without the gentle waves of his hair to soften it. His eyes were the truest emerald green I'd ever seen.

Following his example, I removed my boots and buried myself in a sea of teal and gold cushions.

"For such a short amount of time, your absence has been long *ma chere*." His French accented his English, so that it was delightful for the ear.

"Five years is quite a while."

"Ay me. Sad hours seem long," he said, a hand to his heart and a smile on his face.

"I'm sure you managed, Romeo."

"We did, we did. But it was not as much fun. Nero is far more temperamental without you around."

I raised an eyebrow at him. "He's temperamental enough as it is."

"I know." He smiled and rolled his eyes. He stared at me, and the smile faded, almost imperceptibly, like the waning of the moon. Slightly uncomfortably, he shifted his eyes to a teal cushion he was clutching, and promptly became absorbed in pulling on a loose thread. His hands were fascinating to watch as he picked at it. They were slender fingered, almost the wrong side of thin, gently getting wider at the knuckles, and pale as a lily. His nails were long and glassy, and the slow movement of his hands mesmerised me.

I sunk down into my own pile of cushions and stared.

At some point, I fell asleep. I knew this because I woke up to see Asher sitting with my feet on his lap at the other end of the sofa.

"Ah shit, how long was I out?"

"Not long at all. Don't trouble yourself," Carlos said coolly. I turned my head to find him leaning against the mantelpiece on the far side of the room.

"It's not like we're waiting for you or anything," said Asher. I kicked him.

It was odd how quickly you slipped back into old acquaintances. I realised I had missed this motley trio. I just wish there was a way to be friends with them without having to have anything to do with Nero. I can dream.

"Here comes the big man," Asher murmured, and shifted as if to get up.

"Stay, you're comfortable." He smiled and obeyed.

The doors opened and the King walked in. The resentment I felt for him flared up, and I went rigid in my position of repose on the sofa.

"Get off her," he said to Asher, almost as if he were bored. Asher immediately leapt up and moved to stand behind the sofa Jean-Pierre was lounging on. I tucked my feet in and Nero slowly sat down where Asher had been.

"You can put your feet back."

"I'd rather not."

"You really are still nursing that old wound, I see."

I clenched my jaw and ground my teeth until I thought I could speak without shouting. "You tortured Guillaume. What part of that am I meant to forgive and move on from?" I didn't kick Nero, but I badly wanted to. I wanted to kick him in his pretty little face and break his pretty little nose. I was so furious I was choking to death the pillow I had been hugging. So much for staying calm.

"Woah, Feebz, chill. Even I can feel that all the way over here." Asher said.

"Feel what?" I snapped.

The Hand exchanged a look. "That hot, choking anger, Phoebe," Carlos said slowly.

I looked back at Nero. "Then I hope you choke." He frowned. The three vampires rubbed their necks as if experiencing discomfort. Asher, the only one in the room besides myself who needed to breathe, started to gasp as if he couldn't get enough air. I liked it, that power. I could just sit back and watch him die if I chose to. I honestly think I would have done had he not looked at me. What was wrong with me?

"Jesus, I'm so sorry Asher!" I jumped up from the sofa and ran to him, spilling cushions everywhere. He was rapidly gulping down air.

"What the hell was that?" he asked between gasps.

"I don't know, I'm sorry." I was shocked at myself.

"I'll forgive you Feebz, just don't do it again if you can possibly help it."

"I can't promise on that one." I meant it, because I had no idea what I'd done. Fortunately he laughed, which led to further choking. After that minor fit, he eventually straightened up from his somewhat undignified doubled-over stance.

"Interesting." Even with that one, simple, word, Nero managed to shift attention wholly back to him. If the world wasn't staring at him, then he was bored. Egotistical son of a bitch.

"May I ask what, *sire?*" I said sarcastically.

"Concern and apology, apparently genuine and sincere, for Asher. It's intriguing."

"I'm not some science project. I'm not something to study, Nero."

He sighed. "I'm aware of that, Phoebe."

"Good. So you're also aware that I'm not going to that bloody ball of yours."

There was an extended uneasy silence as I glared at Nero. He stared back calmly over his steepled fingers. I tried to ignore how beautiful he was and concentrate on being angry. I admit it was a little difficult.

"Why?" he asked.

"Because I hate you. I avoided Court and I stopped being friends with your Hand for five years all so I wouldn't have to see you." I laughed bitterly. "Ironically, I should be thanking you; seeing as you made me what I am today."

Everyone exchanged confused glances.

"Care to explain?" asked Jean-Pierre.

"I was sixteen when you tortured Guillaume. Young. I'd always loved vampires, never found one I didn't like. You made me hate them. Not vamps in general, just the bad ones like you. I found Hammer. He hated some of you guys too. We found Predator, Scarlett, Cannibal, and I brought in Jade, and *voila*, the Hammerhead Sharks were born, and I took the name The Raven."

"A group of killers, born of vengeful hatred against the vampire King of England. How poetic."

"Don't flatter yourself. There are plenty of asshole supes

out there to piss all seventeen of us off enough to want to specialise in killing you."

There was silence, tangible and fragile, that would shatter in the hurricane of a whisper. I sighed, and walked to the door. No-one made a move to stop me.

"Want to know why I hate you so much?" I said to Nero, hand on the door, without looking behind me. I took his silence for a yes. "Because before you did what you did to Guillaume, I thought I loved you."

I left, and pulled the door shut behind me. There was the silence of the grave on the other side of that door, and it screamed through my head all the way home.

4

I slept until mid-afternoon. My constant alarm – the phone – rang. Hammer.

"Hello." I sounded as groggy as I felt, and had to clear my throat.

"I take it you were up working all night."

"Yeah, what's the problem?"

"Problem?"

"There's always a problem. My job is to sort out problems; often terminally."

He chuckled. He was, apparently, always up, and wide awake. I didn't understand it. "Wisdom when you've just woken up. Nice, Raven."

"I aim to please."

There was a pause.

"I'm not calling with a problem; more of a puzzlement."

I had just woken up, I was groggy, and I was therefore thoroughly confused. Hammer continued. "Cannibal got a call half way through the night." When Hammer was away,

Cannibal manned The Desk. "It was from your friend Lord Sol."

"Really? What did he want?" I asked, all golly gosh what a surprise, little old innocent me. Hammer knew we weren't on speaking terms if we could possibly manage it, and I don't think he fell for it for one minute.

"This is the odd bit. He just asked Cannibal to say 'thank you'. He wouldn't say why."

Sol had asked me not to tell the Sharks, so I wasn't going to. "I just asked someone who owes me a favour to help him out. It's not merc business. He probably phoned you because he has no other way of contacting me." He did actually have my work phone, but I'd sneakily turned it off, so maybe he phoned HQ because he couldn't get through. Damn.

"How did he contact you in the first place?"

"Ran into me outside The Red Fang." Literally.

Hammer knew I wasn't telling him everything, and he knew that I knew that he knew. But we had reached a stalemate; I wasn't going to tell him any more.

"Fine." He hung up.

Seeing as I had the phone, I called Sol. I knew he was dead for the day, but I phoned and left a two word message: you're welcome.

I went to the kitchen and made tea, which was the most important part of any day. When I was settled on the sofa, I rang HQ.

"Hammerhead Sharks, Cannibal speaking."

"Raven."

I could almost hear him grin down the phone. "Hey Raven, going to tell me what actually happened with Lord Sol rather than feeding me the same bullshit you fed Hammer?"

"Nope."

"Damn. Worth a try. What can I do you for?"

"Do you still find that funny?"

"Yes."

I rolled my eyes down the phone at him. "I'm calling to see if there's any work."

His voice turned mock-serious. "It's a tough economic climate out there, Raven. I'm afraid all our mercenary posts are filled, you'll just have to go down to the job centre."

"If I was at HQ right now, I'd hit you. Let me rephrase; have you got any jobs going for me? Hammer woke me up so if there are day jobs I might as well do them."

"Raven, you will never be in want of work."

Sadly, he was right. Some of the other mercenaries were jealous that I got asked for so much, but honestly, I'd trade them popularity and infamy for a day off.

The next two weeks passed in painful monotony. I did two or three jobs every 24 hours, sleeping when I could. I visited Jade and Tamara – Torturella and her girlfriend – who lived round the corner from me. I helped Guillaume out. I polished and sharpened my weapons. I sat at home and drank tea.

I didn't hear from Nero.

Every time the phone rang I was apprehensive; and my phone rings a damn lot. I was happier to hear I'd got a difficult 'capture alive a mental vampire' job than to get a call from the King or his henchmen.

One afternoon, too early for Lucille to be up, I was bored, and not a little lonely. So I got on my bike and drove to the Concrete Palace.

Predator greeted me by the door on his way out. He was the silent, serious type, but he always gave me a smile by way of greeting. He and I had been in the game for the same amount of time, and we had a lot of respect for each other. It was nice to be respected rather than ogled.

Shamrock hug-tackled me as soon as I got through the door, then proceeded to inform me that I was his bitch, and I needed to carry him to Hammer's office at the other end of the building. Seeing as I often treated Shammy like a five-year-old child, I obliged and gave him a piggyback. It was in this highly dignified manner we entered Hammer's office. Cannibal, Scarlett, and Spider were in the outer room. Hammer was sitting behind his desk, pretending the doorless, almost windowless, almost paint-less partition made it a separate room. Cannibal burst into laughter at the sight of me carrying a demented Irishman who was several inches taller than me.

"Special delivery," I announced, and plonked Sham down in Cannibal's lap.

"Didn't think I'd ever see that," said Spider as she cleaned her gun.

"You always did make an entrance." Scarlett was smiling at me and shaking her head. The Scarlet Belle was one of the original six of us, so she was very used to my occasionally insane behaviour.

"Well, I have got a reputation to keep."

"Raven," said Hammer, "seeing as you're here now, we'll have our little meeting."

I sat down on the floor next to Spider. "I wasn't aware you were waiting for me."

"It's not urgent, so I didn't phone." He re-directed his attention at all of us. "I got a call from the BBC wanting me and five of my Sharks to appear on the news and discuss 'the safety of Britain against malignant supernatural forces'. They specifically asked for you, Raven."

"How many times do I have to tell them that it's never going to happen?"

"More than you have, apparently," interjected Belle.

"Anyway," Hammer continued, "If you five want to do it, fine, if not, I'll ask the others."

"You mean you picked us out?" Shamrock asked proudly.

"No. You lot just happened to be within shouting distance."

"Surely," said Spider, "If the Hammerhead Sharks are going on TV, the originals should do it." Shammy's face fell.

"Torturella won't for personal reasons, and I can't, so that's two down," I said. Jade had said she'd never publicly expose herself in case something happened to Tammy. I don't blame her. "And I just saw Predator on my way in, he's shattered so I think we should give the guy a break."

"Fair enough," said Scarlett. "Well, I'll do it. We probably need Cannibal so we don't look like we're being prejudiced against the supes."

Cannibal qualified as a supernatural. He was a drow after all. Plus, though none of us would admit it, having him there made the rest of us look tough, as he was a supe, and by implication if we could kill a guy who was seven foot four and about two feet wide at the shoulders, we could do anything. I mean let's be serious, he even made Hammer look small, which was no easy thing.

"Very true, we don't want to appear non-politically correct." I said. "Well, Ace would do it, and Shammy's dying to."

"I don't particularly want to," said Spider. "And I know Coal won't. Butcher probably would but he'd be bored, and wouldn't particularly bother to hide it. Pierce might. Unless it's at night we can't have Vlad or Roo or Leech. Tin Man... just no, you don't want a sociopath on there."

"If you did it at night, Leech could do it, and then I wouldn't be the only girl," said Scarlett.

"God I hate the bullshit of political correctness." I sighed, and leant my head against the wall. "I'd phone Ace, see if he's up for it. He looks like a mercenary, he's a good face for us."

"What, with a giant Ace of Spades tattooed over his left eye?" said Cannibal, smiling.

"Exactly."

"Alright, I'll phone him." Hammer went through the partition and was reaching to pick up the phone when it rang. We all stared at it, then Hammer shrugged and picked up. "Hammerhead Sharks. Hammer speaking… You have a job? … Well can I ask who's calling? … Shi—of course sire."

He held out the phone to me and indicated I should get up. I walked over to him. "Vampire King of England for you." There was anger in his eyes. Hammer knew why I had become a mercenary. He knew it was Nero's fault.

"Hang up," I said instantly without thinking.

"No, Raven. As much as I dislike it, he's royalty and I'm not going to get my ass kicked because he's a jerk." He knew the King could hear him, but he said it anyway. He was grinding his teeth together, the muscle in his jaw jumping. I looked at the phone as if it would bite me and swore repeatedly and rapidly under my breath before putting the phone to my ear.

"Hanging up isn't very courteous, Raven." His voice made me want to melt, but I resisted and focused on hating him.

"I know. Sorry." I wasn't very sincere, but it was the best he was going to get.

"Are there supernaturals present that can hear my side of the conversation?" I glanced over at Cannibal.

"Yes."

"Good, you have a witness then."

"Please, Nero, just drop it. Forget what I said, and forget trying to get me to come to your stupid ball. Nothing will change the fact that I still hate you."

"Be mine at the ball and I'll forget that small thing you said when you left that morning."

"You are one sly, persistent bastard aren't you? It's not enough to ask me in front of a full Court, you have to ask me when someone I care about can hear and talk me into it. To top it all off you ask me as blackmail. If you really want me to be there, you are going about it all the wrong way. So stop trying." Pissed off, I slammed the phone down.

I looked back at the room, and everyone was staring at me.

"Please don't tell me that was actually the vampire King of England," said Scarlett.

"It was."

"And you just called him a bastard," said Spider.

"'Fraid so."

"Nice one," said Shammy helpfully. I went and sat back next to Spider, and cradled my head in my hands. I had a bitch of a headache coming on. Why does Nero and a headache always coincide?

"What I want to know," rumbled Hammer, anger barely concealed in his deep voice, "is why you were at Court."

I cursed as I realised I'd put my foot in it. Nero didn't leave the Court, unless he was going to the Court of a different country, so to have been invited to his ball, I must have been to Court. Sometimes I hated that Hammer possessed an abundance of logic and rational thinking. "Personal business Hammer, not your concern."

"Anything to do with Sol?"

"What's it to you?"

"What's it to me?" he asked low and dangerously. "It's that you went to the fucking British Court and spoke to the King. The King!" he exclaimed, his voice getting louder with each word. "The one man that drove you to this life of hatred and murder! It's all his damn fault and you saunter in there to have a chat and get invited to a fucking ball!"

I leapt up from the floor. Hammer was way out of line. Not everyone knew why I had started the Sharks with Hammer, and I'd wanted to keep it that way. "You have no right to pry, Hammer, or to make judgements like that! Keep your goddamn opinions to yourself. You've known me five years. If you'd known me twenty I might think you had a right, but you haven't and you don't. You're my boss, not my friend, and you're certainly not my damn father!"

I stalked out of that office like I was going to hurt someone very badly, very soon. I punched a wall and didn't realise I was being followed until Cannibal spoke.

"Jesus, you left a crater in the wall. You shouldn't be able to do that." He paused. "I've never seen you yell at Hammer like that."

"You too?" I swung round abruptly to face him.

"We're not here to have a go, we're here to be your friends, Raven, for what it's worth."

"Well it's worth about bugger all isn't it? We don't even know each other's real names, and I don't want to know, but it's not exactly a trusting relationship is it?"

I started to walk away again. "That's cruel you know," he called after me.

"Life's cruel. Get over it."

"Specific parts of life are cruel Raven. You, for example."

I stopped in my tracks, torn, but I resolved on not turning around and not replying. I just walked right out of there.

5

Nightfall, and the blissful company of Lucille. I badly needed her advice.

I waited in the kitchen, clutching a cup of tea as if my life depended on it. I never watched her get up; it seemed like an invasion of privacy. I'd sit in a different room, usually drinking tea. I'd hear her moving around in the bedroom, and no matter how quickly she had to be off for work, she would, without fail, come and see me as soon as she was ready. So, I waited in the kitchen until Lucille came in.

She was dressed in a smart grey pencil skirt suit, with a crisp white blouse on underneath. I frowned, because that meant she had to go to work tonight. I had been hoping it was one of her nights off, but the world never seems to give you what you need, exactly when you need it. One concession Lucille did not make for her work attire was her hair. She always left it loose. As far as I could tell it had never seen a knot in its life. Though Lucille assured me it had, I didn't believe her. It fell in a silken waterfall, straight, fine hair, to just below her waist. It was pale gold, a colour I'd never seen anyone else with; even Guillaume's hair was a slightly darker shade than hers, and Sol's was multi-hued like a calico cat done in shades of gold. Her skin had paled a little over time and was a delicate porcelain. Her eyes were almond shaped, and a soft silvery-pale hazel colour. Everything about her was delicate and elegant.

"You have a problem." She said it as a fact, not a question, as she walked in. Her glassy-nailed hands put a mug of blood into the microwave to warm. It hummed cheerfully as I sighed in response.

"You're going to work, I don't want to burden you before you do."

"Pfft." She waved her hand in the air as if to dismiss the idea as ludicrous. "Come on, out with it."

"You might want to sit down."

She obliged, but her eyes kept darting to the microwave. After just getting up, she was starving. It had taken centuries to get this much control; newborns went mad for blood whenever they woke. I waited, silently, until she had the mug of steaming blood in front of her. She looked visibly better after the first sip, and I knew now she'd concentrate.

I looked at her, and pondered how upset she was going to get at my mentioning Nero.

"It pertains to a certain individual who is somewhat loathsome to you," I said slowly.

"Spit it out, Phoebe."

I shuffled uncomfortably in my seat, and stared into the remains of my mug of tea. "It's Nero," I said softly. Everyone seems to think if you say something softly, it hurts less. It doesn't. She stiffened and the silence left in the wake of the microwave was highly uncomfortable.

"What about him?" Her voice was strained, and when I looked up her jaw looked tight, like she was clenching her teeth.

"He asked me to be his plus one at his ball."

She got up and walked away from me, over to the counter, her back an arc of tension. Absent-mindedly, she got my Bowie mug out of the cupboard and put the kettle on. She made me a fresh cup of tea, took away my empty mug, washed and dried it by hand. Then, and only then, did she seem ready to sit down and talk again.

"You're between a rock and a hard place, and you have to take an unpleasant path. You have to go." Ms Lucille Delacroix, vampire ambassador for England, advisor to the Prime Minister, could not do what she did if she wasn't supremely reasonable.

"But I hate him. I don't want to be on his arm for a second, never mind an evening."

"He's the King, Phoebe. He's my King. And as much as I hate him too, Kings have to be obeyed. I won't hold it against you, neither will Guillaume." She sighed, and looked not a little sad. "I really don't want to know how you got yourself into that one, but Guillaume might, so be prepared to explain to him."

I knew Lucille well, and I knew that right then, she was angry with me. Part of her hated me for getting close enough to the King to have been asked. I felt like I'd let her down. It felt like a betrayal.

She got up and left to finish getting ready for work. There were a number of classified documents in the house that she had hidden with one of my weapons stashes in a hollow 'wall' that was actually a storeroom. The documents were contained in a chest that was padlocked and chained to the floor. I heard the chains and keys clank as she retrieved whatever paperwork she needed for this evening. The Prime Minister relied heavily on her. She was not only advisor, but also poster-girl for the British vamps, a shining example of just how *good* vampires can be.

I was five and unhappy when I first met her and her brother, Guillaume. It had only been a year since the world had found out that the monsters under the bed existed, and there was still a lot of fear and a lot of hate. That night, there was a riot that was keeping me awake. It had reached the top of the road and rather than taking the route down the main road, it had decided to make its way down my quiet little street. I was living with parents who had adopted me as I was abandoned at birth. They'd also taken in a boy called Jacob, younger than me, who was adopted too. They were foul to both of us.

Out of the group of vampires that were fleeing the mob of sweating, shouting mortals, two of them scaled the wall of my house and came in though the open window. My child's brain told me they should be breathing heavily from all the running, and that they should be frightened, but in the light of the moon they were composed and beautiful. I'd thought they were angels, what with their gold hair and creamy skin.

Thinking I was perfectly safe, I asked them if they had come to take me to heaven. I was slightly disappointed with the answer, because heaven would have meant an escape from that dreadful house, and my infant mind thought my real parents were there. It was a few years later I realised that they may have just abandoned me, rather than died. I was a cynic by the time I was eight; or so Lucille said. She wasn't of a bloodline that could have children, seeing as only two of the ten Council vampires' bloodlines could have biological children, and so she had become very maternal towards me that night, and had, apparently, vowed to Guillaume to keep me safe. I saw them almost every night after that, and if they couldn't come, they left me a note. They really were my guardian angels. Especially when I was thirteen... all that mess...

My melancholy reverie was broken by the sound of the door shutting as Lucille left. I sighed, a noise to express my woe and confusion. She didn't work every night, and there were occasionally nights when I'd done all my work during the day and she had a night off. I looked forwards to those nights. Tonight, I knew Hammer wouldn't phone, not after that argument. At least I could get a good night's sleep.

The problem with insomnia is I don't sleep. Not like normal people anyway.

After debating whether to knock myself out with my sleeping pills or not, I decided on the latter and came up with a better plan. It involved less sleep, but how much was I really going to get?

I went back to my room and got changed into work-appropriate attire. Except this time, work wasn't killing big bad beasties; it was waitressing. I couldn't put off telling Guillaume; I didn't want him to find out second-hand from Lu. So, I'd decided to butter him up by doing a shift for free, and without him asking me to. I was even going to be doubly nice, and wear a dress.

The Red Fang staff all had to wear branded clothing. Not being a regular, I didn't (wouldn't) wear the standard issue uniform black shirt with the Red Fang logo. I wore whatever the hell I wanted, as long as it fitted the colour scheme. Any patrons who asked why I was in different uniform were told I was the most special waitress, and so was dressed differently. A lot of the others didn't like it, but when I pointed out that I was making their nights easier and not taking any of their wages, they didn't seem to mind so much. I even left them my tips.

The dress I chose was a deep red, strapless, with a black ribbon underneath the bust, and a skirt that ballooned out. It was weightless. It also had an under-dress. Aforementioned under-dress was essentially a glorified holster. I could fit guns and knives in, and because the dress was floaty and light and meant to stick out, no-one was any the wiser. The straps of the under-dress were thick and black, like the ribbon on the red dress, and so became the straps of the whole outfit. The red dress attached to the straps by poppers. This meant the under-dress took the weight of the weapons, and the red dress didn't pull or hang at a funny angle. It had large pockets in the side that were actually just holes, so I could slide my hand in easily and draw a weapon. Better paranoid than dead.

It was one of my favourite inventions.

Seeing as I was in sillily high heels and a stupidly short dress, I did a rare thing and took my car. Some of my friends didn't even know I owned a car, because bike was by far my preferred method of travel. I listened to The Eagles' *Life In The Fast Lane* as I drove along too fast. The employee car park was practically empty this early in the evening. Guillaume's vampire employees weren't that old, and so they weren't early risers. There was, however, one car I did recognise. Jasper was a Were, friendly, young and perpetually chipper. He generally had the effect of improving my mood due to his infectious cheer and relentless optimism. He was the bright and breezy summer's day to my winter thunderstorm. I was selfishly pleased he was working tonight, not because he'd cheer me up, but because he might put Guillaume in a good mood.

I was clearly unexpected when I walked in the back door. The cook jumped, and Jasper did too – on me. He gave me a big bear hug, making me wonder, not for the first time, if he shifted into something other than a wolf at the full moon.

"Didn't think I'd be seeing you tonight." He grinned, and it seemed to make the very air a little bit warmer. It struck me that he was like the opposite of Carlos: warm, cheerful, sunny; and alive, let's not forget that one.

"Guillaume's not expecting me either."

"You are the only person I know who calls him by his full name."

"Me; and his sister." He chuckled.

"I'll go man the bar and get Guy to come back here."

"Thanks J."

He left, smiling, and the clouds closed back in behind his sunny wake. My momentary optimism lessened, and disappeared completely when Guillaume appeared moments later. He was wearing a Red Fang t-shirt (which I appreciated the snug fit of) and black skinny jeans.

"Phoebe, I thought J was joking when he said you'd turned up. What're you doing here?"

I shifted uncomfortably and glanced down at my hands. It was odd to see no magpie tattoo on my left wrist and no scars. I'd glamoured them away, for my scars tended to make customers uneasy.

"What have you done?" Guillaume asked in the bored yet chastising tones of someone who's done this many times before. I half expected him to chuck me under the chin.

"I can't tell you now. You'll freak. I'll work 'til closing, then I'll tell you, and you can come back to the flat and yell at me." I couldn't look at him. It was cowardly, but I kept my eyes downcast.

"Feebz, I can't imagine you doing anything that would make me angry enough for you to not only feel the need to do a shift, but to wear a dress too. Not that I mind, the view below the hemline is rather spectacular I must say."

He was his usual smiling, teasing self. If anything that made me feel worse, but I gave him an uncertain smile and followed him to his office. Just because I wasn't a proper employee, didn't mean I got away with not wearing the logo somewhere. I had a name badge with a fake name on it, and a black cuff with the logo printed on it in red. I clasped it round my right wrist, and then headed out to the front. In his office, he'd told me that they had a private party in for the first two hours, and then he opened for general business.

The private party took up the entire back section of the restaurant. I was talking to J over the bar, putting drinks onto a tray, when I felt eyes boring into my back. I ignored the strong urge to turn around, and the even stronger urge to draw a weapon. I remained outwardly calm. There was something about the feeling that alarmed me. I gently let my metaphysical shields – a must in my line of work – down a fraction, and realised why I was so uneasy. Whoever was looking at me was insanely powerful. They weren't quite as powerful as Nero, but they were in the same league. They were perhaps a few centuries younger, and that made all the difference with the vamps, but whoever they were, they were still a great force to be reckoned with.

I made sure I didn't look up as I walked over to the centre table so as not to make eye contact with whoever was staring. As always with the supes, the people around the table were arranged in terms of rank. With my shields down even just that small amount, I was getting power signatures from everyone at the centre table. I located the starer without even having to look up. As I leant across to give a vampire his blood cocktail, the vamp sitting next to him inhaled deeply and took hold of my arm. He had gripped my lower right arm, he could feel the triple claw scars there, so for him, the glamour broke. It's always risky when glamour breaks, not just because they see what's underneath, but also because they realise you've been working magic on them. Fortunately, his mind was on other things.

"She smells divine, Guillaume. Is she on the menu?"

I reigned in my instantaneous anger and was very polite

as Guillaume came over. "I'm afraid not sir, we don't do live feedings here. It's against the law." Technically, it wasn't; it was just heavily frowned upon.

"Which law?" he asked, disbelieving.

"My law," said Guillaume as he reached the table.

"Let her go, Clive." The voice was male, authoritative, and powerful. I recognised the same power in his voice as I had in his gaze. I rammed my metaphysical shields back up instantly.

"Yes, my Lord," Clive said with as much unwilling respect as he could muster. Clive the vampire wasn't a name that rolled off the tongue easily. I'd have pitied him if he weren't such a jerk.

I finally looked at the powerful man. Why, why are they always beautiful? If power corrupts, and absolute power corrupts absolutely, than why did that rule not apply to their faces? All the powerful men I knew were bloody gorgeous. It was very distracting, which made them even more dangerous.

His face was handsome, *very* easy on the eye. He had dark tan skin, darker then Nero's, which made the sharpness of his very high cheekbones somewhat softer. His hair was jet black and shiny, brushed straight back so it fell in a sleek waterfall down the back of his skull to stop just below his shoulders. The occasional strand of hair had the tendency to curl. His eyebrows were as perfect as I have ever seen eyebrows be, an odd thing to arbitrarily notice, but not as random as you might think. The main focal feature of his face was his eyes. Yes, his nose was straight, and yes his lips were delicate and soft-looking, but his eyes… his eyes were yellow. Rimmed in a smoky line of pitchest-black kohl, he had eyes the vibrant hue of citrine in sunlight. It was a honey yellow, golden almost, but somehow radiant. I was quite taken aback.

"Thank you sir," I said, giving an appropriately low bow.

He was obviously head honcho here, and I hadn't had my rank declared. I was trying to be Phoebe tonight, not The Raven, so I couldn't pull rank and show any less respect than a peasant would their King. A beefy Scandinavian-looking vamp on his left grunted, glaring sullenly at me from an icy blue eye. The other eye was hidden by a curtain of straight blonde hair that fell across his face, making it nigh impossible in the low light to see what he looked like. I took his grunt as permission to leave, so I stood and turned to Guillaume.

"One moment please," the yellow-eyed vampire said. I turned back. "You have piqued my curiosity. May I talk to you for a short while?"

I looked at Guillaume, who nodded, and took the empty tray off me. "Of course," I said.

I expected to have to stand near him at his table, but he rose. As he got up, so did everyone in the restaurant. He was clearly their master in some way or another. With a vaguely annoyed look, he waved in their general direction. The Scandinavian was the first to sit down, slouching low in his chair like a petulant child that didn't want to be there. Everyone else followed suit and sat back down again.

The vampire led me to a table far enough away that none of the vampires would hear, but they could still all see. I wasn't sure if it was so they could see him, or so he could keep an eye on them. Guillaume took over at the bar, and told Jasper to ask if the party wanted anything. With everyone (bar Guillaume) comfortably out of earshot, he seemed satisfied. He pulled a chair out for me, which I sat in, puffing out the skirt of the dress so gravity wouldn't reveal the weaponry underneath. He sat in the chair next to me and gave me a warm smile.

"I don't wish to alarm you. I thought you'd feel safer if we were somewhere that everyone could see us."

I nodded and thanked him, playing the part of defenceless waitress quite well. Or so I thought.

"From what I have heard, though, you need little protection." I noticed Guillaume go still behind the bar. I felt ice run through me in a sharp jolt, and I too fell still; well, as still as I could, being human and all.

"I'm not sure I understand."

He smiled again. It was a very nice smile. "Explanation is in order, I know. I have seen you recently at Court. I particularly admired your thinly veiled hostility towards our King when he asked you to attend his ball." The smile on his face became bemused. "Raven." The ice that had shot through my blood seeped into my bones. I think my heart stopped for a moment.

"It's impossible for you to recognise me. Who are you?" I asked, quietly but urgently, deeply worried that someone, anyone, could recognise me without me first altering my glamour to make it so, or without being a Lord of a Court.

"Oh how rude of me. In my intrigue I forgot my manners. I'm Bastien, Lord of Thurudīn Castle in No Man's Land. You've worked for me before I believe." Ah.

"Dylan Forbes."

"Precisely."

I didn't even bother to conceal my surprise. It was too overwhelming. The Lord of Thurudīn Castle. That explained his power, and with power and rank like that, I guess it made sense that my glamour didn't work on him. It was disturbing, though. I could accept it, but I didn't have to like it.

"Is there something you want, sire?" I asked at length.

"Please, just Bastien." He had laughter in his voice. I think he was amused by my shock, and my politeness. If he'd only seen me at Court when Nero asked me to the ball, he'd have only seen me at my least respectful. "There is something though. A job, or two. If convenient, can you meet me at my club tomorrow night? I will get someone to phone the Sharks."

"Of course. Which club?"

With slender, glassy nailed hands, he passed me a business card. "The Chained Beast."

6

I was thrown off balance by Bastien's interruption to my evening, and momentarily forgot about my predicament. As soon as I remembered I had to tell Guillaume about Nero, a searing wave of guilt passed through me.

Bastien kissed me on the hand when he and his private party left. Such gentlemanly manners put the behaviour of the horror that is The General Public in a worse light than usual. However, guilt-driven, I worked hard and was pleasant to absolutely everyone, even a group of wannabe vamps who, in their imitation, dragged through the mud everything the vamps were trying to stand for. Guillaume frightened them a bit and kicked them out once they got rowdy.

At closing time, Jasper gave me a big hug that was much needed. It steadied my growing nerves a little bit. Guillaume came back to the flat with me, seeing as he had clothes and a coffin there if the argument took all night, or rather, morning. I was hoping it wouldn't.

Dreading getting back to the flat, I drove slowly for me, hands tensely gripping the steering wheel. Guillaume gave a sidelong glance that told me he'd noticed, but he didn't comment; he knew me well enough to wisely stay mute. When we got back to the flat, I warmed up some blood in the microwave, which he took from me with a boyish smile on his face.

Unfortunately, it was time to tell him.

"Guillaume," I began slowly.

"*Oui ma cherie?*"

"I've spoken to Lu about this, and she said to tell you the full story. It was greed really that caused it; my deadly sin."

Confusion was plain on his face at my cryptic opening, but as I continued to tell him about Vittorio, then Sol, then Nero, his face turned from confused, to alarmed, to angry, and finally settled on an ice cold, bone-deep hate with a dash of anguish thrown in there just to twist the knife.

"Lucille said I had to go," I finished quietly, something inside me dying at seeing that look in his eyes. I felt dreadful.

"She's right," he said bitterly "He's still the King of England." I didn't, and probably never would, know the full extent of torture Guillaume suffered at Nero's hands. Whenever he was reminded of it, there was an alteration in his demeanour that told you he had been a broken man, and would probably never heal.

"I'm so sorry," I said inadequately.

We sat in brooding silence for what seemed like the chasms of years.

"It wasn't me who wanted you to never see Nero again you know," he said unexpectedly. Not knowing how to respond, I stayed silent. "Lucille's just over-protective. She was more upset about it than I was, especially because she couldn't see that it wasn't Nero's fault."

I was confused and alarmed. "But he was the one who tortured you."

"Yes, but he only did it because The Queen told him to."

"I wasn't aware Nero had a wife." I'd certainly never seen her at Court. I was just getting more and more confused.

"He doesn't. The Queen I refer to isn't his Queen, she's everyone's Queen. She is to vampires what Gaea is to the fey; she's the mother, and in our case she is also the first of us, the only vampire to be born, not bitten. She made the Council. It was she who told Nero to torture me."

Sometimes, I forgot that the British Court was only the glittering tip of the iceberg of vampire politics.

"How do you know she told him to?" I asked slowly, my brain trying to wade through all the information it was being given.

"Because Nero told me. He kept apologising for what he was doing, but he told me The Queen had said he had to. If I were a child of the moon I wouldn't have understood, but I'm a vampire, and I have to answer to the same Mother Queen as he does, so I understood. I don't blame him, not really. He's been an easy target for my anger, but really it's The Queen's fault. But I'm betting she has very good reasons," he added hastily.

He didn't really seem to be angry with The Queen either, and I wondered who his cold hatred was directed at. And then I realised; he hated the memory of his suffering, he hated the torture itself, rather than either of its instigators.

"So, will you hate me if I have to keep going to Court then?"

He smiled at me, a smile that was sad, and made him look very old indeed despite his youthful face. "No my darling Phoebe. I could never hate you."

I found myself wanting to cry. I had been keeping my

distance on the sofa in case Guillaume got angry, but instead he looked lost. So I moved over and slid my arms around his waist, leaning my head on his chest, and I held him like that. He kissed the top of my head, wrapped his arms around me too, and we stayed like that until I fell asleep.

7

I woke up at about half six, so I'd been asleep for less than two hours. Guillaume was still up, and Lucille was back. He'd put me in my bed and made sure I was comfortable, but he'd left the door open. From what I could see, though bleary eyed and sleepy, he and Lucille were arguing.

"You weren't supposed to tell her," Lucille hissed. "The Queen swore us to secrecy!" She was jabbing a long-nailed finger into his chest like she meant to use it as a weapon.

"She had to know. It's been ruining her life and making it more difficult. She felt so dreadful just for him having seen her again that she came in to work! She needed her sleep far more than that. I'm not going to keep something from her if it means it's detrimental for her health; I love her too much for that."

"You just don't think, do you Guillaume? You're all heart and no head. I'm going to have to tell Her." I don't know how, maybe it was a moment of sleep-deprived brilliancy, but I knew that that was capitalised.

"Fine. She'll resolve it; The Queen always has some sort of answer."

He looked grim. I was torn between jumping out of bed and demanding to know what the hell was going on, and staying silent so they'd never know I'd heard. I opted for the latter, and feigned sleep until there was silence. Lucille came in and got Guillaume's coffin out. She put it on the floor in the living room, and then shut the door. She didn't even check on me as she went to bed, just angrily got in her coffin and shut the lid.

I felt the dawn rise, and didn't get back to sleep. As I lay awake in bed, I found myself wondering if I could trust my guardian angels. I wasn't so sure I could anymore.

The moment beyond which Lu or Guillaume would be awake passed, and so I got up, restless. Ironically, I wanted to go and see Nero and see if he had any answers, but he was a day's long stretch away from being awake.

I showered and got dressed, then headed over to the Concrete Palace. I needed to be away from those two, peaceful coffins with their precious charges. They suddenly seemed like predators, ruminating in the darkness.

Hammer was in his office, as usual, with a pile of papers on his desk, as usual. He gave me a grim smile, I glared. He said sorry, I said sorry too. I sat down, he talked. It was details of the jobs Bastien wanted doing, or as many details as His Lordliness was willing to give to anyone but me. I had to feign surprise at getting yet another job from the King of Thurudīn Castle, and attributed it to my excellent work with Dylan Forbes. Unfortunately, Bastien wanted to meet me as soon as night fell at The Chained Beast, so I'd have no chance of getting hold of Nero tonight without having to go through Court. Hammer slid an envelope across the desk to me.

The paper it was made from was thick and creamy,

and had 'Ms Raven' written on the front in an exquisitely beautiful hand. The card inside, however, was entirely different. It was the same business card he had given me the night before for The Chained Beast. It was black and shiny, with silver lettering. On the back, in the same handwriting, but this time in a normal biro as opposed to a quill, were instructions to follow when I got to the club. It was all very straightforward really.

I spent the rest of the daylight hours in the firing range. People came and went, but I think the determination with which I was shooting things put any of the Sharks off talking to me. At one point, The Tin Man came up behind me and just stared as I shot targets. I ignored him as best I could, and he left without saying a word. Creepy guy.

I was thinking too much, and the more I thought, the more I wanted to shoot things. Thank god for my job, or I might be one of those spontaneous killer types that just goes out and shoots a load of people because they're pissed off at the world. I might even find that thought amusing if it wasn't such a likely occurrence. Eventually, I felt the sun begin to set. Maybe it's spending too much time with the vamps growing up, but I was very attuned to solar and lunar movement. Whatever it was, when I went outside there was the first darkening painted across the horizon, so I headed to the club.

The darkness had set in when I got there, and so had the line. People were desperate to get into the undoubtedly glamorous interior. Almost everyone there was wearing patent leather, or something shiny and silver. The material must be expensive, because there seemed to be very little of it, like there were clothes enough for one hundred people, that three hundred people had to share. I got bizarre mental images of the line outside the club in the jungle, tearing shiny bits of clothing as they wrestled for it and sticking what bits they won to their bodies in an attempt at decency. Or maybe they just preferred being indecent.

The Chained Beast, as the name might suggest, was infamous for being a lycanthrope club, but it was owned by a vampire, it seemed. A Were of some kind was on the door. He didn't feel like wolf. Perhaps he was a werelion. He was waiting until he got the go-ahead to let people in. I, naturally, walked right over, skipping the queue. There were grumblings and glares, but I had spent all day shooting targets, I really didn't give a shit about pissing a few people with bad dress sense off.

"You can't come to the front of the line Miss," the Were said. It was an upper-crust English accent, which reminded me of Mr Darcy. The image that went with the voice was all wrong: leather trousers and a fishnet, long-sleeved top through which you could see his many bodily piercings. I was disappointed; give me Colin Firth on the door any day.

"I think you'll find I can; I know the owner. Monsieur de la Sang has asked me to come tonight."

He frowned, and it made his eyebrow ring wink in the lamp-light. "He hasn't told me of this, one moment." He stuck his head round the club door, and yelled for 'Pierre'.

The man that appeared was missing something: the first half of his name. It was none other than Jean-Pierre. I tried not to gape like a goldfish as I noticed his attire. I think the only thing he was wearing was glitter. Silver. Iridescent. Glitter. A quick sweep from head to foot informed me that he was, in fact, wearing tiny silver hot pants that didn't leave much to the imagination. Several women screamed as he came out of the club, and there was a lot of swooning going on.

"Either someone painted you in glitter or you've been to a primary school art class," I said, looking him up and down in mild astonishment. Even his shoe-less feet were glittery.

His palms and the side of his fingers were bare, but the tops of his hands were glittery, and his nails had been painted a dark silver that was almost black. His eyes were framed in smoky eye-shadow of the same colour, so they seemed to burn, the emerald green irises fiercely bright. A slightly darker glitter was used to accentuate his eye sockets and his cheekbones; it looked like you could cut things on them, they were so sharp.

"Ah ma cherie," he breathed as he saw me, looking me up and down too, lingering a little too long on my chest. I guess the low neckline wasn't helping.

"Eyes are up here, *Pierre*." I said his name sarcastically. He just chuckled low, and moved in to kiss me on each cheek as was usual for him. I could feel the soft imprint of the shiny silver lipstick and a few bits of glitter cling to my skin. He was obviously feeling very pleased with himself tonight, because he stole a kiss, a proper kiss, smearing silver all over my mouth in the process and getting glitter in my hair as he ran his hands through it. The kiss was dazzling, as for that one startled moment in which my eyes were open, I was blinded by glitter. As I pushed him away, a woman from the crowd looked at me as if I was mad. It wasn't the kiss I objected to, more that fact that Jean-Pierre was getting me covered in shiny shit.

"Next time, wait for an invitation," I said, trying to wipe the silver and glitter off my face.

He chuckled. "Ah, but then I'd be waiting a very long time."

"Damn right. What the hell are you—?" He leaned in and whispered before I could say 'doing here'.

"They don't know who I am. I am Pierre, werewolf. Don't spoil this for me, Phoebe." He said my name almost as if it was a threat. My real name being used against me? Surely not. I laughed.

"No worries darling, I'd never do that to you. I'm here to see the big man, gonna let me in?"

Despite the confusion of the Were on the door (I learnt he was called William, how terribly British), 'Pierre' took me through into the currently empty club. There were a few dancers milling about. Their outfits looked like the '*Underworld*' equivalent of Jean-Paul Gautier's '*Fifth Element*' designs. Regrettably, none of the dancers were Kate Bekinsale or Milla Jovovich.

Inside the club, it was all black and mirrors. Glitter-balls hung from the mirrored ceiling, casting squares of light on the polished black floor. The poles in the middle of the stage were very shiny chrome. All the staff were in something that was shiny in either black or silver, though so far Jean-Pierre was the only one I had seen who was coated in glitter. The guests standing in the line outside would look out of place in here if they were wearing anything matte. I looked out of place myself, as I wasn't really one for shiny work wear, but it didn't matter because I was being swiftly led through that mirrored paradise by a glittery hand.

"This stuff is highly impractical you know. Why the hell are you here dressed like this anyway?"

"I work here, when Nero lets me off the leash. Your Maker has a little more power over you than your master, so Nero has to agree to it."

"I bet he just loved that."

Jean-Pierre laughed. I noticed he was leaving a trail of silver on the floor from his feet. At least he'd never lose his way home. I'm sure glitter was easier to follow than breadcrumbs in the dark. If Hansel and Gretel had gone out coated in glitter, it would have been just dandy.

Some of the dancers gave me filthy looks like they thought I was being taken into a back room somewhere so

Jean-Pierre could have his way with me. I wasn't, of course, but it wasn't exactly an unpleasant thought if he was as good in the proverbial bed as he was at dazzling kissing; though I could do without the glitter if I'm honest.

Eventually, we reached a dark wooden door that opened onto a flight of steps. You could tell this part of the club had been around long before it had served as the underbelly of The Chained Beast. It had a weight to it that only age could give. Candles glittered down the stairs, sitting in their black wall-mounted candelabra. It was such a contrast to the club that it looked wrong for a fleeting moment. Truthfully, I was more at home with the candles than with the glitter-balls. That dimly lit stairway was almost beautiful.

Jean-Pierre shut the door behind us, and suddenly we were alone. Taking advantage of the solitude, he wound his arm around my waist and buried his head in my neck. Hungry lips searched along the skin until he found the big throbbing pulse. I felt fangs elongate and push against my throat through his soft lips.

"Get the fuck off me Jean-Pierre." He drew back and the sight caught my breath in my throat.

He was literally glowing. His skin had an ethereal light to it like some internal fire was burning. His pupils had reduced down to the tiniest of pinpricks, making his irises an almost unbroken wash of silver-green, not his usual emerald colour. His brown hair seemed darker next to that pale skin, hanging in soft curls to his shoulders. I'm sure the effect would have been better minus the glitter.

His eyes held that hunger that only vampires get. It had a lot more sex in it than the eyes of a starving man, and a lot more hunger than the eyes of a lascivious man. His gaze burned into me like he could consume me with his eyes alone.

I glared at him. "Why this sudden lust? You've never

had trouble keeping your hands off me before. I never even thought you wanted to get your hands on me in the first place." Jean-Pierre, though he enjoyed an innuendo almost as much as Asher, never pushed the issue. He was a gentleman. Or so I'd thought.

"Nero imposes many rules and restrictions. You are off limits when I am under his control. But Bastien isn't nearly so restricting. This may be my only chance to taste you, your blood and your body. You are a craving I've been longing to sate."

What do you tell someone when they say they crave your body and your blood? Hell if I knew.

"Maybe later." I was only half joking. So sue me, he's beautiful, and he's always been kind to me. And did I mention he was beautiful? What a deadly combination.

His eyes burned more intensely for a moment, a flare of emerald in the silver-green. "You actually mean that," he said.

I nodded. "You've always been gorgeous Jean-Pierre. And since I just found out you can give a good kiss you have me intrigued."

He smiled, flashing his fangs at me. "Then I cannot wait for this business to be over, but just in case this takes all night may I ask one thing?"

I hesitated, which seemed to amuse him. Mustn't trust the vampire. "What?"

"May I have one more kiss, Phoebe dearest?"

"Asher's taught you well I see." I frowned. "I don't see why the hell you'd ask me to do that."

"Can you just humour me this once? It's just a kiss, ma chere. To satisfy my curiosity."

"Well, I've never been asked to kiss someone because they're curious. I assume you mean a proper kiss?"

"That depends how you define a proper kiss. But I am French," he added, smirking. I gave him a scathing look.

"Fine, if you'll leave me alone after this then I'm perfectly happy to give you a kiss."

He smiled, then the smile changed to a smoulder, and he moved in. I had my back pressed to the banister and the wall behind. It was less than comfortable, but I tried to ignore it. He gave me a long, deep kiss, which I responded to as if I'd been desperately in love with him. It would have been rude to give him a cold kiss after his asking so nicely.

"Mmmm, scrumptious," he said, his voice low and no-where near as teasing as his words, as he finally pulled away.

Then a new voice interrupted, and it sounded pissed off. It rumbled low, not low like Jean-Pierre's, more like gravel, or a particularly irritated mountain. "If you're quite finished, Master Bastien is waiting."

Good thing I don't blush easily.

The figure was just a shadow at the bottom of the stairs, so I couldn't make it out, but his voice was definitely masculine, and the figure was definitely huge.

We went down the steps. It seemed to take forever because the impatience of the waiting man was like a little bundle of energy that buzzed through the air.

When we finally did reach the bottom of the stairs, I didn't get a look at the man's face because he turned his back to us and started walking. Something soft brushed my face and I froze. It took me a second to realise it was his hair. It was an icy gold waterfall down his back hanging to his waist. The colour was strangely familiar. His shoulders were huge, broad things that made him look top heavy, but somehow it didn't look bad on him. He was covered from head to foot in black leather, not the shiny skin hugging and flesh revealing affair that most of the people upstairs were wearing, but a no-nonsense, I-will-break-your-neck-and-enjoy-it, well worn, heavy duty kind of leather. It covered his back in a thick hide and the smell of well kept leather wafted back to me with every gigantic stride he took. He must have been six-seven at least. His legs were clad in leather too, the same thick stuff. It looked like it should have been difficult to walk in but it wasn't. The trousers were too tight for him to have had a gun at the small of his back, but I was betting this vamp didn't need weaponry to slay his foes. Maybe a look would be enough, though I'd be able to tell if he was a gorgon. The lack of him being a woman and having snake hair was somewhat of an indication he wasn't.

We were led through a series of passageways, cold and slightly damp like a cave, gently sloping downwards. Every passage was identical, designed to confuse your enemies. It was a good idea. Who needed doors to keep enemies out when they couldn't work out which way was right or left anymore? I think if there had been no gravity you wouldn't be able to tell what was up or down either.

"We're here." The masculine voice was deeper and richer up close. He pushed forward the only door I'd seen since the one at the foot of the steps and suddenly there was light. Golden light. Hundreds of thousands of candles littered a space so vast it couldn't possibly be underground; no-one would bother to dig that deep. But they had.

Chandeliers made of wrought iron hung from the ceiling, holding their precious charge of miniature flames. Everything was edged in gold from the stucco cream walls to the black material upholstery on the chairs. Though chairs was not quite the right word. They looked like they could swallow two people comfortably, one sitting on top of the other, because the backs went up higher than I'd ever seen.

Bastien was sitting in what had to be a solid gold throne, or at least gold plated. Jean-Pierre's silver glittery-ness looked out of place in this golden cavernous room. Shimmering as he did so, he walked off in the direction of a plain wooden chair. There was no throne for him here.

"Mademoiselle Raven," said Basiten, smiling. "I'm glad you could come." He took my hand in his and placed his lips ever so softly on it, looking up at me as he did so, just like he had done when he left The Red Fang. That one touch of his lips was enough to make me feel his power again. It swirled over me and, unlike most vamps I'd met, it was warm and golden, and felt safe. It was an odd sensation. He sensed my confusion and smiled.

It is always worth remembering to breathe when you are looking at a vampire. I'd forgotten that momentarily.

This cavernous room was brighter than The Red Fang, and I could see that what I had thought to be tanned skin actually had a gold sheen to it, as if someone had applied a thin layer of paint to his skin. His citrine eyes looked gold. Trick of the light? Perhaps.

"Bonjour Bastien. Ça va?"

"Ah, even more delightful, she speaks French. You get curiouser and curiouser Raven." I was mildly surprised that he knew Alice in Wonderland. Okay, not mildly. It improved my opinion of him somewhat.

"Can we get down to why I'm here now?"

He chuckled, and it gave me shivers, the good kind.

"Jean-Pierre warned me you did not... what is the delightful idiom? Beat about the bush?"

"Jean-Pierre's right." I flashed him a grin. Bastien smiled back. The tall guy had moved to one of the stupidly high backed chairs, and sat so low, one leg propped on the other, that he was practically curled over himself. The icy gold hair looked rich and colourful in the candlelight, and it fell over his face so I still had no idea what he looked like. It was in that glance, I realised he was The Scandinavian who had been sitting at Bastien's side at Guillaume's.

"Indulge me. I'd like to know you better before I give you my proposition."

I didn't like that, but I didn't really have a choice. I said nothing, so he smiled and proceeded with whatever plan he had.

"Did you enjoy the view on the walk over?"

I hadn't expected that.

"Oh yeah, stone that looks identical wherever you go, a damp chill to the air and a muscle man that won't speak a word to you, or even look at you. It's just fantastic. If Jean-Pierre had been standing in front of me and not behind, the view would have been just dandy; if potentially blinding."

He threw his head back and laughed. The sound hummed through the room; a golden note in his golden sanctuary.

"I meant the view directly in front of you on the way over."

"Oh, you mean Mr 'I'm the strong and silent type'." He nodded, amusement sparkling in his eyes. "I can't complain about that view. I always appreciate a man who wears leather for utilitarian purposes rather than for flashing as much flesh as possible."

"You can't have much liked my club." He was still amused, thank god. I was hoping I hadn't offended him. Seeing as he wasn't wearing a stitch of leather, I was safe. His shirt had to be silk, the sleeves billowing around his arms, coming in at the cuffs, and the trousers were black jeans that clung very tight.

"It's not so much the leather, there's just too many damn mirrors. Good if you're in there for an ambush, bad if you're paranoid and jump at shadows."

"My, my, I think you're the first person to notice that."

"Do I get a gold star?"

He looked puzzled. Best keep the quips to a minimum. Don't want to confuse head vamp in his own lair. He might get pissed off.

"Why did you want my opinion of your bodyguard's ass in leather?"

He looked startled, and turned to the glittering Jean-Pierre.

"You are right, no matter how much you told me of her she would have still caught me off guard. I've never met anyone like her."

I turned to Jean-Pierre. "Talking about me behind my back's not very polite sweetie." I gave him a sickeningly sweet smile but my eyes told him that I didn't like that he'd been discussing me with this vampire. I didn't know the vampire in question well enough yet.

He avoided my gaze and instead addressed Bastien. "You certainly won't meet anyone else like her."

Thurudīn 's lord smiled, and turned to The Scandinavian.

"Edouard," He crooned like he was about to enjoy this. Edouard needed no other prompting. He unfolded himself from the chair in a long fluid movement that seemed impossibly graceful for such a big guy. I had guessed wrong. He must have been hunching over in the passageways to get here because he was brushing seven foot. Jesus.

He turned to face me, one half of his face visible, the other hidden by a curtain of that icy golden hair.

"Show her."

"Show me what?"

"You will see." Those three words reminded me too much of Gollum leading Frodo into Shelob's lair. If a giant spider came out of the walls, I was going to shoot Bastien right between his pretty gold eyes.

Nothing that bad happened. Edouard just pulled his hair away from his face and looked at me.

Looked at me with the only good eye he had.

There was a claw mark down his face, a tear or a rip that had gone deep and taken the eye with it. It had been stitched up in a long line from underneath his hair down his face to his neck. It was a big fucking claw mark. He had some minor slices on either side of the big one, that melded into it to make it a triple pointed single scar, with one thin line trailing over his nose. His eye must have been sewn shut when they'd stitched up the wound, but you couldn't really tell he'd ever had an eye there; it was just scar tissue and a slight depression.

I'm not sure what reaction they expected, but it clearly wasn't the one they got. I took a step closer and lifted my hand to his face as if to touch it, but decided he might not like that, and I'd like to leave with both my arms still attached.

"What gave that to you?"

Edouard looked surprised with his one good eye, which was as blue as blue could be.

"Dragon." His low voice rumbled out the word rather than him saying it. It was like listening to thunder speak.

"Wow." I paused. "You're insane to go against a dragon. They're no fun."

Everyone asked a question at once. Edouard's was 'how do you know?' Jean-Pierre's was 'you've fought one?' and Bastien's was…

"He does not repulse you?"

"To answer Ed and Jean-Pierre, I've seen one, I haven't fought one. To answer you, Bastien, no he doesn't. Not in the slightest."

"Everyone recoils from him, yet you do not. Why?" There was a sort of curious anger to his voice.

"I've seen worse. Hell, I've even got worse. Taking out

an eye is gruesome but… let's just say I've seen more of the inside of my body than I care to." I turned to face Edourard, my eyes for him alone. "What did they use to stop the scar from eating at your face?"

He looked even more confused. I was almost relieved to see that all the muscles in his face still worked, as both eyebrows managed to plunge into a frown, though admittedly one was just a ridge of shiny scar tissue.

"How do you know I needed anything for it?"

"To leave a mark like that, all the claw marks melded together, they had to use something to burn the poison out, or your face wouldn't be nearly so scarred. You look like someone took acid to you, which means you went against a greater dragon, which means you're even more insane than you look."

"Impressive."

"You like her," Bastien said.

"I do," Edouard rumbled in reply.

I resisted the urge to say aw shucks, that makes me feel so warm and fuzzy inside. Point for me.

"Show me," Bastien said, turning back to me.

"What?"

"Show me your scars that are worse than his."

"Not as gruesome, but deeper."

"Deeper then. Show me."

I hesitated. It wasn't so much that I was bothered about him seeing them, though letting beautiful men see deformity was always risky if you had any plans of that persuasion. It was that it'd flash a large number of weapons, and I'd have to strip.

"We know you have weapons, we'd expect no less of The Raven, so if their concealment is your worry then do not. I can smell the metal on you."

That was a bit weird. I knew vamps could smell gun oil but smelling metal was just strange.

"Fine."

I think I even surprised them by how much weaponry I was carrying. I would have set a metal detector berserk.

Over my back I had a double knife sheath, though they were more like small swords in their length. They were positioned for a cross draw and hooked over the ends. They made me look a bit like Riddick, but fortunately I was not bald. There was a gun at the small of my back because my other shoulder holster was broken, and it's not that comfortable to wear with the knife sheaths strapped on. My other gun was in the still intact shoulder holster. There were also knives tucked into the top of my leather trousers at the sides; two on each side, but they didn't see them, because I only needed to remove my top.

"Well, I knew you came well armed, but I think we underestimated you. My apologies. Who would you prefer to disarm you?"

That was an easy one. "Jean-Pierre; as long as he doesn't get glittery shit all over them."

Bastien smiled. Jean-Pierre came over to me and took all the knives and guns, then removed the holsters. His hand brushed the raven tattoo just once before he moved away, but I could feel that stroke as if his hand was still there. Edouard was looking at me like he wondered what I would taste like.

The top I had on was a plain black scoop neck, but that meant you couldn't see the scars at the back. I was almost wishing I'd worn my halter-neck now, though that would have made the knives and guns uncomfortable.

"Off," Edouard said, and his voice was gruff with something akin to hunger. His eyes were gazing at my chest, but not the way Jean-Pierre had been earlier. It was because he could see the silvery scar line from jaw to half way down my breast.

Bastien also looked hungrily at me. I was glad I couldn't see Jean-Pierre's face.

I sighed, and lifted the top up and over my head, dropping it on the floor. At least I had nice underwear on. Red satin with black lace, you couldn't go wrong.

I turned slowly so my back was facing Edouard and Bastien. It meant Jean-Pierre got a good look at my front while the others studied my back.

Bastien actually gasped.

I knew what they were seeing. I hadn't been able to see my back very well, even after I'd healed, so they had taken a picture of it for me so I could see; I like to know how badly I'm injured. There were three deep gouges taken out of my back, and a fourth shallower one. If it had been a normal wound they'd have filled out with scar tissue and I'd just have some pretty shiny lines. But this had been a highly infectious breed of shifter – werewolf. They'd got a claw-full of my back. I'd been fighting the Were in front of me and could do nothing about the one behind me. He'd been a powerful sod and could shift his feet and hands larger than normal size in half-wolf form, so the scars took up all of my back rather than just a hand-span stripe. They'd stayed like canyons on my back because to stop me from getting lycanthropy they'd had to treat it with silver. Some smaller wounds could be treated by placing silver shards in the wound, stitching it up, and taking them out later, letting the skin heal over the fresh wound. This hadn't been one of those wounds. They'd got a witch to bind silver leaf to the gouges, which moulded perfectly to the scars and would never come off. It was more than one layer to ensure it killed the infection. I'd been out for a week in which they had to feed me the blood of supernaturals to keep me alive, and a silver supplement, like an anaemic taking iron. A vampire had tried to suck the disease out of my blood, and in turn I'd had to have blood to keep me going. Fortunately for me the vamp hadn't been a maker like Bastien. If it had, I'd be a hell of a lot more avoidant of sunlight right about now.

I knew Guillaume had taken my blood, but I didn't know what blood they'd given me back, or who'd given it.

Underneath that thin layer of silver the skin was white. No blood flowed near it. It freaks me out sometimes when I think that a little bit of me is dead, really dead. I was thankful for the silver on my back though. Without it, spine and nerves would have been exposed, and that is never a good thing. They're still not sure how I survived it. They wanted to do a blood test. It came back that I was a vampire, but that was just from all the blood I had swirling round my veins. It was without a shadow of a doubt the most horrible and excruciating experience of my life.

If I were human I would have died. Makes you wonder who your parents are in a situation like that. I'll let you know, soon as I find them.

"What… did this?" Bastien's voice was low, almost a whisper.

"Werewolf," I said, matter of fact. I'm used to people staring, commenting, I'm used to hearing horror in the voices of people who see my scars. If I forget to glamour them away, or if I'm having a defiant day, I scare people shitless when I go on holiday.

I slipped the top back on, and when I turned around I saw pity in Bastien's eyes. I have no idea what Edouard's good eye was telling me.

"Don't look at me like that," I said to Bastien, angry.

"Like what?"

"Like 'poor human, how horrible'. It's over now; I don't give a shit. If anything, pity is going to piss me off. Now, I think by following the rules of fair game you owe me a favour for that. You will owe me a favour anyway for whatever job you want me to do, 'cause I'm guessing it's big, so let's get down to business before you owe me a whole host of favours, or before I decide to say no." I couldn't help being angry, my back scars were a touchy subject for me.

There was no teasing after my little rant; it was all seriousness.

"I apologise for asking you to do that." Bastien said. "In return, I will be happy to owe you a favour. I also deem the jobs of enough worth to merit a favour each."

That made me a little tense, hesitant, to ask what he wanted, but I did anyway. No good mercenary turns down a job.

"What do you want me to do?"

"You know I am king of Thurudīn ."

"Yes." It was a pretty damn impressive castle. "Last time I was there, I asked to speak to you and I was told you were otherwise occupied." I gave a short laugh. "Actually, I was told that just because I have a pretty face doesn't mean you'd take me to bed. I think they thought I was making some move." I laughed again, more at myself than anything else. I was upset that Bastien had seen my scars, I'm not sure why, and laughing beat the hell out of crying. I'm a mercenary, I don't cry. Sure.

"Why were you there?"

"I was called in by a friend, one of your weretigers, to sort out a particular shifter that was having trouble with authority."

"Bane," Edouard said in that low voice of his.

"She sorted him out?"

"Apparently so."

"I had wondered how that had happened. Well, I guess I owe you yet another favour."

"It's alright, your tigers owe me a debt for that, not you." I grinned. "So, what's the job?"

"Right, yes, back to business." He smiled. "I am holding a party of sorts… for The Council and our Dark Queen."

I blinked once. Twice. "Fuuuucking hell. You're having the top of the top over for tea?"

"Nero is set to entertain at the Sunken City sooner than the Council can all arrive, but those who can make it will be there. It means, however, that the duty of host falls to me, being the next step down in the hierarchy, as it were."

"Right. Where exactly do I come in?" I had a feeling I wasn't going to like my piece on the chessboard if the other side had the Council and The Queen.

"All the Council will have their own protection, as well as my castle's guards. However, one of the guards of Kyvernaw, seventh Council member, was struck by a curse when defending his master. He has become a crazed thing, and is killing close by. Very bloody murders. Kyvernaw understands that this looks bad, and the Queen requested I sort out the problem, because it is on my territory that he was attacked."

"Shit, you mean Master Death was on his way here when he was attacked? They've got to be pretty pissed off."

"*Exactement.* Now I have to prepare for the arrival of the Council and the Queen, and I will need all my people to help me. This is why I am asking you to take care of his servant."

Great, a bloodthirsty, insane vamp to kill. Huzzah. I hated revenants. They were a bit like zombies, they didn't have any inhibitors, so they used all their strength, even if it meant they shattered their bones or popped their joints, and they were hungry *all the time.*

I didn't bother saying that it was a difficult job and I could die. He understood that, and so did I, so instead I asked something more practical, "Do you want his head?"

He looked slightly startled. "I hadn't thought of it."

"The Council will see it as a sign that you can carry out what you're asked. The Queen may think better of you for it. I tend to take the head and the heart and burn them, scattering them over different bodies of water, but I can burn the rest and give you the head; or the heart if you wish."

He looked at me thoughtfully, then his gaze shifted to Jean-Pierre. I turned to look at him in all his glittery glory. He was smiling, amused by something.

"What?"

"You. You've just been told you've got to take out a revenant vamp, and you talk easily about doing it clean enough to keep the trophies. You never cease to amaze me."

"Get used to it. It's gonna be a bitch to decapitate him cleanly, but I can always cut him in half lower down then neaten it off, make it look pretty."

"Damn." That was Edouard. I turned to look at his cold blue eye.

"Hey, I'm an artist at heart."

I know, I know. There is something very wrong with me. I've always known that. I've also always known it's not necessarily entirely my fault. Exactly why I was so strange is something only people I'm biologically related to could tell me. I didn't think I'd be finding out any time soon.

Edouard and I had a prolonged staring competition, but his gaze was so piercing I got uncomfortable, and turned my attention back to Bastien. "What's the other job?"

"Ah, yes. Because of the problems on my territory, I would like you to head up a team of extra bodyguards on the night."

I blinked at him for a few seconds. Tons of answers swarmed my brain. Unfortunately for me, my brain had little choice, and my mouth chose to say, "Are you insane? You want me there with the entire fucking council *and* the

Queen? I'm human, you've got a whole army of Weres to do that."

He didn't seem to mind me swearing at him. "I know, but none of my people think like you do, or would be able to handle a situation as you do." He hesitated, and dropped his gaze to the floor as if he couldn't look at me.

"What?!" I was pissed off now. "Tell me or so help me god—" I delved into the top of a boot and drew a gun, a new compact kind that Predator had built – it fired thin wooden bullets, "—I will turn you into a colander."

His eyes widened, and Jean-Pierre cursed.

"It will hurt your feelings, but seeing as you are so insistent I will tell you." He sighed, not at all perturbed by my slimline weapon. I hated it when people didn't take me seriously when I was threatening them. "We all know you are not human, Raven, you need to stop fooling yourself."

He seemed to imply that a human couldn't do either of the jobs he was asking me to do. I clenched my teeth and shoved the gun back where it came from. I wanted to be angry with him, but I'd been thinking the same thing only seconds before.

"Fuck."

A few moments of silence passed, in which I felt all their gazes on me like hot pokers, branding me.

"I'll do it, on certain conditions."

"Name them."

"One, I get to wear whatever the hell I like. If I dress in assassin chic and look like a bodyguard, people are less likely to mess with me. Two, keep the Council members away from me. You can count the second as one of my favours; I have no intention of getting even more involved in vampire politics than I already am with Nero."

He thought about it for a moment then said, "I am fine with both, but the latter may be difficult."

"I don't care how you do it, just do it, or it's a deal breaker."

"Fine. We have a deal, Raven."

A human would have insisted on shaking hands, but he was a vampire, and he was old school, so I took his word for it.

8

My business meeting with Bastien hadn't taken too long. He'd offered me three quarters of a million for both jobs, so I hadn't bothered haggling. Edouard phoned Hammer, who was informed of the price agreed on. I'd love to have been there to see his reaction. The whole time, Edouard stared at me like I was the most fascinating, and equally the most confusing, thing in the universe. It was slightly more off-putting considering I was re-dressing myself at the time.

As I left, Jean-Pierre detained my hand. "You're still beautiful you know," he said softly.

"What?" I asked, completely puzzled.

"The scars, they make you no less beautiful."

"Thanks," I said uncertainly. "As much as I appreciate the compliment, and as much as I know you hoped we could have a little rendezvous in private, I have to go and see your other Master."

He smiled, but it didn't reach his eyes. "I guess I will always lose you to Nero."

"He's not won me, so you can't have lost, Jean-Pierre."

"I know who has won you," he said softly, after a moment. We were in the twisting labyrinth of corridors, far from anyone who could hear, so I stopped in my tracks and turned to face him.

"Do enlighten me."

"Asher."

I frowned. "I'm not in love with Asher."

"Perhaps not, but he has bedded you."

My eyebrows rose sharply. "And did he tell you that?"

"No. It's just something I picked up on, something in the way he looks at you, and how comfortable you are around each other."

"We've always been comfortable around each other."

"Not like you are now. You forget, I have not seen you for five years, I notice things that were not there before."

"I guess I have no choice but to own up then. "Yes, Asher and I have slept together."

"Last week?" he asked.

I smiled at his suspicion, he just looked so damn *earnest*. "No. A long time ago. The first time I came back to the Sunken City after what Nero did, the first day visit. I was seventeen, I didn't have as many scars or as many woes as I do now. It was just the once, Jean-Pierre, so don't… I don't know… get jealous because you're curious, and he already knows."

"I am rarely jealous of Asher, Raven," he said, as if Asher was so beneath him it didn't even occur to him to feel envy. I didn't like the tone he used, but I could tell it was a defence mechanism. I was not going to stroke his ego, and nor was I going to argue with him. So I headed off and hoped I was going in the right direction.

When I eventually re-emerged into the reflective world of The Chained Beast, the music was at full volume and the dancers were in full swing. I wove through the throbbing mass of people to the front door, and gave William a smile as I left, saying 'bye Bill' as I walked past. He scowled, and did his best to ignore me, and the looks my talking to him had earnt him. My irritating deed done for the day, I headed off to see the King of England. Whoop de fucking do.

The Sunken City was teeming with life; and death. Staircase thirteen was manned by two Weres; one a tiger, and one a wolf, if I was right. They were both fairly young, but it seemed to me that the weretiger was training the werewolf.

"Evenin' gents," I said as I pulled up on my bike. I don't think they were expecting to see anyone, as it wasn't a public staircase. "I'm here to see Nero. He's not expecting me, but he's hoping I'll turn up."

They looked very confused. The tiger spoke. "Who are you?"

"The Raven."

There is always a moment of stillness, of shock, after I make that declaration.

"Seriously?"

"Seriously. If one of you could carry my bike down, I need to see Nero as soon as possible."

"Of course, Raven." The tiger took my bike, which didn't surprise me. Power comes with age, and he felt the older of the two. From their lack of argument, I got the impression that Nero had told them to let me in whenever I turned up. It was both useful, and unwanted.

We walked down the steps in silence, and I pretended that I didn't know they were whispering to each other and sharing furtive glances. I walked down those stairs like I owned the place. At the bottom, the tiger put my bike down, and I started up the engine. I knew it was a pedestrianized area, but I'm The Raven, and I'm not exactly known for my adherence to rules. I revved the bike, smiled a little sinisterly at the two Weres, and then drove off at a suicidal speed. If the crowd had been human, many of them would have died, but they had more-than-human speed, so they stepped out of the way. I enjoyed it, driving through the outskirts of the city. It was beautiful to look at, to take in at a leisurely place, but I didn't have time to do that tonight, and I certainly wasn't going to walk. I was feeling too lazy.

I arrived at the Court in record time, and roared into the courtyard. The guards looked more than alarmed. I think me blazing in there on a bike was a bad security risk.

I dismounted, and told them who I was; I don't think it put them at ease at all. Once they knew, though, they let me in right away, promising to look after my bike until I asked for it again. I walked in through the corridors of the Court, now so used to the glares and snide comments that they slid off me like water off a duck. The usual announcement took place, the usual crossing of the floor, the usual kneeling bow. My hair fell down in a golden-brown waterfall of curls that I could just see Nero's feet through when he reached the bottom of the stairs.

"Speak your piece," he said softly, as if afraid I was going to say something horribly hurtful. There was that cautious tightening around the eyes that spoke his fear. I stared right into that painfully handsome face, and felt a little bit of my heart melt. All these years I had been hating him for something The Queen had ordered done; and all these years he'd maintained his loyalty to his Queen by keeping his silence. Dammit. I hate finding out that people I dislike intensely are actually innocent, or at least not to blame. It makes hating them harder, and it makes me in the wrong. I don't like being in the wrong.

"I have come here to apologise, King. My last acceptance of your generous offer to be on your arm the night of the ball was less courteous and genuine than you deserved. And so, I am here to make a truthful, formal acceptance of your proposal, that honours me with the attention it gives. For that night, I shall be your Raven." It was a pretty speech, full of flattery and humility, but one I did not see the reaction to, as I gave another sweeping bow. I never had been one for curtseying.

Nero's hand appeared in my vision, drawing my hair aside. "Stand, Raven." I obeyed, and as my eyes met his, I smiled. It was the first genuine smile he had got from me in over five years.

He was still unsure. "Truly, you will be mine?"

"Truly, Nero." Guilt over how I had wrongly hated him for years gripped me then, and made me commit a small act of insanity. I stepped forward, closing the gap between us, and kissed him. It wasn't the lusty, tongue-probing sort, but the gentle, chaste kiss of a wedding, just a warm press of lips.

There was uproar. Nero's executioner, the burly scarlet haired Blair, stood up as if to make for me, but the King himself pulled me to him and hugged me tight. That was our reunion, the open wound of the past years scabbing over to leave raw, new skin in its place. Once Nero had made it clear that what I had done was a good thing and not bad, the tumult faded a bit. While everyone was quieting down, he murmured in my ear, "If you would wait for me in my quarters, we can speak further." I nodded, smiled, and began to walk up the steps. There was a door to his rooms at the side of that topmost platform. I walked over to it, and paused to look back at Nero, feeling slightly less guilty now. As I did, I saw something that baffled me.

There was another throne on the top platform.

It stood a little back from Nero's and was silver and black, the cold colour not matching the rich gold room. I was about to look at the figure, frowning in a puzzled manner, when

Nero caught my eye, shaking his head ever so slightly. Even more puzzled, I didn't look back at the second throne, and instead retreated into the velvet dark of the corridor.

I found my way to his rooms fairly easily; I just to had to go where there was a higher concentration of guards. They all let me past without questioning to see if I was who I said I was. To be honest, I didn't get many people claiming to be me, because people could recall their appearance afterwards, and they were immediately written off as liars. And shot if I found them, and come on, I'm The Raven; I always found them.

The rooms were as beautiful and comfortable as I remembered them. I sat on the big sofa again, and managed not to fall asleep this time. Nero appeared in record time; barely fifteen minutes had gone by. I rewarded his haste with another smile as he walked in. I could get used to this liking him again thing.

"Raven, I…" he trailed off, seemingly at a loss for words. He stared at me like he was hungry, and I wasn't quite sure which hunger it was.

"I'm sorry, Nero." The surprise on his face was complete. "I know now that it wasn't your fault. Guillaume, I mean."

That seemed to get his attention. "You do? How?"

"He told me. I went to see him, to tell him I was going to accept your offer to attend the ball with you. I felt I owed him that much at least. He saw how much it grieved me to think I was hurting him by saying yes to you. And so he caved, and told me. I know now I've been hating you for something that you never wanted to do. I'm sorry, Nero," I repeated. His eyes were shiny with the silvery slick of tears. One fell, clear as crystal, and then a red, bloody one followed. He wiped those ruby drops from his cheek, and walked closer. He sat down on the far end of the sofa, and I put my feet in his lap.

He smiled, and it was radiant.

I came to realise that the reason I'd rushed over here was to heal the hurt between us. I'd meant it when I said I'd been in love with him before what he did to Guillaume. Sure, I was sixteen and naïve, and it had been an adoring, besotted kind of love, but it was love nonetheless. I'd never *love* love him again, but I could grow to truly like him again, and I was satisfied with that.

"So what am I to wear to your grand ball, my King?" The sarcasm was back, but it wasn't meant to insult this time, merely to tease. It was refreshing to be nice to Nero again.

He chuckled, an old familiar sound. "Anything you like, but preferably a dress. As ravishing as you look in leathers, they're not exactly ball wear."

"Do you have a preference in colour? Am I to match the decor?"

"I'd rather you wore whatever colour you wanted. Lots of the Courtiers think they have to wear teal, gold or black, or their own House colours, and it ends up in a monotonous array."

"Isn't that a contradiction?"

"Probably, cara mia."

I smiled. "It's been a long time since I've heard you speak pretty endearments."

"I never thought you would forgive me, you have no idea how much it has brightened my disposition, Phoebe." Despite the archaic phrasing, it was one of the nicest things he'd said to me, and I looked at him in flattered wonder.

I stared, at that soft mouth, at that beautiful straight nose, and at his rich teal eyes. It was like his eyes were the ocean, the bright hue of the Mediterranean Sea in sunshine, deeper and darker in the middle were great beasts of long ago move slow and sluggish, sentinels in the dark water. I stared, and that sixteen-year-old self peeked out shyly at the man she'd been obsessed with, the man who was looking at her like she had grown into a woman more precious than diamonds and more beautiful than a Da Vinci. My heart sped up, my breathing quickened, and my freshly healing heart, with the petals of that old besotted love falling like red rain, surrendered to that gaze. I was drowning, drowning with no hope of rising to the surface again, and not really wanting to.

9

I awoke in a four-poster bed with the tell-tale signs of tangled sheets and a distinct lack of clothing. The naked man in the bed was also an indication; just because he was dead now, didn't mean he had been during the night.

My stomach fell through the floor, and proceeded to practice the art of Celtic knot work.

I'd somehow always expected Nero to be paler and colder when he died for the day, but the only thing that really gave away that his animator had cut his strings was that he was utterly still. I didn't remember the previous night at all, and was certain that I hadn't been drinking. Shocked at myself, I scrambled off the bed and stared at its dead occupant.

Asher chose that moment to walk in.

"Jesus fucking Christ!" he exclaimed as he entered. He made no move to look away, and I was frozen, making no move to cover myself. "Did you sleep with Nero?" he asked, though the answer to that question was fairly obvious, wasn't it?

"I don't remember, Asher, I don't remember." If it had

been a different member of The Hand, which it of course couldn't be, I would have covered myself immediately. But it was Asher, and Jean-Pierre was right, I was *very* comfortable around him. I was taller, and more filled out than the last time he'd seen me naked, and I certainly had more scars and tattoos, but it was still just Asher. "He must have… he must have rolled me." In shock, I slumped down onto the bed, and pulled the sheets up to cover myself. Asher came over to me, concerned, managing very well to ignore the glorious sight of his King, naked and dead, on the bed behind me.

"He can't, Phoebe. Believe me, it's not for lack of trying, but he can't roll you. He's never been able to."

"But he did!" I said, my voice rising in desperation.

"Okay babe, calm down." He sat next to me on the bed and hugged me. My mind was spinning, and I stayed rigid in his arms, until, bit by bit, I relaxed against him. "Feel better?"

"No, but I feel saner.

"Isn't saner better?"

"Not always."

We sat there for a few minutes more until I could think rationally. As soon as I could, I got up and picked my clothes up off the floor. My top was on the sofa, plain black. I would probably never be able to look at a black scoop neck tank top again without being reminded of the empty space of last night. Asher helped me get dressed. I felt like a child, but was glad he was there, taking care of me. He even helped fasten the holster. When I looked at his face, his jaw was clenched, and the pulse was jumping in his neck. His eyes had washed out to faded silver with a hint of blue in them, not the light spring skies blue I was used to.

"What did that to you?" he asked, voice low and growling as if it would crawl inside you and hunt for vital organs.

"What did what?"

"Your back."

His pupils spun down to tiny specs of black. He looked like an angry wolf. Oh. Of course, Asher hadn't seen the scars before.

"One of your kind," I said softly. His glare became steelier.

"Who?"

"I don't know. They're dead though. Cannibal hunted him down."

Jealousy flashed in his eyes. "He should have brought him to answer to me. None of my kind can get away with hurting people I love without having to answer to their pack leader."

"He may not have been in your pack."

His eyes bore into me. "All the werewolves in Britain are my pack, just because they are subdivided doesn't make them any less mine."

I often forgot that just as Nero was vampire King, so Asher was werewolf King. Asher had his Bastiens and Sols aplenty in his Kingdom, but he was the ultimate authority. I had never fully realised that before.

"Easy Asher. Calm down. Breathe."

He glared at me, but did so. Eventually his eyes became blue again. I'd never particularly thought of his eyes as warm before, but after that silver spectacle, they were as warm as a forest fire.

"I'm sorry Phoebe," he said slowly. "I just hate the thought that I can't make him pay for that."

"He's already paid with his life. It's so sweet that you're that protective, but I can take care of myself." He just looked at me. "Of course I get into scrapes, that's inevitable, but I always come out of them too." He just gave me an empty smile. "I've agreed to go with him to the ball, that why I was here yesterday," I said eventually.

"Were you in the Court room?"

"Well… yes. Why?"

"Did he tell you who the man in the second throne was?" I shook my head. He seemed to have an internal battle with himself. "Then I have no right to tell you, but try and avoid him if you can. Now, go home. Sleep. Kill something, I don't know. Just don't stay here."

There was an urgency in his voice that brooked no argument, and after his anger at my old wounds, I had had more than my fair share of being freaked out for one morning. So, I picked up what possessions I'd had with me, namely weaponry, secured them about my person, and got the hell out of there.

10

Work continued as normal. I got no more phone calls from Nero, and only made the odd one or two to Bastien to sort out details. All other clients were relatively low-key. Not all my jobs were to kill things. People wanted me to find things, find people, talk to people, heal past hurts, get them information. That was what you did when you were a mercenary: anything.

Hammer was less friendly because it had become widely known that The Raven was to be on King Nero's arm at his annual ball. He felt it was a betrayal. I couldn't explain to him why I had forgiven him, so it would probably be a wedge driven between us forever. Contrarily, Cannibal was being nicer. I was letting out some aggression on the firing range when he brought me a cup of tea. It was such a small gesture but I was startled. We became closer after that.

The day of the ball arrived. Jade came over to help me get ready, seeing as Lu was still asleep. Tammy was meant to be coming too, but she was out raising the dead. I guess that's what you get for being a couple comprised of a mercenary and a freelance necromancer.

I had a dress picked out for the evening, one which displayed my scars. I was The Raven, they were to be expected, so there was no point wasting energy on glamour to hide them. I wasn't ashamed of them (I repeated to myself) so I decided they would be a showpiece. The dress was the deep red of rubies, silk satin, and entirely backless. It was a halter-neck, with a sort of draped neckline. It looked like the material had been pinned at the neck, and left to gather in an arc covering my chest and hanging nearly to my waist. The back was similar, but it being a halter-neck the drape hung from the front, and curved round to the small of my back at its lowest point. It meant that my silver scars were glittering and bare for all to see, set in my honey skin like a piece of macabre jewellery. To further emphasise these, my hair was pinned up, which was where Jade came in.

She gathered the hair on the top of my head in a small beehive, which is difficult when your hair is curly. She left long curls to dangle down my back and over my shoulders. It took a lot of pins and a lot of hairspray, but after an hour's struggle it was secured in place as best as it ever would be. I wore black satin gloves that came up to mid-forearm. My earrings were long, elongated triangles about a centimetre wide at the top, and tapering inwards, the triangles long enough to just brush my collarbones. They were jet black like the gloves, and polished so they were very, very shiny. I left my face bare of any make-up but smouldering kohl eyeliner that was applied in a band so thick it was almost eye shadow. My eyes looked very blue bordered by all that black.

One reason I liked the dress, a reason why I like many of my outfits, was I could fit weaponry under it. There was a small knife sheath secured around the front of my ribs with tape, so there was no strap round my back, attached to one of those ludicrous yet ever so practical stick on bras. Of course, you always had to reinforce the damn things with your own tape, but it was better than going bra-less. The knives themselves were accessible by diving down the front of my dress and pulling one out. I also had two more knives above each hip in an odd holster Belle and I had come up with for backless eveningwear. I could slide a hand under the fabric hanging at the sides and get a knife out. They were all very solid steel, but with a higher silver content than usual for my fighting against the nasties. I had some knives that were steel with silver inlays, so if you pressed them into the flesh of a lycanthrope or vampire, they left a swirly pattern. Yes, I'd tried it; it worked beautifully. Naturally, though, you had to get rid of the body so the mark didn't stay or they'd be able to track the kill back to your knives. Pity, it was pretty. They were too long to fit under the dress, so I had my plain Jane knives on me for tonight.

The major downside was that I could no way in hell get a decent sized gun under there. I had an ankle holster, but they tended to make you alter the way you walked slightly, which was noticeable if you knew what to look for; and seeing as the word 'ball' implied dancing, I could not afford to wear two to balance out the weight. I put one gun in my large red leather bag. I was not a woman to use a pathetic little clutch bag into which you can fit lipstick and travel-sized perfume and that is it. I knew it was a posh event, but I was damn well having my big bag. I also knew that you could get shot in the time it took to get a gun out of a bag rather than whipping it out of a holster, but I just didn't feel safe leaving the house with no gun at all. Call me paranoid, but it's better that than dead.

"Do you think you've got enough weaponry?" Jade asked as I put the gun in my bag. It wasn't sarcastic; it was a genuine question. She'd known me long enough to have witnessed or had described in detail every attempt on my life, and so she knew just how careful I had to be. Torturella could afford to go out of doors with just the one gun or the one knife. I could not.

"I think so. I'd love another gun but there's no point having two in the bag, it might make drawing time even slower."

She nodded in an understanding fashion, then said, "Well, you're set to go."

I smiled, and thanked her for her help. Even I had to admit I looked good. I was particularly proud of my exposed back, an odd thing to be a favourite feature, but I was mostly proud because normally I hid the back scars. Today, I would flaunt them, and not see them as an imperfection.

My car was parked in the space they usually left my bike in. Blaze had become responsible for all my vehicles, and so I was more than happy to give him the car keys and trust him to treat it nicely. He met me at the top of the stairs, and took it down to the garage. I think I'd only been to the garage once myself.

Blaze wasn't the only one who met me.

The sight that greeted me at the top of staircase thirteen was wondrous, to say the least. The Master's Hand were to be my escorts through the city to where I would meet the King on the steps to the main Court entrance. Usually a relatively quiet spot, the courtyard would be teeming with honoured guests and people so important to the vampires they were almost deities. I knew at least two of The Council would be attending Nero's ball. And as much as I knew many members of The Council were famed for their beauty, I was struggling to imagine something more delectable than the Hand in that moment.

They looked positively scrumptious.

Carlos was dressed entirely in silver and white. He was

wearing an old-fashioned tunic in the style not of earth, but of Otherworld, the realm in between where the elves and fey came from. It had a stiff rising collar, and parted all the way down the middle. It was fastened with plaited silver thread wound round solid silver buttons. It was the pure white of fresh snow, with that sunlit sparkle to it despite the lack of any sunlight shining on it, or any glitter in the fabric. The large, folded over cuffs of the sleeves were silver and looked like satin, but again they glittered in ways fabric did not, like dawn glancing off the frost. In very fine, very pale silver thread, there were snowflakes embroidered along the edges of the garment, so he had a band of silver down his front where the two halves met. I could have sworn it moved, like gentle snowfall, but I must have just been staring too hard. His trousers were of the same silver as the cuffs, cut in a perfect, straight line, a little too long so that they creased where they rested on his white leather shoes, giving the impression of snow shovelled close to a wall. His skin didn't look warm against all that white and silver; it looked pale as ice. His hair, which I knew for a fact was uniform grey, was completely silver. It wasn't just the bleach of the moonlight, because like the cloth it glittered in ways hair just didn't. The entire effect, albeit in a different colour, reminded me of the clothes Green wore, our only elf mercenary. It made me wonder what Carlos' origins were. Funny, I'd never thought to ask before. Then again, he could have killed someone for the outfit.

Carlos was smiling, something I could not recall him ever doing. I vaguely wondered why, but I still had two more of The Hand to gaze at.

Where Carlos reminded me of winter's kiss upon the earth, Asher reminded me of all that was male. There was just such masculinity to him that even the floaty shirt couldn't make you think of him as any less male. He had on dark brown leather trousers that clung to his skin in a delightful way. They were high waisted, and from slender waist to narrow hips were bands of brown leather with a panel in the middle which held gold eyelets and brown laces, fastened in a criss-cross pattern. I moved my gaze lower, noticing how well the trousers clung to his thighs, baggier at the knees, to disappear into well-loved brown leather boots with the same large turnover tops that Nero so favoured. I could see that they laced all the way up the back, just like his trousers did at the front, a perfect compliment. A large triangle of chest was exposed, and I must admit it was a lovely view. The billowing-sleeved shirt was a pale cream, which made his skin look almost golden. The wide neck meant it was very close to falling off his shoulders, but it dipped down enough in the middle to defy gravity. There was a triangular section cut out from the middle, in which there were more gold eyelets and this time thin gold laces, left loose to expose golden skin though the gaps. His hair was tied up with a chocolate brown ribbon, and its golden loveliness was spilled over one shoulder, the gently undulating waves of his hair trailing over his collarbone. It was longer than I remembered it. His eyes were the purest sky blue I had ever seen, even when they were muted by the moonlight. Sunshine and summer skies.

I couldn't contemplate anything being more beautiful than Carlos and Asher in that moment, but I hadn't even looked at Jean-Pierre yet.

When I did, my breath caught in my throat.

His trousers were the black equivalent of Asher's, but with silver eyelets, and they were patent leather. They clung like a second skin to his slender thighs, and graced the curve of his hip as if poured on. I had never seen him in such snug trousers, and just how slender and graceful his legs looked encased in all that leather was astounding. It was more obvious in these trousers than when he had been covered in glitter. The shirt he wore was a deep emerald green, and had a sheen to it, so that it was never quite the same emerald colour, like when light plays off all the facets in the crystal and dazzles you with how many shades are trapped inside. It had the same billowing sleeves as Asher's, but the neckline was entirely different. Although wider than a t-shirt, it was much closer to his neck than Asher's. The main difference was that it hung in a long curve so low that the neckline stopped only a centimetre or so above where the trousers began, meaning the ruffled fold that hung from the neckline covered the very top of the lacing on the trousers. His skin looked like it had been carved from perfect white marble, and the chest the shirt revealed looked sculpted in a way I hadn't noticed when I had been blinded by the glitter. His eyes were rimmed in black like mine were, and it made the emerald colour of his irises shine the more brightly for it.

I almost felt weak at the knees just staring upon so much beauty. If I were the kind of woman who swooned, I most certainly would have. I managed not to fall over, but equally, I couldn't move towards them. It was as if I was paralysed in the face of such gorgeousness.

Jean-Pierre gave a low chuckle, a masculine sound that came from the knowledge that I found him desirable. Wicked humour sparkled in his eyes, and they held such vitality that for one glittering moment I forgot he died at the dawn, for he was so alive. Asher was grinning, but instead of his usual boyish grin, it was more sultry, more seductive, and seemed to suggest we could have a very good time indeed if I would but ask. Carlos' smile was that of the thawing frost, and there was a heat in his eyes that had certainly never been there before. I'd always thought Carlos was cold, but he was a man underneath his cloak of winter snow, and he was beautiful.

"I'm speechless," I finally managed to say, gazing at the trio, my heart mourning that I couldn't have them all.

"That look on your face," Jean-Pierre murmured, voice

lower and more purring than usual, "I would give anything to see that look on your face again. Desire. It is wondrous to be truly desired."

"Never mind her desiring us," Carlos said, "How about us desiring her. I have never seen anything so beautiful in my life, and it has been a long one."

Asher ruined the moment but saying coarsely, as was his way, "Sweet Jesus, I'd have you right here on the rocks, Nix, but I think we've got some ball to attend."

That made me laugh, warm and joyous, which released the tension the paralysing desire had created. "Oh Asher, you certainly have a way with words."

With that we proceeded down the stairs and into the city, where a sleek black limo picked us up to take us to The British Court.

11

We had guards all around us as we arrived near The Court in our very stretched limo. They were there to keep back the sheer press of people. A mob of plebeians with a generous smattering of reporters surged when we arrived, pressing the security guards to the side of the car. You'd think they'd have more guards than this. Blaze came bounding over in a barely there outfit of ripped denim shorts and what I can only describe as an open leather waistcoat. It was for the masses; you wouldn't mistake him for anything other than a Were. He shoved his way through the crowd, followed shortly by five or six other Weres, all of different flavours, but all physically imposing. With bared teeth and snarls, people backed off so the car could get through, but Weres were an attraction in themselves, and people just got crazier.

Eventually, the limo crawled round to the foot of the steps. Our uniformed chauffeur got out and opened the door. Jean-Pierre got out first, then Carlos, then Asher. He turned around and held out a hand for me, which I took, and got out the car. I was almost blinded by photographers. I thought that was because they knew who I was, but they evidently didn't. I was just a woman with The Hand until someone spotted my raven tattoo and screamed at the top of their voice "It's The Raven!" That I had a massive raven tattoo on my right shoulder was the one piece of information I'd let out about my appearance. The reporters descended like hungry sharks, and even the supernatural guards had a hard time keeping back the overwhelming press of bodies. One man got past, and took a blinding photo of my face. Jean-Pierre broke his wrist, and his camera.

"It doesn't matter," I said loudly enough that my voice carried to the nearest reporters, "The pictures won't develop anyway." I meant in terms of my glamour, but it wasn't until I was walking up the steps that I realised people might think I'd just threatened the life of every reporter there. I wasn't bothered enough by it to want to clarify.

Jean-Pierre took my arm, and Asher and Carlos fell into natural bodyguard positions on either side and slightly behind. I felt better away from the crush of bodies at the foot of the steps, but the flashbulbs were just as relentless. I didn't think the feeding frenzy could get any worse, but then the King himself appeared at the top of the stairs with his entourage of Robert DeBois, Juillet Silverfox, and Blair.

I walked up those steps fairly gracefully despite the heels, but I faltered a bit when I saw Nero, and in spite of myself, and all the past years of hurt, I found myself smiling. He had on the same pair of trousers as Jean-Pierre and Asher (I was sensing a theme) but in matte black. The turnover-top boots were shiny with polish, and had gold lacing up the sides. He had the same shirt on I'd seen when I'd first re-appeared at Court, but this time in gold not teal. He was also wearing and honest-to-god cape, black, with a dark gold lining. A tan hand appeared along with a gold shirt-sleeve from that cape, and extended towards me. As I reached the top, I put my hand in his. He used it to pull me towards him and pressed my body against the front of his, then bestowed upon me a fierce, crushing kiss that made my knees melt. I was glad he held me firmly by the waist or I'd have been back down all those stairs again, slightly less elegantly.

The next morning, on the front page of most of the papers, would be a picture of Nero embracing an unidentifiable woman, because, mysteriously, a trick of the light seemed to have shrouded the woman completely in darkness. The freakish thing was, it happened to every camera. Weird.

After that earth-shattering kiss, I was glowing. Literally. I looked down at my hands and there was a faint light pulsing beneath my skin. Baffled, I was escorted inside by the King and his six most trusted men; and woman.

We caused uproar when we walked into the Court complex. It wasn't the carnivorous attacking of the reporters outside; it was uproar of a different kind. Fear and respect reigned in these walls, and both made people scurry out of our way, bow as low as they could, comment on our astounding beauty, remark on the superiority of every facet of our beings. I thought they'd run out, but they never did. I hadn't walked through the Court with Nero before, so this was new to me, but the others brushed off the compliments with cold smiles and the barest of nods as if completely unimpressed. I couldn't do that cold rejection, so instead I stuck to what I was good at: being sultry and being scary. Most of the men we passed, and some of the women, looked at me in a predatory way, something between the desire for touch and the desire for food. Those I found handsome I gave a winning smile, those I found less so I gave them the empty smile of a sociopath that made more than one person shiver. I was glad to be on Nero's arm, because those lusty men had no claim to me as I was already claimed, but equally I wanted to be recognised as a power in my own right.

The scars helped with that.

People who saw my back gasped, one person even shrieked. When I turned to look at them and gave them that cold smile, they fled. Jean-Pierre laughed, and the sound was sinister to the ears of the frightened, and exciting to the ears of the aroused. The air was thick with fear and lust, it was almost like wading through honey, if honey could give you power over the people around you. You can always scare someone into doing something if they are truly afraid, and you can always use the promise of sex as a powerful persuasive device. Either worked for me, as both came easily. Before we were even at the end of the corridor, I was being addressed before the Judge Juror and Executioner. It was a sleight to them and praise to me, but they were all grown up enough to not take offense. Well, I wasn't sure about Blair, but he could just deal with it.

When we entered the Main Court I realised something was different, but it took my dazzled eyes a few moments to work out what it was. The throne at the end, Nero's throne, was mostly hidden by the longest banquet table I'd ever seen in my life. The silver throne I'd noticed the other day was next to it, and then a plain black one was on the other side. Apparently, the black one was for me. Nero told me that whatever colour I wore, he figured it would go with black, because I always wore black. I'd have argued if he hadn't been right. You can never go wrong with black. There were three more thrones next to mine, silver, gold, and black, for the Hand. The three on the other side of the mysterious silver one were red, purple, and dark brown. The mismatched thrones looked odd empty, but I'm sure when all the occupants were seated, each one would match their throne perfectly. Nero matched his gold and black throne with particular perfection today.

The outer ring of banquet tables were lavishly decorated with the colours of the House of the Court they belonged to. The platform round the edge was filled with more tables than usual for the most important members of each House. At the foot of the steps that led up to the outer platform were two more rows of banquet tables down the long sides of the Court floor. There was still floor beyond enough for a hundred people or more to dance on, even with the extra tables, which tells you how big the Main Court was.

There was applause, cheers, and shouts of 'Mother Dark save the King' as we walked along that long stretch of floor, almost like a catwalk, on display. The cry was their version of 'God save the Queen' because to them, their god was the original vampire, The Queen, also known as The Dark Mother.

When we were nearly at the foot of the steps that led up to the highest platform with the long table on it, a man appeared in front of us in the blink of an eye, and everyone dropped to the floor in a bow. I was a little slower in my dress, but I was down and bowing low. Even Nero was almost flattened to the floor, which made me wonder who the hell this man was.

When I risked a glance up, I realised he was the mysterious man in the equally mysterious silver throne, who Nero had told me not to look at when I had noticed him.

It was Nero who spoke first.

"My lord, and Maker, Decorus Mortuus, we thank you for gracing our Court with your presence. We are but your humble servants."

The man laughed, and it felt like velvet rubbing along my insides where no hand should touch. Dear God, that voice.

"Stand Nero, both child and old friend of mine. Stand Nero's Hand, His Judge, Juror, and Executioner. Stand, mighty warrior, Raven." The way he said my name made me shiver, in a good way.

It was only then that I looked up into the face of Decorus Mortuus, third member of The Council, The Queen's Beautiful Death.

12

And boy was he beautiful. The Queen's Beautiful Death was the first who was able to create the gorgeous vampires we're so used to seeing now. Before him, they'd been bloated, oozing things, bound by curses galore. The tale went that his first child, the first vampire he'd made, had been beautiful, and free of many of the curses that had plagued vampires for years, apart from the curse of the sun, of course. And so, he had mixed his blood with the other elders in a golden cup, occasionally thought to be the fountain of youth, from which they all drank. It beautified some of the council who were less so before, and it passed into their bloodline the beauty that Decorus Mortuus could bestow. Of course, not everyone's vampires were as beautiful as his; nothing could quite match true beauty.

I realised I had been staring for quite some time, and he'd been staring back. I came to myself with everyone's eyes on me, and considering it was a full Court and a ball, that was a lot of pairs of eyes. Feeling my staring had overstepped boundaries of propriety I lowered my head again and curtseyed. "A pleasure, my lord," I said, and when I raised my head, he was right in front of me.

"Enchanté. And really, the pleasure is all mine." If possible, he was even more beautiful up close. He had wavy black hair, glossy and sleek that looked thick enough to grab handfuls of it and luxuriate in the rich sensation of it falling through your fingers. His skin was a creamy white, delicate and perfect, without a single blemish. He had a pink, kissable mouth, with full lips balancing out nicely and softening the sharp line of his high and haughty cheekbones. His eyes were ringed in black, and the irises were pure silver. He was wearing the same poured on leather trousers as Nero, the patent version like Jean-Pierre's, that clung deliciously to his skin. He even had the same boots on. However, his shirt was not the same. It had the billowing sleeves that I'd come to find usual, but the neckline was entirely different. It was as if the wide neck of Nero's shirt had been gathered at the top to form an oval framing the pale flesh of a smooth sculpted chest, the ruffled edge hanging down to soften the oval outline. The neck was fastened together with a silver pin, which had a ruby bigger than a two pence coin nestled in the middle of it. I wanted to reach out and put my hand on that invitingly framed chest, the gap in the fabric just about big enough for me to lie my hand flat across his skin.

I didn't succumb to that desire, but I did shiver when he brought his lips to my hand, rolling his eyes up to stare at me as he did so. He smiled at the shiver, and I could see his perfect canine teeth, sharp and deadly, and exciting. He took my hand and placed it on Nero's arm. I was glad, because I craved to touch Decorus Mortuus in a way I wasn't used to. I huddled in against Nero's body, sliding my arm through his. I think the contact surprised him somewhat, but he didn't move away. Decorus Mortuus chuckled, then said low, and somehow seductively, "Let the festivities begin."

I turned to face Nero completely, almost hiding away from the Council member that I so badly wanted to touch, as if out of sight really could be out of mind. Nero was staring over my head at him, not glaring, but with something I couldn't quite comprehend flitting through his eyes, his arm slid round my back and hugged me tight, and I snuggled in against his chest, noticing for the first time how good he smelled. I don't know why, but Nero made me feel safe. Odd.

There was a gasp from behind me. I glanced over my shoulder to see the beautiful Council man with his eyes wide and his mouth a-gape.

"Such scars as I have never seen!" he exclaimed a little theatrically. I turned round so my back was pressed against Nero, immediately on the defensive. Where had my former confidence gone?

"They're an old wound, I forget they're there sometimes."

"How did you get them?"

"Excuse me for declining to regale the Court with gruesome tales but this is not a matter for open discussion, not even for you Monseiur Belle Mort."

His eyes flashed dangerously. "The last person who called me that died, Raven."

"Was that a threat or a statement?" I was good at threats; oddly, they made me feel at ease. Shows what a fuck up my life is.

"Merely the latter. If your scars are for private discussion only, we will have plenty of time over dinner." With that parting threat, he mounted a few of the stairs and spoke to the entire Court. "We are here to enjoy ourselves in the grand British Court, and so, enjoy ourselves we shall."

Everyone applauded, though I had no idea why. Perhaps it was a formality. I didn't clap, because my arms were preoccupied being wrapped around Nero's waist. Decorus

Mortuus unnerved me, and I think I just wanted to be held.

I looked up at Nero to find him staring at me. Again, his eyes were unintelligible, as if fathoms of ocean separated me from his deep thoughts. When he spoke, he finally said, "May I have this first dance, Raven?"

"You may, Nero." I caught myself smiling. What the hell?

As if by magic a song came on, floating across the air via speakers I hadn't known existed. I instantly recognised the opening to the song, and stared at Nero in shock. Love Over Gold, by Dire Straits, was playing. I had mentioned loving it to Asher perhaps a year ago. Nero smiled, and by the time Mark Knopfler started singing, we were in the middle of the Court floor. We danced, even I have to say, beautifully. I always had been able to dance, even before all the mercenary training. It was no dance in particular, just movements that felt natural. I didn't realise until half way through that we were the only two dancing, and that everyone was standing around watching with something akin to amazement on their faces. I sought out the precious few people I knew, and found the Hand gathered at the foot of the steps, staring. Once I knew where they were, my gaze kept coming back to them, lost among a sea of people.

The song finished, and Nero pulled me back into the embrace of his arms. I kissed him on the neck, forgetting how sensual that is for a vampire, and he gave a small moan, muffled as he buried his head in the few strands of hair that fell over my neck. I smiled, and we walked off the dance floor to thunderous applause. Apparently, the King always had to open the dancing. He knew if he'd asked me to dance with him while everyone watched, I would have said no, but he hadn't. He'd just asked me to dance, and I was glad he had.

At least, until my eyes strayed to Decorus Mortuus, still

atop the stairs. He had hostility glinting in those silver eyes, and I felt my blood run cold.

"Is something the matter?" Nero murmured as the Courtiers poured onto the dance floor, and we reposed in some vacant chairs.

"Is he really your maker?" I asked, to avoid saying what I wanted.

After a long pause, Nero said, "yes." The word was clipped, and almost harsh.

"You don't like him much?"

"He can hear."

"Let him."

Nero sighed, and tried not to smile. "He insisted you be here, so he could meet you, which is why your refusal was so vexing to me."

"Vexing, am I?"

"Immensely."

"Good to know."

We stared out at the dancing couples. Everyone was beautiful, the women all swirling skirt, the men all leading man.

I glanced at Nero, and realised what was wrong with this picture. Infatuation. I remembered then, I remembered the night I thought I'd forgotten. I remembered falling into his eyes, and forcing myself to forget some of what I had seen there.

I also realised that I had let him roll me. I'd wanted to be rolled by him, completely, but I hadn't realised the consequences. No, I hadn't realised that at all.

Completely unnerved, I excused myself, and told Nero to dance with Juillet. He said something like she had never danced at a ball and wasn't likely to start, but I was weaving my way through people to try and find Asher. After much searching, I found him leaning against a wall in discussion with an attractive woman. I hated to interrupt, but I was too selfish not to.

"Asher, I'm so sorry to intrude, but there's a slight emergency."

"Emergency?"

"Yes." I looked at him, and I think he got what I meant.

"Of course. Just before you rush off, this is my sister, Petra. Petra, this is —"

"The Raven. I know. It's wonderful to meet you, but right now, I think Asher should shut up and you should go and sort out your emergency."

"You are so his sister."

"'Fraid so," she said with a grin.

"Come on," Asher said, and we walked away. I gave Petra a little wave over my shoulder. She smiled and waved back, then went off to talk to someone else.

"Have you had a revelation with regards to the memory blank?" Asher asked hurriedly as we rushed through the crowd to try and get to somewhere private.

"Yes. Completely. None of it pretty."

"Really?" He asked with a leer in his voice. "Not even th—"

"Shut it!"

He obeyed. We finally made it into a quiet room. I groaned when I realised where I was. It was Nero's Hall of Horrors. Pinned to the wall were body parts, bones, and personal items of vanquished foes. Some of the body parts were left to rot, but the special ones were preserved by magic. There was a heart impaled on the wall with a sword that I knew for a fact had been bleeding down the wall for the last six centuries.

"Nice room choice."

"I was just thinking that. Maybe we could get something like this at the Concrete Palace."

Asher smiled, and just waited for me to get to the point.

"I let him roll me," I said suddenly.

"Shit. What?"

"I let him. I didn't realise the side effects it would have."

"What side effects?"

"Affection. Trust. Loyalty almost. I know I loved him when I was sixteen an foolish, but I'm twenty-one and a murderer now, my heart melts for no man."

He didn't give me the expected reply of 'not even for me' but instead said, "Shit," again. "You've seen who he's descended from. Beauty is an attractive thing, and Nero carries in him, as one of the first Made by the Third Council Member, some of the beauty that makes him so attractive. Jesus, Nix."

I glared at him for his slip-up. I didn't want my real name said anywhere near the Main Court.

"He wants to talk to me over 'dinner' about my scars."

"Who does?"

"Councillor Beautiful."

He frowned, then said, "I can't follow your train of thought. It's a crazy train."

"Apologies, my mind is screwed up." I paused, debating. Finally, I agreed to confess to Asher. "I don't love Nero, Asher. Not really. It's almost like… like I've had him now and that's that, curiosity satisfied. But because of being rolled by him, I feel safe with him, I just don't want to be his lover. I want… I'm getting very intense cravings for Decorus Mortuus," I said very quietly, in the hope no-one else would hear.

"You sure know how to pick them," he said, but wearily, not teasing.

"Am I a bad person?"

"You kill people for a living."

"Fair point."

"No, you're not."

I just looked at him. "Maybe it would be nice to hear that when I'll believe it. Let's just get back out there; I'll deal with the big man at dinner." I felt my mouth make a small 'o' of horror as I realised something. "I'm going to have to sit next to Nero all evening and pretend. And I'll have to talk over him all the time."

"Nero's not so bad, darling." He even managed to look sympathetic.

"You're his lackey, and you didn't let him roll you and therefore completely fuck yourself over."

"Touché."

We glanced at each other, sighed, then headed back out into the throng of people.

13

The bell tolled. Not for 'whom' but for dinner. Dinner with vampires is… interesting. It involves a lot of trays of heated up blood, and the occasional live donor, donating directly into the glass – it was too posh a do to have it go from vein from mouth. I was glad Asher was seated two away from me, because a lot of the people at the head table were vamps, and everyone hates to be the only one eating in a crowd.

Dessert was brought to the main table. For the dead ones among us, it consisted of a sweetened blood, like dessert wine, which must be strange. I found out, moments later, that it was indeed very odd, as several vamps couldn't stomach it, and spat it back out; Jean-Pierre included. Thank god I was wearing a red dress already.

"Nice one," I said sarcastically. "If you want I can go and mix you up a blood cocktail."

Decorus Mortuus leaned in so he could see me around Nero. "And why would you know how to do that?"

"I do bar work, occasionally."

He laughed. "Really? Where?"

"I can't tell you that I'm afraid."

"Why, would you be inundated with customers?" He smiled at his own wit, as if expecting me to agree.

"No, because men with guns and all sorts of weaponry would come and try to gun me down. I'd hate to ruin a perfectly good bar." He wasn't deterred.

"What a delightful life you lead, Raven."

"It gets me by my lord."

"Please, call me Mort."

Mort; one of the conjugations of the French for 'to die'. I smiled. "I thought you were French, but you've had years to hide your accent so I wasn't quite sure. It's a clever abbreviation, Mort."

"Why thank you." He gave a wide smile that showed his perfect canines. I had to look away, because those teeth, so dangerous, didn't put me off. He was inviting in his very essence, and that was what worried me.

"If I go and make Jean-Pierre a blood cocktail, would you like one too Mort, Nero," I turned, "Carlos?"

"You're not a servant, Raven. Let one of the staff make it," Nero said.

"They'd make it wrong. I make a mean blood cocktail, I've got good at it." I gave him a winning smile, and he agreed to let me go. No-one complained that I might poison the most powerful vampires in the room.

"Do you think other people might want one?"

"Probably. If Jean-Pierre comes with you he can help you make a batch."

"Good idea, sire." Again I found myself smiling at Nero, but couldn't seem to stop myself. Inside I was kicking myself repeatedly. I was also having great difficulty not smiling at Mort. Jean-Pierre and I got up, and left the Court in the direction of the massive kitchen.

I let out a breath I didn't realise I'd been holding as we

got further away from the Main Court. Jean-Pierre didn't comment, and instead said, "It's nice of you to give me an excuse to leave," he said. "Give me people to beat up and I'm happy as a cat with cream, but ask me to attend a social event on that scale and I get bored by the tedious monotony of Uninteresting People."

"Funny that, I'm almost exactly the same." I moved on to more pressing matters. "What do you reckon, Blood Bellinis?"

"Isn't that made with blood-orange juice?"

"Not the way I make it."

Half an hour later I was still in the kitchen. The first batch of Blood Bellinis had gone out and been so popular they'd asked me to make more. The mortals started to complain that the vamps were getting all the champagne, so I stared making Bloody Hells; you don't want to know what's in them.

I found I was shaking, and it just kept getting worse. Champagne did not help steady me. I had no idea what was wrong. "Phoebe, sit down, you're paler than me," Jean-Pierre said, a frown creasing the perfect sculpture of his face.

"I'm fine. I just… I just…" and I burst into tears. Jean-Pierre held me, and rocked me while I cried.

"Shush cherie, it'll be alright."

I wiped my eyes, and was thankful for waterproof make-up – with that much eyeliner it would have been a disaster.

"I'll give you the condensed version: I slept with Nero, I let him roll me, he now makes me feel safe, but I don't love him. I'm ridiculously attracted to Mort."

"Oh mon petite chou," he sighed stroking my hair, "how do you get yourself into these situations?"

"Wish I fucking knew," I replied, feeling more myself now I was cursing rather than crying.

I started drinking more after that. Kir Royale was a particular favourite, so I made myself a bowl of it and just kept on going. Maybe I could forget everything again if I just kept on drinking. That's always a bad idea, but when you feel like shit, bad ideas seem like good ideas. I stayed in the kitchen, and didn't head back out to the ballroom. The kitchen staff had been giving me a wide berth since the crying session, which most of them heard, if not actually saw.

Apparently, my company was being missed, as Jean-Pierre, who had taken the last lot of drinks out, returned with Mort in tow. My heart ached at the sight of his perfection.

"Madame la Ravenne, you are dearly missed at the top table. The tedium is unrelieved without you there." I was certain I had never been called Madame la Ravenne before, but it sounded strangely familiar. "You never did tell me about your scars."

"I suppose I didn't did I." I sighed, tired of the whole thing. "Shall we head back out and find ourselves a private corner and I will tell you all."

Mort's eyes burned into mine. "I would love nothing more."

Jean-Pierre shot me a warning look as he held the door for Mort and me to pass through. Mr High Council offered me his arm, and as soon as I took it butterflies did cartwheels in my stomach, and my heart sped up.

Nero asked me to dance with him again, but Mort saved me the trouble of politely declining, as he said he had detained my attentions for a while. It was a relief, but then again, being so close to Mort probably wasn't a good idea right now either.

We sat down in the corner of the room in sumptuous chairs. There was a couple nearby but Mort shot them a less than pleasant glare so they scuttled off to leave us be. We had our own little bubble to ourselves – or our own disaster zone.

"So Raven, how many scars do you have in total?"

I had to think about that. "Seven."

"Where?"

"Right calf, left knee, right forearm, left elbow, left shoulder, left side of my neck, my back."

"That's quite a collection."

"Comes with the job," I said shrugging.

"Was your back a… work related injury?" he said it with a small smile, but those silver eyes were serious.

"I guess you could call it that. It was a raid on a werewolf pack who were trafficking their youngest members for sexual purposes."

His eyebrows – perfect arches – rose sharply. "I knew the wolves were less refined than a lot of the other shifters, but I wasn't aware Asher could let his kingdom slip so."

"He didn't, he employed us. If the Hammerhead Sharks dealt with the issue, it would mean there could be no pack feuds afterwards. Only if Asher himself had personally dealt with the clan would there have been no repercussions in the werewolf community."

"Wiser than I guessed."

"Indeed."

We sat there in amicable silence for the span of a minute or two. Apart from having to resist the urge to kiss him, I was very comfortable sitting there in the corner with him, surveying the scene. After a while, he spoke again.

"So how exactly did it happen, the injury I mean."

I sighed; this was a frequently told story. "The fight got ugly when it became apparent the pack leader had brought in rogues to supplement his numbers, expecting an attack from us. I was in a fight. There were three werewolves in front of me, which is an overwhelming number even for me, so I had no chance to defend myself against the one behind me. He was a powerful shifter, with the ability to make his paws larger than usual in his half-man form, which is why the scars are so wide and deep. I was in hospital for a few weeks while it was treated with silver and magic. Thankfully, I don't turn furry once a month, so it must have worked."

"I'm sorry for your suffering Raven."

I gave him a hollow smile. "It's Phoebe."

"Phoebe. I've always liked that name." He didn't sound shocked that I'd told him my real name, and it was nice, nice to just be normal with someone. Though, I guess The Raven and Decorus Mortuus sitting down for a chat about a werewolf attack isn't that normal, but for me that was about as normal as it got.

"You know Mort—" but I didn't finish my sentence, as my work phone rang.

"Hello?" I said.

"Raven."

"Oh hey Cannibal. What's up?"

"Can you come into work? You've just had a load of jobs pile in all at once." I sighed, and shot a mournful glance at Mort which I hoped he didn't see. I didn't want to leave him.

"Who calls himself Cannibal?" he asked softly.

"Are you with someone Rave?" Cannibal asked.

"Yeah, I'm at Nero's ball."

"Oh sorry to call you. Who are you with, it's not Nero."

"No, it's not, it's… um. I'll talk to you later. I can be there within half an hour if you want me to keep the dress on. If not it'll be an hour or so."

"Go home, get changed. Do you need to sleep?"

"No, I'll be fine."

"Okay, well… see you soon I guess."

"Yeah."

"Raven?"

"Yes?"

"Are you okay?"

"I'll see you later Cannibal." I hung up.

"Work, I presume," Mort said. I nodded. "No rest for the wicked."

I said my farewells to Beautiful Death, and walked off in the direction of the doors. Asher detained me. "Are you leaving?"

"Cannibal called and asked if I could come in."

"Doesn't he understand you need to sleep?"

"He asked me if I needed to, I said no. He trusts me to know if I need to sleep or not."

"Fair enough, but I'm not letting you go home by yourself. Blaze will drive you."

I was too tired and dejected to even argue. I glanced behind me as I left the Main Court, but I couldn't see Decorus Mortuus anywhere.

I went to work exhausted, but did a couple of the easier jobs before admitting I needed to sleep. By this point, I was thoroughly depressed. When I went home, there was a werewolf with a shock of red and orange hair asleep on my sofa. He was wearing my Nightmare Before Christmas pyjama bottoms, Jack's face smiling manically from fifty faces. They were long on me, and ankle-swingers on him. I was so tired I didn't remember offering them to him, but I must have. I vaguely recalled him saying something about getting donor blood on his clothes.

The kitchen was my first port of call, and by the time I had boiled the kettle for tea, Blaze was awake. With sofa-ruffled hair, he yawned a hello. He looked very cute all sleepy, which isn't something I thought I'd say at a man going on two centuries. Then again, he looked twenty-two. Ah immortality.

"You want a cup?" I asked.

"I'd love one." His voice was gruff with sleep, and despite the long kip, he still looked shattered.

"Do you need feeding too?"

"No it's alright I don't want to be an inconvenience."

I smiled. "Blaze, you looked out for me at the Court for all those years, you will never be an inconvenience. I have bacon and eggs I think, I might even have beans if your lucky."

He grinned, "Anything you got sounds good."

We kept up small talk while I cooked him breakfast. He mostly whined about long hours he had to keep, and how little sleep he got.

"Ask Asher for a break."

"Are you kidding? I can't just go up to my king and complain he's working me too hard."

"Fair point. I just think of him as a pain in the arse rather than a King. I forget it a lot."

Blaze grinned, and wolfed down (no pun intended) the food I put in front of him. He was such a nice guy; it made me regret my years of Court aversion.

"You can stay a while longer, get some more sleep, and I'll take you back later if you like. I'll tell Asher you were chauffeuring me around as I was so tired. He can't blame you for something he started."

"It's a tempting offer, Phoebe, but I should get back. There's always a hell of a lot to do after a ball." I was a little disappointed, I enjoyed his company.

"Oh, okay then. I'll take you home." I gave him some of Guillaume's clothes to wear. To be fair, he just left them at my house and never wore them, I doubt he'd miss them much.

After I'd dropped Blaze off at the Sunken City, I phoned Carter, a tiger in the employ of Bastien. Actually, he was the very same weretiger who had asked me to sort out Bane. I called in my favour with them, and asked them to help out with the clean-up at The British Court. I think Carter was relieved to finally know the nature of the favour he owed, and that it wasn't anything that would get them killed. They were instructed to tell the staff clearing up that Lord Batsien had sent them. I left a message with Bastien to tell him to confirm this if anyone asked.

My good deed done for the day, I went home to pass out.

A dream. An argument.

"You of all people should know I am not the kind of woman who, after but an hour's interview, can be presumed wooed and won!" I was yelling at a man who was obscured by shadows in the corner of the room, moonlight from the window hitting only his gleaming, silver-buckled shoes. I could feel boning of a particularly snug corset pressing against me, and hear a full skirt of many layers rustling along the floor as I paced angrily over 18th century carpet.

"It takes more than that!" I continued at my unreasonable volume of outrage. "To be so presumptuous shows a hateful conceitedness which I thought had been got rid of, and which, if reappearing, I wish not to be reacquainted with. You may consider yourself henceforth dismissed from this room and all further interviews if you intend on continuing in this manner."

The man moved forward from the darkness, and my betraying breath caught at the sight of that perfect visage, cheekbones and jawline thrown into sharp relief by the harsh moonlight.

"Please leave." My dream-self sounded less certain than when it had been shouting indignantly.

I blinked and he was directly in front of me, backlit by the silver light. "I will leave now, my lady, and return only upon your wishing me back. You will always be able to find me." He paused and drew a hand gently across my cheek, so lightly, so softly, the sensation of which lingered after the hand was removed. "Ma cherie..." he breathed mournfully. There was another eye-blink, a slight breeze, and he was gone. To my surprise, but apparently not to the surprise of my dream self, one crystalline tear tracked down my face to land with a tiny sound upon my gold satin bodice.

I woke up, disturbed, but I was still exceptionally tired, so I tried to fall back asleep. Eventually, it worked.

I kept dreaming. Every time I closed my eyes I would envision something set in a time long since gone, with the cast of characters that surrounded me daily. Even Lu and Guillaume were in them, but most of the time all I was focused on was where Mort was lurking, apprehensive of the moment when he would appear.

Another troubling aspect of these dreams was the effect they had on me. I found myself thinking in an archaic fashion, and made a mental note not to talk like that when I went back into work.

It was the afternoon when I next went back into work. I felt a little revived after a few hours' sleep.

Hammer was in when I got back, and the look on his face made me wish I'd stayed at home all day. I didn't have to, but the truth was, I didn't want to sit around with only myself for company, thinking about pale skin and silver eyes.

"So. How was the ball?" Hammer managed to squeeze

out through clenched teeth. He was trying to keep his voice neutral, but he was failing.

"Fine. I sat next to Nero for the dinner, disappeared to the kitchen to make blood cocktails, went back out, and Cannibal called."

They exchanged a glance.

"Spit it out. Are you pissed off with me because I was on Nero's arm?"

Cannibal said no. Hammer said, "That, and other things."

"What's that supposed to mean?"

"Who did you meet at the ball?" Hammer continued, ignoring my question.

"Loads of people. Of course I know the Master's Hand, and I met Asher's sister, and I was sitting at the head table with Robert DeBois, Juillet Siverfox and Blair. They're all fairly high profile people. Nero's a given."

"What about the two Council members that were there?"

Well, shit. I knew he wouldn't like that.

"There was only one. Decorus Mortuus."

There was silence to that comment. They looked at each other, then me, and then back again.

"Two Council members were definitely there. Master Death was also present." Cannibal sounded concerned.

"Well, Mort had a throne next to Nero. I didn't see any other Council member." They exchanged a glance again. "That's starting to piss me off."

"Raven, are you aware that no mortal has met any member of the Council and not gone under their power in some way."

"I wasn't but I am now."

"You don't seem concerned."

"That's because I know I haven't come under Mort's sway

in any way," I lied, panicking deep inside. "Jean-Pierre was with me most."

"Do you know whose line Jean-Pierre is?"

I shook my head. "I know his maker, but not the Council member they're descended from. May I ask, why all the questions?"

"You may. Decorus Mortuus is one of the oldest Council members. He's known for being very persuasive. This," he said, flinging the morning's newspaper across the weapons table at me, "isn't something I would have thought you'd have done."

"You don't even know that's me," I said defiantly, indicating the picture on the front page of Nero and his mystery woman, obscured by freak darkness.

"I don't have to. No other woman I know, who was on Nero's arm that night, who was at that ball, can produce a glamour that obscures any records of physical appearance. You try and tell me that's not you."

"Are you angry I didn't shove the King down the steps when he grabbed me in front of a crowd of reporters, or are you angry that I had a chat with Decorus Mortuus? You really think I wouldn't notice the Tin Man skulking around like some bad-tempered shadow."

"I wanted to make sure you were safe!" he yelled.

"No you didn't! If you did you'd have sent Belle. Tin Man doesn't give a shit about anyone!"

"At least he'd tell me the truth and not lie to cover your ass! I know you danced with the King! I know you spent a long time with Decorus Mortuus all cosy in your corner!"

"You're not my father Hammer," I growled out.

"If I were I'd be ashamed of that!" he yelled, his anger bursting forth in a scalding tidal wave.

"You have no right to be!" I yelled back. "In case you don't remember, my birth father abandoned me and my adopted

142

one I shot in the head! I've never had, and never needed, any kind of paternal concern, so I certainly don't need it from you."

"Yes you do, because how you behaved at that ball was a betrayal to the very reason we started doing this!"

I took two deep breaths, and then thought, to hell with it. "You know what Hammer? I had a nice time at the ball, I plan on reacquainting myself with the people I lost because of Nero, so fuck you very much."

With that parting shot, I stormed out, ignoring Cannibal's shouted pleas for me to come back, with the empty promise that Hammer would be reasonable.

I turned my work phone off. Let the jobs pile up, or let them go to the others. That should cheer them up, as what do mercenaries work for if not money? I was happy not to see any of them for a while. The only pang of guilt I felt was when I realised I was meant to be babysitting Coal's children the following night so she could do some night work. She didn't phone and intrude; she just left it.

I held onto my anger, because if I wasn't supremely pissed off, I'd be crying my eyes out. I was so angry because Hammer hit too close to home. I knew Nero had rolled me, and I suspected Mort had done something, which scared me. Truthfully, Hammer was my father figure. I'd spent hours of my life torturing myself over the fact that I'd been abandoned, and wondering how things would have been if I'd grown up in a normal family. With his accusations he brought back the memories of killing my adopted parents at the age of thirteen, firing bullets into their heads until you couldn't recognise them. I hadn't thought what that would mean for Jake. He'd gone into a home, and I'd got Lucille. It didn't seem fair.

Speaking of Lucille, I avoided her like the plague. I went out at night, driving my bike aimlessly until the dawn rose to be certain I wouldn't see her. She left me notes, but I never responded. I just wanted nothing to do with the Sharks or the vamps for a while.

The third night I went out riding my bike, I didn't come home.

14

Everything was dark. My head really hurt, and I had a gap where my memory should be. Again.

But this time I didn't come round in a four-poster bed with a beautiful man next to me. Instead, I was in a tiny room, in darkness, with the only light coming from under the door. The light was the harsh, white kind that I expected would burn my eyes when I got out of this damn room. If I got out of this damn room. I felt grimy floor against my face, so I tried to sit up. I got just over half way, when my movement was restricted by a chain around my throat. From the way it was tugging, it felt like it was attached low on the wall. I moved my hands to touch it but they were manacled as well. I had a certain amount of movement, but not enough. This was bad.

I slumped down enough to lean against the wall, without pulling on the chain, but it bent my spine painfully. Panic clawed its way up my throat as I realised that I was not only chained, but I was also unarmed. I don't now why I had expected someone would chain me up and leave me with my weaponry, but to be without the familiar weight of guns and knives was unnatural to me, and shook me more than waking up in a dark room did. The last time I'd been unarmed was probably in a hospital bed. Sleeping doesn't count because I even have a gun holster attached to the headboard of the bed, and a knife sheath on the bedside table.

I resisted the rising panic, because I knew if I opened my mouth, I would scream; and I wouldn't stop. My mind couldn't think clearly, and that was definitely a problem.

After forcibly slowing my breathing, I calmed a little. When I could think, the first thing I did was wonder where the hell I was, and where my weapons and bike were. They were more precious to me than my brother. No, really. Considering last time I'd seen Jake, he'd stabbed me, that wasn't all that surprising; what can I say, he doesn't see killing his 'parents' as me doing him a favour. I do.

Blind in the darkness, I tried to figure out what state I was in. I realised that where the chains and manacles were attached, I couldn't feel anything except when they tugged, which was why I hadn't noticed they were on immediately. They must have had some sort of numbing agent on them, which was bad, because it meant they were manacles of the worst kind. They were the ones Jade used on her worst enemies, the kind that had spikes on the inside that speared your skin. Maybe they were hoping I'd do myself some damage, and start screaming when the pain kicked in later. Or maybe they were normal manacles and I was numb from lying on my arms. Yeah, and pigs can fly.

I subdued the panic yet again, and made myself angry with the people who'd done this to me. Anger was easier. I frowned, and there was a sharp pain in my head. Something thick and warm trickled into my eye. I lowered my head to my knee and wiped the blood off because I couldn't get my hands up. I evidently had a head wound, and now I had frowned, and it had started bleeding, it'd be a bitch to stop. I tried to stretch my legs out, but found my ankles were chained as well. I felt my mind go still and cold, the mind-set I was in when I killed people, as I decided that whoever had chained me here was going to pay dearly.

As I wiped my eye on my jeans again, I heard a snuffling sound, and the light was blocked in bars as something moved along the foot of the door. That *something* growled, "Fresh blood," then there was the sound of a lock turning. And then there was light, blinding, burning light.

"She's awake!" someone yelled. I couldn't see anything because my eyes were refusing to adjust. When they did, the guy had moved enough into the room to be mostly a silhouette; a silhouette that filled the doorway. I pressed myself against the wall and glared. There was a chuckle, then a switch was flicked, and a crappy, flickering electric light came on.

I instantly knew who this man was. More precisely, I knew he was a werewolf, and that his name was Blake, and that his brother and been nicknamed Ritson because their eldest brother looked exactly like Blake Ritson the actor, but didn't hold with nicknames. What Ritson's real name was, I'd never heard. I knew that, three years ago, Blake and Ritson had been minor players in a werewolf sex trafficking plot, which I'd busted in on. I knew I'd killed over half the pack.

But most of all, I knew that the head of the clan that had been trafficking Weres for sex was the bastard who had scarred my back. The dead bastard. I was sensing a theme.

"Long time no see. Still handsome as ever," I spat at him, and he laughed. His face was so square the mind almost thought it was wider than it was long. He had an army crew cut, and some lovely knife wounds on the side of his head that had been a parting gift from me. He also had very long canine teeth, thick and yellow, and amber wolf eyes with an unnatural piercing yellow at the centre, and was a lot bulkier than the last time I'd seen him. His hands were claws with long yellowing talons. I'd have said he was in half and half form, but I knew a stuck shifter when I saw one. "Spent too much time running around wolfie-boy? Can't fully change back now can you?"

All humour faded from Blake's eyes. He leant out the door and yelled again. "Why didn't we gag this bitch?!"

It was my turn to laugh. Despite being a little bit more butch and even more ugly, the same things still pushed his buttons. How well you could Change was a point of pride to a shifter, and the better ones could shift at a moment's notice. Blake was obviously a terrible shifter, and I expected he'd be a lackey for life.

"As lovely as it is to see you again, can I ask what the hell you want with me?" I said it with a sweet smile on my face. Something flared in his yellow eyes.

"Sure you can, Raven, but I'm not going to answer." He gave me a wide grin, which was truly hellish with those teeth, and crossed his arms over his broad chest. He couldn't quite cross them properly because of all the muscle. He tried to stick with it for a few moments, but it was evidently uncomfortable, so his arms dropped to his sides again, and he leant sullenly against the doorframe.

"You and Ritson were such weedy little things last time I saw you. Now you just look ridiculous. Where is Ritson by the way, we might as well make this happy reunion complete." Blake moved to one side, and Ritson was standing behind him, no wolf eyes, no claws, and weedy as ever. But he wasn't the same. His eyes were strangely empty, his expression blank as a wandering wolf. I realised then why Blake had bulked up so much: Ritson was the wolf, and Blake was his muscly trainer. Ritson actually had a leash on him. As he slowly crawled, on all fours, into the room, someone appeared behind him holding the other end of the leash.

She was at least six foot seven, and as butch as they come. She had long, blonde hair, which did nothing to soften the harsh, fatless lines of muscle. I could see just how muscly she was because she was completely naked. A lot of shifters go around naked because any clothes you wear get ruined when you shift, but the Weres were less for that than a lot of the other shifting clans. I was betting anything she was to be part of my punishment, or whatever the hell this was, and was naked in preparation for a shift. That was bad news for me. I've got nothing against them (in general) but I did not want to be furry once a month.

My attention was brought back to Ritson when he started licking the blood off my forehead. A low rumble started up in his chest, like a great purring cat. He sounded like he should shift into something other than a wolf, which I knew he did not.

"Heel!" a high, feminine voice said, the kind that pierces your skull. Ritson, a big wolfish grin on his face, scuttled back to the naked woman, and sat at her feet. She patted his head like he was a pet, and he nuzzled her hand. "You're going to pay for what you did to Jeremy," she said menacingly in my direction.

My first thought came out as words. "Who the fuck is Jeremy?" Bad choice.

"Oh like you don't know you little bitch!" she shrieked. With jerky, furious movements, she handed the leash to Blake and stalked in, like a wolf hunting prey, not as graceful as any of the cat family lycanthropes I'd met, but not human all the same. Humans, not even catwalk models, could stalk like that. She took two strides and was right next to me. With a crushing blow she pounded her fist into the side of my head, knocking the other side into the wall. There was a blinding light, stars danced across my vision, and more blood flowed down into my eyes. I realised my head was numb from the shock, so something must be hurt badly. More blood rained down my face as she made little slices with her nails. They were shallow, but head wounds bleed a hell of a lot. Ritson whined and made an effort to get to me, but Blake had his beefy-clawed hand around the collar, and there was no way Ritson was getting free.

She'd crouched in front of me, and was so close now I thought she was going to tear into my face with her teeth. She was stupid, and obviously very angry to be that stupid. I tensed, but she didn't have enough time to move away. I head-butted her in the face and enjoyed the cracking sound as her nose broke. "Back off bitch!"

"You whore! You filthy vile little cow!" She started yelling all sorts of insults at me and, although she had backed off when I'd hurt her, she was advancing again. Blake grabbed her, trapping her arms by the side of her body. She struggled, and he tried to calm her down by saying 'easy, Selma' over and over, but he'd never been that bright. He'd let go of Ritson.

He ran at me like a famished thing, while the blonde fought with Blake and yelled accusations that he thought that I, chained up, was more dangerous to her than she was to me, an insult to a shifter any way you look at it. Blake evidently thought I'd best her because he kept his death grip on her.

When Ritson reached me he lapped at the blood on my face as if he were starving. His tongue was normal, human, but he was rough and forceful, and after the first few licks began to force his tongue into the cuts, widening them, to get more blood. I used my knee to manoeuvre him away from my face, and he complied. His eyes were yellow, yellower than Blake's, a piercing icy colour. Yellow was normally warm, but somehow his eyes seemed cold. Dead. Glazed.

"Ritson!" I hissed in his face, and nudged him in his hollow cheek with my knee. Warmth filled those eyes, shortly followed by fear. He screamed, and backed away from me on all fours. He froze when he hit the blonde's legs, looked up her no-longer-struggling body, and screamed again. His head swung from me to her, and eventually he noticed his brother. He fell still when he saw him.

"Blake?" There was a trembling to his voice. "Blake why do you look like that? Why do I have a leash? I thought The Raven said she was going to leave us alone, and what's Selma doing? What's happening Blake?" Ritson was every part the petrified younger brother; he wasn't an animal anymore.

Wide-eyed, his brother replied. "You haven't spoken in three years Ritson." His voice was a low rumble, and I realised that he too, was afraid, but not of me.

"What? I've always been able to *speak* Blake. I'm not an animal."

I scoffed at that, and three stunned wolves turned to face me. I felt some explanation was in order. "They put you on a leash, Ritson. Your brother's been dragging you round like a pet."

"I'll never take you at your word," Ritson said, shaking his head, eyes going wide with fear. He seemed confused by how long his hair was, a shaggy dirty mess around his face. He was looking at me with such fear that I had to, *had* to, act on it. I lowered my head, rolled my eyes up to look at him, and smiled.

He shrieked, got up, and ran away. Selma, wicked bitch of the West, stalked over. The blood was still dripping down my face. She wiped some up with her finger and then licked it. Her face changed as she tasted the blood. "What the fuck are you?" That was a question I'd never been able to answer.

I leant in, and whispered. "A trained killer who is going to wipe the floor with you, you little bitch."

She punched me again, in the stomach this time. I guess I had that one coming, but I got the last laugh, because I vomited blood onto her face. It got in her hair, streaking the blond with red. Her face was a bloody mask of shock. I enjoyed it for a moment, before the world swam in front of me and grey streamers went across my vision. She slapped me so hard it stung, and I was betting I had a red imprint of her hand on my face. "You pass out, and I'll let them eat you."

"Don't you want to punish me for… what's he called?"

"Jeremy." She hissed.

"Yeah. Him. You won't let them eat me because you want me to suffer, not to die."

She didn't answer, or maybe she did, but I didn't know because I promptly passed out.

The next time I woke up I was in pain. A lot of pain. The lights were on, and I looked at myself for the first time since I'd been holed up in this poky room. The reason I had passed out had been blood loss. I had lost so much blood because my arms were opened from wrist to elbow. I could see bone glinting through the wet, red sheen. My vision swam, and I felt sick. I'd seen worse, hell, I'd inflicted worse, but the sudden knowledge that my arms had been sliced to the bone and that only now could I feel them made my stomach churn in unpleasant ways. I finally looked at my wrists. I had been right about the manacles. They had holes in them, in which sat four-inch spikes. The end was flat, so the torturer could push them in, but the end that went against the skin was frightfully sharp. I could feel them in my flesh, and I swallowed to try and stop myself from being sick. Overthinking things sometimes made me feel more ill than the reality of seeing something. Swallowing, however, was a bad idea. I could feel the spikes digging into my neck, buried too far in. It should have killed me. Add all the blood loss and the beating, and it was nothing short of miraculous that I wasn't a corpse on the floor, werewolf food. I could feel bruises beginning to form on my face and stomach. The scratches had stopped bleeding though, even the ones that Ritson had widened with his tongue.

I moved my head and gave a grunt of pain as the choke collar bit into more of my flesh.

They had left me without a guard, but Selma, hearing me, sidled round the corner, still naked, but clothed in dry blood. I knew it was my blood on her face, in her hair, and at least some of it under her nails was mine too, but the blood that had dripped over her chest and run down her pale body, trailing over the swell of her thighs, new paths started on her calves to collect in pools on her feet, and making her arms slick from fingertip to elbow, was not my blood. At least, I didn't think it was. Blake appeared a moment later, dragging what I thought was a dead Ritson on the end of the leash. He slid along the floor in a pool of his own blood. A second later, I saw why there was so much blood. He'd been gutted, and his intestines were trailing father behind him than I cared to look in a long, glistening loop, the grime from the floor soiling a part of him that was never meant to see the air. Grey fogged my vision again, but from nausea, not blood loss.

It took me a few moments to realise why I couldn't stomach all the blood and guts as much as I usually could. I was finding it difficult to concentrate, to retreat into my mind enough to find that cold, dark place where I was truly a sociopath. Currently, I was thinking with the emotional part of my brain, when I really needed to be completely detached.

Selma clicked her fingers, and two wolves came in, both in half-man form, slightly more human and slightly more clothed than the wolf-men you see in films. They manacled Ritson to the wall next to me so his slick, bloody shoulder was forced to rub and slide against my bare, scarred one. He whimpered, and took a deep breath. He reminded me of a shark, getting the scent of blood in his nose, because he sat up straight like someone had passed an electric current through him, and cold, yellow eyes looked at me as he slowly turned his head.

He had normal manacles on, not the spiked kind, and the chains on them were much longer, so he had a lot more movement. He didn't seem to care anymore that he was bleeding profusely, or that his entrails had left a glistening wet line along the floor and out the door like some gruesome path to follow. He looked at me intently. He wasn't raving and bloodthirsty like he had been when Blake let go of the lead. He was hungry, and it was a dark, base hunger. His eyes showed it, that mixture of lust and starvation permeating his gaze, like food and sex were the same to him. They probably were.

Making sure he kept his eyes on me despite the shaggy hair, he lowered his head to my left arm, which he had grasped and raised a little. I had, finally and blissfully, gone to my cold, dead place, and so I knew it would hurt me less to let him touch my arm than it would to try and jerk away. I just stared back at him like the arm he was holding was someone else's. I felt the pain, but it was being received in a different part of my brain that I'd closed the door on for the time being.

In a very sensual movement, he lowered his head over the wound, and locked his mouth around it. His tongue probed the deep gouges all the way down to the bone. I was distantly aware that it was very painful. He fed at the wound like it was more important than life. I glanced away from him to see Selma looking on with anger, Blake with disgust, and the two half men with puzzled curiosity.

I heard an odd sound, like something heavy and wet

dragging along the floor. I looked away from Ritson's face, to see his intestines slithering back into his body as if by their own will. It was almost funny. No, it *was* funny. I laughed to see those thick pink snakes slinking back across the floor like chastised schoolboys caught lingering in the playground. Everyone but Ritson went still when I laughed, and it made everything even funnier that they looked at me like I was a true psycho.

To avoid a hysterical laughing fit, I looked back down at Ritson who had stopped sucking at the wound. To my surprise, it was filling out with perfectly healed flesh. I watched it fill back in with fascination. A low growl brought my attention back to Ritson's face. His eyes were changing colour again, becoming warmer, more like citrine in sunlight. He laughed, surprised, and looked at me inquisitively.

Everyone jumped when he spoke. I was cold and still and detached.

"Why aren't I afraid of being chained? And why aren't I afraid of you?"

"You always did ask a lot of questions. I remember them being more to the line of 'why are you hurting me' and 'why should I have to pay for my pack-master's crimes'." Selma's eyes flashed dangerously at that. I think I'd just worked out who Jeremy was.

"I like to know the answers to things."

"As do we all Ritson. I have a question for you. How have you healed my arm and yourself and come back into your sanity?"

"It's the blood. Your blood, it—"

Blake finally couldn't take it anymore. "Don't answer her Ritson! She's the one that broke your mind and sent you mad in the first place!"

"I'm not your pet, brother of mine." He sounded cold, and detached. He sounded like me. "I won't be treated as one any more. I remember these past three years, and I don't like any of it."

This was crazy. What had started out as my punishment for Jeremy, who I was betting had been Selma's mate, and who I would also bet was the packmaster who had given me my back scars and been subsequently hunted down by Cannibal, had turned into Ritson's glorious return to sanity, and discovering he didn't like he brother one jot. Blake was silenced.

"As touching as all this animosity is, I would like to leave as soon as possible because you are wasting my time and costing me money. Whoever the fuck Jeremy is, let me pay for my crimes against the bastard and let me leave."

Selma gave a loud wordless scream of anger. "The only place you will ever see other than this room is hell, because that will be your punishment for killing my husband!"

"Husband? Who'd marry you?"

She rushed forward, but found Ritson was in the way, which, oddly enough, stopped her.

"Out of the way!" she shrieked, high and shrill. She seemed frightened by him, and made no move to strike him. He stared her down, and it was clear that he didn't answer to that voice anymore.

"No, Selma." He said her name like it was a fatal disease.

"Ritson, let her close." I stared at Selma as I said it, and to her shock, he moved.

Blake started yelling, asking if Ritson now answered to 'that bitch'. His words often came out as growls. He really shouldn't spend so much time gallivanting about as a wolf. His yelling, and Ritson's cold, scathing returns meant they didn't pay attention to our conversation.

"I'm guessing Jeremy was the pack-master when I slaughtered nearly half his sex-trafficking pack on behalf of abused werewolves everywhere." It was sarcastic. I wasn't aware I could be sociopathic and sarcastic at the same time. Interesting.

"He was," she hissed in answer.

"So you're also aware I paid my price for that."

"You paid no price."

"He took four gouges out of my back and I was in hospital for three weeks. His lycanthropy was so infectious I had silver pumped through my veins, which hurts, and a witch had to bind silver to my scars for fear the leftover wound could still infect me once the silver left my bloodstream. Believe me, I paid."

"It warms my heart to hear you underwent such suffering, but you killed Jeremy after that, and it is for that crime that you must pay with your life."

"I didn't kill him Selma."

"Then how is he dead?" She didn't expect an answer, but I gave her one.

"Because someone who cares about me hunted him down and killed him because he was so incensed at the injury inflicted upon me. So, bitch, you've got the wrong man if it's the death of Jeremy that's being paid for."

A flicker of uncertainty passed through her eyes, then changed to resolve.

"Fine. As payment of your debt to this murderer, you can stand in their place and fight me, one on one, with no weaponry."

Triumph flashed in her eyes. I think she expected me to cower.

"Done."

Selma smiled, thinking me overconfident, and stalked out the room. Blake and Ritson fell silent as she left.

"What happened?" they asked in unison.

"I'm going to fight Selma. She's going to die, and I'm

getting the hell out of here." I reeled off that list like I was telling them what I wanted from the supermarket. It was inevitable. My mind couldn't comprehend events turning out any differently; and that, of course, is always a dangerous thing.

15

I was un-manacled from the wall. The spikes had to be pulled out of my flesh one by one before the shackles themselves could be removed. They left the choke collar for last. As they pulled out each spike, I could feel it sliding through my flesh, a dragging sensation as it slowly inched its way out of my airway where it had been deeply buried. The spikes were slick with my blood, and seeing as they were crudely made they grated and tugged at my skin as they came out, making the sensation all the more horrible. Blood dripped down my neck, slow and sluggish, as I struggled to breathe.

Ritson moved in, a question in his eyes, and when I didn't object he nuzzled into that warm blood and cleaned it off in long, slow, sure, licks. It was distracting, and when he was done I could breathe again. I didn't waste time marvelling that I was alive, I was just thankful for it. The holes at neck, wrist, and ankle, all burned. I never had liked the feel of cold iron against my skin, and I'd just had it buried in my flesh where nothing should ever touch. Ritson repeated the lupine cleaning of the blood at my wrists, and that same deep rumble of enjoyment started up in his chest. When he had cleaned one wrist, I idly stroked his hair, getting blood in it, but he rolled his eyes up to look at me, and smiled. The change in him was dizzying, or maybe that was the blood loss. I'd seen him as a beast on a leash, a broken and petrified man, and now, he seemed fine, and he also seemed to be on my side. Surely he should still recoil in fear from the woman who had broken his mind?

"Here," Ritson said, offering me his still bleeding shoulder, a little awkwardly seeing as he was just as chained to the wall as I was. "I have a theory. I've taken your blood to reclaim my sanity, maybe now you need to take my blood to reclaim your strength."

It seemed reasonable. I'd been dealing with vampires since I was five, so blood didn't bother me. In my line of work, there weren't very long life expectancies, but I'd have been dead long ago if I hadn't had the blood of supernaturals pumped into me to keep me alive. They didn't always set up a transfusion; sometimes you just had to take it straight from the source, wound to mouth. The thought of drinking Ritson's blood, therefore, was not completely abhorrent to me. I was vaguely aware that the detachment was helping with me being completely calm at the prospect of drinking the blood of a recently amnesiac psychotic wolf. I was involved with the supernatural creepie-crawlies enough to know the power blood held, not just for vampires, but all kinds of supes. Who knew, maybe Ritson's blood had in it a power I needed.

I lowered my head slowly, partly because of the neck wounds and partly so Ritson could watch me, and laid the barest of kisses on his shoulder. His eyes fluttered shut for a moment, and when he opened them again they were more yellow, and his gaze was more intense. Like he had done to me, I picked along the wound, and opened it up a little with my tongue. He made a small pain noise, which a dark part of me liked. Seeing as the dark part of me was the driving force of my brain right then, it encouraged me to probe deeper into the wound. I rolled my eyes up to look at him, and his eyelids were fluttering like the pain was good. I drank in his blood and I did feel better. Stronger. The vamps said the only blood they prized higher than lycanthrope was fey, but that still made lycan blood pretty damn good.

When I'd finished, I looked up at Ritson. His head was resting against the wall, his posture relaxed, and his eyes closed.

"Have you practiced that?" he murmured without turning his head.

"Not recently." I grinned, and my sociopathic self found it odd that I was grinning. "Unchain him," I told Blake. Oddly, he just did it. No fuss, no fight. The half-men, who had until then been watching me curiously, tensed, like they expected Ritson to rip their heads off. Nothing that bad happened. He opened his eyes, and looked at me. Slowly, he unfolded himself and stood, then looked down at his stomach wound.

He had a dark line across the soft flesh of his stomach, but other than that you'd never know his entrails had just been crawling across the floor in some macabre dance. "I wish I could bottle your blood if it heals like that."

"I'm not entirely sure I should be taking the credit for that. I thought it was your doing," I replied, craning my neck up to see him from my vantage point on the floor.

He gave a grim smile. "I've never been all that strong in any walk of life, so it must be you, especially as you're wound free too." I looked down at my right arm, the one that Ritson hadn't drunk from and healed. The skin was as smooth as it had been before the wound; which wasn't very seeing as my forearm bore a triple scar from slashing werewolf claws. I touched my face and it bore no remnants of the cuts Selma's nails had made. Every wound but the ones inflicted by the manacles were healed. It must have been the blood exchange, some bond formed, for it to have had a healing effect like that. I thought that kind of healing only ever happened with the fey, but I wasn't going to question it. I was healed and that was good.

"Selma will see you now," one of the half men said, shifting his weight nervously onto his other foot. I wondered if he had a direct line to her, like some of the telepathic vamps and shifters had, or whether he was just unnerved and wanted the hell out of the room. I retreated further into the cold, dark centre of my mind. It can't be healthy, fracturing the mind into so many cold, dead pieces, but without giving over to that darkness, embracing the side of me that enjoyed hurting people, enjoyed proving I was better, stronger, that thrived on all the death and terror… if I didn't have that part of myself, I would not be alive today. Either that or I'd be in a different profession, and I couldn't exactly see me working a desk job.

The pain left in the manacles' wake was suddenly insignificant. Sure it hurt, but what's a little pain between you and the person trying to kill you? I'm sure pain was pretty much the only thing on Selma's agenda for me tonight, possibly including death there somewhere at the end. Even that thought didn't scare me. I might die tonight. So how was that different from any other day? Let's face it, I get angry quickly, I lack manners. I would put money on my death not being some heroic act, trying to slay a murdering vampire, or kill a dragon, it would be because I rubbed a supe the wrong way, they'd smack me upside the head for my impudence, and I'd get internal bleeding in the brain. Or something to that effect.

Ritson extended a hand to me. I like to get up under my own steam, no matter how badly beaten I've been, but there was an understanding between us now, a bond, and taking his hand didn't bother me. Normally I felt patronised by the gesture, but today it was a practicality.

Everything creaked; joints clicked like they were going to start up their own percussion band. Practically, but inelegantly, I had to arch over backwards, cracking my back to release the tension of having my spine curved so severely for so long. It hurt, but it felt so much better too. In fact, the release of tension felt so good, I clicked my wrists, elbows, ankles, neck. I had one shoulder that I could dislocate at will, so I stretched my back out, popped the shoulder out and in, and felt better for it.

Selma had loved Jeremy, her slimy good-for-nothing asshole of a husband, a sex trafficker, a creep. She wanted revenge, and it seemed like she preferred to serve it hot. What can you do? Ours is not to reason why, ours is but to do and die.

With some very nervous wolfmen, and a zenned-out Ritson, I went out to meet the mongrel bitch.

The tiny room opened out onto a narrow corridor as grimy and filthy as the room had been. The floor still bore the trail left by Ritson's wounds, the blood adding to the grit and grime underfoot. The corridor was just about wide enough for me and Ritson to walk abreast, shoulders touching. Blake was too wide for anyone to walk next to him, so he headed up the group, and the half-men fell behind. There was no way to avoid stepping in the blood on the floor. One of the wolves swore as he skidded a foot or so on a particularly large pool of blood. This is why you wear heavy-duty boots. I was going to say sensible shoes, but thick heeled boots, about five inches high, with a platform, akin to something Trinity would wear in the Matrix, would not be considered as sensible by most. But I'd be damned if I didn't look good.

Eventually, Blake led us outside, to a clearing. It was night-time, black and starless. What had to be the entire pack was standing in a ring around the grass and dirt of the clearing. There were trees around it, shying back from the clearing itself. That alone was an indication that there was magic in this ground. It shivered along my spine and made my skin crawl. Old wolf magic, very old indeed. I'd had no idea the clan had such history. Knowledge being acquired with age was inevitable, and so I felt mild surprise that this clan had been one to traffic their people; I would have expected an old clan to know better. Of course, I could just be being over-generous and they could just all be really dreadful people, or they could have stolen this ground from someone else, and the magic wasn't theirs.

There were fires lit round the edge of the clearing, some behind the ring of wolves, some in front. The pack themselves were in an array of forms, human, half and half, and pure wolf. The wolves were huge, imposing things, muscular and threatening. There was a constant rumble, like distant thunder, that was actually the wolves themselves. They knew blood was about to be shed.

Selma was still in human form, and still bloody. I strode out to greet her in the middle of the clearing, but pushing through that ancient earth magic, that wolf magic, was hard, almost like it was a physical force. It made me more inclined to think that what I was feeling was old earth magic, wild magic, not belonging to the clan at all. Whatever it was, it made it difficult to concentrate. I stood for a moment in the middle of the clearing with my eyes closed, and formed metaphysical shields around myself, greater than the shields I usually wore. They were something else I could do, along with the glamour. If I didn't have my metaphysical shields, I would have gone mad from feeling the earth magic long ago.

Some are more sensitive to it than others. I was definitely in the category of *more*.

"I call a traditional duel, Raven, for the death of our pack leader, my husband, Jeremy." Selma's words made me open my eyes. She was standing just a little over two feet away, trying to invade my personal space. I didn't step back.

"I accept your challenge, and appreciate your forfeiting of your right to shift within this duel." I started to walk away to my side of the clearing, the arena for this fight, but she grabbed my arm and tried to turn me back to her. I just looked at her hand until it fell away.

"I'm allowed to shift. What do you mean by saying I'm not?"

"You declared a traditional duel, and tradition, for the most part, is fair. I'm not a shifter, I can't shift, and so you are not allowed to either. And, as you are stronger than me physically because of your other side, I am allowed to keep a weapon of my choosing." I smiled, empty as a starless night. "I will have one of my knives back, and you will be forbidden to shift, unless you break your challenge and be declared a coward, and thus step down as leader of the pack."

I'd hit right on the money with all my educated guesses, as Weres in the circle began muttering and exchanging glances.

"I suggest that those who claim the rank of second and third in your pack step forward." Two wolves moved out of the ring of spectators, but would not get closer to me. Usually, if you're to be a mediator, you stand an equal distance from the two opponents, but these wolves stayed on the far side of Selma, away from me. This pack was a cowardly shambles. I looked at the wolves, making sure I had their attention. "Do you deem the rules I have stated fair, and in accordance with your traditional ways of duelling?" I asked.

"I do," one said, shortly followed by the affirmation of

the other. Selma glared at them, and if she lived beyond this fight, I was betting they were going to pay dearly for that. I got the distinct impression that Selma was used to getting her way.

"I know you are naked in preparation for a shift, so I am willing to let you go and get dressed if you wish, seeing as you will not be able to shift." It was rude to point out a shifter was naked, because that meant you were judging them by human rules, not shifter, but I'd rather tell her to go and put some clothes on than have someone claim afterwards it was not a fair fight because I had protection from my clothing and she didn't.

"I don't think I will. But in the interest of being fair, I think you should strip."

"I'm not a Were, I don't do casual nudity."

"Then keep your underwear, but your leather trousers at least will give you ample protection, and that," she grinned at me sinisterly, triumph in her eyes, "is not *fair*."

"Fine, though you are being childish, I'll abide by the rules."

She snarled, a truly animalistic noise. I don't think she liked being called a child. I looked behind me to find Blake and Ritson. I went over to the latter, disrobed down to my underwear, and gave him my clothes. As I was getting ready, Selma said, "I am no coward, so when you are prepared, Raven, we shall begin this dance." She meant it as scathing, to show she was better than me, but really she was just impatient.

"You wanted me to disrobe, so you will wait. The night is young."

Blake produced, from about his person, all my blades, and displayed them along his forearm for me to choose one. I'd been carrying five, but my weapon of choice for this fight was the biggest one I carried. It was as long as my forearm, and went in a holster that cut diagonally across my back, the hilt of the knife sticking up over my shoulder for ease of draw. I needed the belt from my leathers to keep the sheath on, so I slipped it out of the loops and wore it round my hips. It had lightning-bolt shaped studs on it all the way round, so it was fairly heavy, and kept the knife in place as best as it could.

I turned to face Selma, and smiled.

Her second in command barked 'positions' at us. We stood in the centre of the clearing on each of our sides, a good six metres between us. She snarled again, and I got the distinct impression that if she'd been in wolf form, it was the equivalent of raising her hackles. I curved my body into an attacking stance, stretching out my back. I could feel the scars shift, and the silver cling to that moving skin. I'd been kept cramped, chained, in a tiny room for who knew how long. My muscles complained, screamed at me, but it didn't matter. The world had narrowed down to Selma.

I vaguely heard a voice say 'begin'. With a wild, high-pitched shriek, that made me think more of a banshee than a wolf, Selma launched herself at me. She sprung straight from a relaxed stance, like she had her more powerful wolf legs in her human form. I was ready for her to land on me, so threw myself onto my back and kicked. It wasn't all that comfortable with the knife, but I got her in the gut. With a satisfying oomph she flew backwards, but unfortunately she flipped in the air and landed on her feet. I was up by then, but she tried to rush me all the same. I dodged sideways and she ran past me. I couldn't see how she'd become alpha, she was letting her emotions rule her, and was flailing around like an untrained puppy. She almost ran into the crowd of Weres.

"Come on. Let's dance," I said, inviting the bitch to fight me properly. She gave the banshee call again and ran at me. This time I didn't dodge, but blocked her, fought back. We grappled, traded blows. She got one in on my head as I got her in the neck. She choked, but I bled and felt dizzy. She took that opportunity to stab me with claws she'd grown on her hand. It was such a subtle change that the pack might or might not notice, and if they did, they might or might not care. The claws bit into the soft flesh of my chest, over my heart, and kept on going in until I had four holes, each one with a finger buried deep in it. She'd knocked me to the ground, but I was still sitting upright. In a flash of movement, I reached my hand to the back of my neck and drew the long knife. It flashed silver in the firelight for one brief moment, then bit into the back of her neck. I couldn't get enough force to decapitate her cleanly from this angle, and even if I could the knife would continue on into me. Instead, I left her shrieking at the relatively shallow wound, and cut her hand off. The fingers stayed buried in my flesh. She screamed and screamed as I, quite calmly, pulled the clawed hand out, hating the sound of my breathing, like that of a stuck pig.

While she writhed on the floor, clutching her brand new bloody stump, I held her claw up in the air, standing as I did so, to show to her pack that she was a coward and a cheat. Even as they snarled and growled, the claw changed back into a hand. Selma made a wild slash at me with her one remaining claw, and began to shift in earnest, seeing as she'd already been outed. I jumped backwards, out of the way, and she gave a howl of frustration. Fur started to crawl more rapidly over her body. I wasn't going to give her the opportunity. With her on the floor and me standing, I had the right leverage to take her head off. The knife wasn't ideal for the job, I'd have liked to have had my swords, but after three hacking blows her head was on the floor. The Change stopped, her body slumped, and her blood mingled with the dirt. I fell to my knees in a jarring movement, and came back into my head as if I'd been on holiday. I wasn't the sociopath anymore; I was just in pain.

"The Raven is declared the winner," a low voice growled. I could see her second in command, a tall dark and handsome man, was in half man form, and seemed to be relaxing from a stance that indicated he had been thinking about interfering.

"Thanks," I said, smiling slightly manically over at him. "Can I ask… what was she… like as a packmaster?" I was finding it difficult to breathe, and was very light-headed.

"Tyrannical, just like Jeremy before her. We didn't like her much."

"Well," I said slowly, the pain really becoming unbearable now. "If you disliked her that much, you get my vote to be next packmaster."

The wolfman smiled at me, and I swayed on my knees. Ritson was there in a flash. The last thing I saw was a mixture of fear, pride, and loss in his eyes. I smiled, took my last shuddering breath, and fell still.

The next thing I was aware of was dirt hitting me in the face. It was unpleasant. I sat up, coughed, wiped the dry earth out from my eyes, and then clutched my head as someone close by screamed. The voice, strangely, seemed to be coming from above me. I looked up and saw the night sky. I also saw four walls of dirt rising six feet on each side. I gasped as magic speared through me from the ground. It took me a moment to realise that breathing didn't hurt. It should have. As I stood up, a pitiful whining howl that had been riding the night air stopped. I was not short enough to be incapable of jumping over a six foot wall. It only came six inches above my head. I gave a little jump, got my arms on the ground, and hauled myself up out of the hole. Gasps, cries, and more screams met me. I was still in my underwear. There was dried blood on it, but no wound to speak of. Even the wounds from the manacles were gone. I knew I'd lost a lot of blood, but I didn't feel weak, nauseous, or unsteady. I was fine. Remarkably so.

Actually, I felt fantastic, full of life and energy. When I looked down at the earth, I saw the hole I'd been in was a grave, six foot deep and cut as neatly as could be done in the rough dirt. The grave was in the clearing where Selma's body had been left to bleed out. The blood would make the earth rich. I looked at the dark bottom of the grave, and suddenly there was light. It was green, and seemed to be coming from each grain of dirt, from each damp clod of earth, from each root. It drifted upwards, towards me, and passed in through my bare feet where they touched the ground. It made me feel warm, and calm. I didn't know for certain, but I could bet it was the wild magic of earth I had felt earlier, and it welcomed me, recognised me, and healed me. No-one else seemed to see it, as they were looking at me, not at the green illumination of the ground. The light faded, and I mourned its going, but somehow knew that the earth had given me a gift. I'd always been told the earth hated killers, that it didn't accept them into the land. The people who'd told me that were evidently wrong.

A giant, silken muscle machine of a wolf bounded towards me. As it got closer, it started to stand upright and turn back into a man. Ritson's change was smooth and perfect. He was utterly naked, but I wasn't distracted by baser thoughts as he came towards me, but captivated by the pure joyful grin on his face. He hugged me tight and proclaimed in a disbelieving tone that I was alive. It was a fact I was aware of.

"Yes, Ritson. Next time you decide to bury me, can you check I'm dead first?"

"You were." This came from Blake, a low rumble. He had a chain on his neck, which Selma's second in command was holding the other end to. I liked this change in circumstance.

"Evidently not Blake."

"As much as I wish to disagree with Selma's pet here," the tall dark and handsome man said, tugging a little too hard on the leash, "You were dead for half an hour. You had no vital signs, and Ritson went mad again, which, it seemed at the time, was proof enough."

"You can't kill me that easily," I said with a grin, ignoring the twisting sensation in my stomach at the realisation that Ritson was somehow now my responsibility. Damn.

"Evidently not," Selma's second replied.

"What's your name? I hate thinking of you as 'Selma's second in command', it seems rude, even though you can't hear what I'm thinking."

He looked a little startled at my bizarre train of thought. As Asher had said, it was a crazy train.

"Roderigo," he replied.

"Nice to meet you, Roderigo. Now, are all my debts with this pack settled, because if anyone else wants to fight me I'd rather get it over and done with now." No-one volunteered, what a surprise.

"I'd say you were within your rights to have killed the members of the pack who where trafficking our men and women, and I say I'm glad Jeremy got what he deserved. I'm also glad you rid us of Selma. She was a terrible packmaster and only got the job because she slaughtered anyone who objected. To me, that's not a debt paid, that a favour done. The Clan of the East Clearing is in your debt."

I smiled, unpleasantly. "That's a very dangerous thing to say to a woman who operates in favours just as much as in money. Are you offering me a favour debt?"

"Yes. I am. I am not lord of this clan, we have no master until it is decided, but at the very least you have my personal promise of a favour debt, from me to you."

"And me," said the previous third-in command. About

twelve more of the wolves chimed in. The rest had clearly been on Selma's side, as had the sullen and silent Blake.

"And me," a voice said softly. Ritson looked at me with pure adoration and thankfulness. That was the moment I though 'oh fuck', but I smiled at him rather than voiced that thought.

"Well, I'd say you're an honourable clan after all. You also have a lot of power here, old magic. I'm grateful to it that it saw fit to heal my wounds, or I'd end up with four silver holes in my chest to go with the four gashes on my back that Jeremy so kindly bestowed." I turned as if to leave, but Roderigo spoke.

"Jeremy inflicted the wounds on your back?"

"Yes. Why do you think he's dead?"

He didn't answer that; he just smiled.

Two hours later I was home. It was just about still dark, but the air had the feel of dawn to it. The wolves had given me a nice classy Tesco bag to put my weaponry and torn jacket in, and thankfully, they'd given me back my bike. Probably because I told them heads would roll if they didn't. Turned out Selma had treated it a little roughly, but with a bit of fine tuning she'd be just fine. I didn't mind too much, because the images that sprang to mind of her doing a Tesco shop were funny enough to keep me in good humour. Or maybe that was the residue of the earth magic. In fact it must have been, because my bike was my baby. That, and I was a pessimist at heart, and I'd just died, apparently. Surely I should be pissed off and grumpy. I wasn't even angry that I had a tag-along follow me home. Ritson had begged me, literally, to not leave me with his brother anywhere near him. I'd told him to live with me. Crazy.

I also wasn't angry at Hammer anymore, and no longer

felt the need to avoid Lucille. The last however many days had put things in perspective a bit.

Lucille, however, was angry with me.

As soon as I got in the door, I saw her. She was sitting on the sofa, arms crossed, and fuming. "Six. Days," she hissed at me menacingly.

"Last I knew it was only two. It's not exactly my fault I got kidnapped by a bunch of angry werewolves." At least now I knew how long they'd kept me for. Four days. God, Selma was a bitch. Thank god she was dead.

Lucille's eyes went wide at the news that I'd been captive and she'd had no inkling. Unfortunately, Ritson decided that was a good moment to appear from behind the wall that hid the living room from sight if you were standing near the door, and vice versa. She must have been really angry to not have smelled werewolf when he walked in the flat.

"What is he doing here?"

"He's my ward. Apparently, I made him go insane three years ago, and only my blood and my presence keeps him sane. So we've got a houseguest. Play nice." I was still feeling far too chipper. When would the earth magic wear off?

"Why are you so relaxed and happy? What's happened to you?"

"Apparently, I died, but the earth saw fit to pump me full of magic and heal me. I've never gone half an hour with no vital signs before."

Lucille went utterly still. There was a look of... something, in her eyes, something I couldn't pinpoint. It turned to resolve, then she appeared faint. "I need to get in my coffin. It's almost dawn, Phoebe."

I stiffened and glanced at Ritson. He was looking intently at me, paying no attention to Lucille whatsoever. "You tell anyone that, Ritson, and you're dead."

"I wouldn't tell a soul. And it's not Ritson. It's Gabriel."

"Nice to meet you Gabriel."

"Nice to meet you Phoebe."

I smiled, but it disappeared immediately. I felt dawn rise, and as I looked at the sofa, I watched Lucille die. She lolled on the sofa, eyes as empty as glass and body limp with death. At least vamps don't get rigor mortis all over again when they die for the day. I sighed, and felt sad that I had hurt Lucille. She was only angry because she was worried about me. The world was slightly less fine and dandy than it had been moments ago. It was a bit of a relief, as I didn't want this magic riding me too long. Me as an optimist was just not something I saw working.

Slowly, as if she were merely sleeping, not truly dead and oblivious, I carried Lucille to my bedroom and put her down on the bed. I moved the lid of her coffin and lay her down inside it. With a kiss to the forehead, I shut the lid on her empty face, and yawned.

"Time for bed said Zebedee," I muttered under my breath.

"Where can I sleep?" Ritson – no, Gabriel – asked softly.

"That depends how… damaged you were. I'm guessing quite damaged."

"I didn't fight anyone, and you healed the wounds Selma made."

"I meant in your head. Will you be okay in the other room or not?"

"I honestly don't know, but I'm happy to stay on the sofa if that will make you more comfortable."

I looked at him for a moment, deciding what to do. Some of the earth magic must have still been in effect, because I opted on the side of kindness, and decided not to be selfish.

"You can stay in the bed with me. I'll find you something to wear." It seemed I was doing a lot of loaning Guillaume's clothes to people these days, but if the man couldn't be bothered to clean up after himself and take his stuff home, I figured I could loan it to one or two random men who stayed with me. Ah what a shambles my life is. Gabriel was smaller than Guillaume, so he didn't have the same problem with the clothes as Blaze had, who was much broader. He wore a t-shirt and pair of tracksuit bottoms that were a touch on the large side, but at least he was clothed and comfortable. I put on my favourite, if a little faded, Nightmare Before Christmas pyjamas, not the ones Blaze had worn. I didn't bother having a shower, or taking off my make-up. I didn't bother with anything. The strength the earth had loaned me ebbed, and I was about ready to collapse into bed.

I slid in on my side, putting one gun in the holster on the headboard and one under my pillow, just in case. Gabriel slid in on the other side of the bed, back to me, keeping his distance. When I told him I know shifters heal faster by touch, he snuggled in against my back and promptly drifted off to sleep. One hand slid around my waist, and he hugged me, whimpering as a bad thought crossed his mind, but it passed and he relaxed. He was like a fragile child, mind broken and remade and broken and remade too often in too short an amount of time. He'd take a long time to heal; I knew that. I also knew that I'd been the cause of his suffering. I may have wished death upon his clan, but Gabriel himself had turned out to be okay, and I wouldn't wish his bestial insanity on anyone. I fell asleep worrying about what I'd do with him, and whether I would be able to keep him sane.

16

It was softly sunny when I woke, late afternoon streaming in through the window. Lucille liked to see the night sky when she was up. Personally, I liked the curtain shut, but to each their own. I was surprised the light hadn't woken me up sooner, it normally did. I sat up slowly, hurting, and turned to see Gabriel fast asleep, clinging to the covers. They were balled in his fists and he kept frowning, occasionally whimpering.

The sight was pitiful. I gently shook his shoulder, figuring half four was as good a time as any to get up. His eyes fluttered open, and he quieted.

"Phoebe?" he asked, uncertain. I nodded. "So that did happen."

"I'm afraid so."

"Wow," he said softly. "What time is it?"

"Gone half four. I'm going to go into work. Do you need to come with me?"

"Maybe. Probably."

I had a lightbulb moment. "You said something about

my presence and my blood keeping you sane. Does that mean you'll have to keep having my blood on a regular basis?"

"I think so. I'm not sure." He looked so guilty, and worried. There was that fear of rejection and abandonment in his eyes.

"Don't worry about it. I'm a donor for Lucille, she keeps my blood in the fridge. I don't donate much, but she doesn't drink much, so she can share."

He smiled, and security seeped into his eyes in the place of fear.

"You really think I'm going to cast you out don't you?"

"Of course not, I…" he stopped. Sighed. Nodded.

"I'm not going to kick you out Gabriel. For better or worse, I fucked you up, and I'm going to try and fix that. So," I smiled, "I'm going to work, care to join me?"

An hour later, we'd both showered and changed. I made a mental note to take him shopping after work; Guillaume's clothes just didn't fit right.

I walked into The Concrete Palace like a returning hero. Hammer still thought I was mad at him, so he was on the defensive when I strolled into his office with Gabriel behind me like a good rear guard.

"Raven. Are we on speaking terms again?"

"Yeah. The last four days kind of put our little argument into perspective. I'm not mad at you, though I understand if you're mad at me."

Hammer's eyes flicked to Gabriel, then back to me. "Who's the wolf?"

"I think this is more of a sit down conversation."

Cannibal had been in the room when I'd come back, which is fairly normal as he was second-in-command, but his usual relaxed demeanour had disappeared.

He walked over to me, and Gabriel drew back. It was

the most dignified cowering he could manage. He was a little surprised when Cannibal drew me into a fierce hug. Makes two of us. "Are you okay?"

"Yeah, I am now, Cannibal. Sorry I was short with you."

"You can't help being short, I'm so bloody tall." And there we were, back to normal. I grinned at him.

"I'll talk to you later, okay?"

"Sure. Have fun with Hammer."

"We will," Hammer said, voice low, so very low, and a little threatening.

Cannibal gave me a mock-frightened face, and shut the door behind him. Gabriel relaxed a bit, but then saw Hammer, and had an internal battle with himself as to how much he could cower, or whether he could just flee.

"Take the sofa Raven. He's here for a reason I presume." Hammer looked at Gabriel, who moved a little behind me, like he was trying to hide. I moved to the drug dealer sofa and sat down. I told Gabriel to sit beside me, and he did. Nice doggy.

"He's essential in the explanation actually."

"Then please, explain." Hammer was not a happy bunny. In fact, he was no kind of bunny at all; he was more like a bear.

"I know you feel like I've… I don't know, betrayed you, by the ball at the British Court. If I could explain it to you, I would. I'm sorry I got angry with you for saying what you thought. You know I'm not the best at keeping my temper." Hammer's lip twitched. He tried to keep it still, but one corner of his mouth ended up pulling into a lopsided smile. The coldness started to thaw in his eyes.

"I'm well aware of your bad temper Raven."

I smiled, but continued with my story. "I was only angry at you for a couple of days. I didn't want to see anyone, so

I went out on my bike to avoid Lucille at night. The third night… well. I was kidnapped Hammer."

"You fucking what?"

"Yeah."

"By who? Him?" he was getting angry now.

"No, no, not him Hammer. He's with me okay, he's one of the good guys. But it was his clan. The wolves we busted in one three years ago, you remember that pack?"

"Raven, that is one job I will never forget, and one aftermath that is burned on my retina."

"Well, turns out the aftermath wasn't over. You know the head of the clan was the bastard wolf that did my back, the one Cannibal killed?" I paused, Hammer nodded. "His mate, Selma, became packmaster. She had a vendetta."

"Shit."

"Do you remember those unwilling, uncooperative, little oiks who were low down in the pecking order?"

"The brothers?"

"Exactly. Voila," I said, indicating Gabriel. "One half of the gruesome twosome. I'll get to that later. I woke up numb and chained to a wall. I had several wounds, but I couldn't feel them." I sighed, and I sounded tired. "Torturella's favourite manacles, the ones with the spikes, they used that kind. Neck, wrist, and ankle. There was a numbing agent on them, so I didn't feel them 'til I next woke up. Turned out Selma wanted to make me pay for killing Jeremy, even though I told her it was Cannibal not me."

I was getting tired of the sound of my own voice. Gabriel had relaxed a bit, and sunk down on the sofa, moving a little closer to me. I sighed, and continued. "She challenged me to a duel. This was the fourth day I'd been there. I had no weapons, and my arms had been opened from wrist to elbow."

Hammer looked startled. "I shared blood with Gabriel," I

glanced over at him and he smiled, though to reassure him or me, I don't know. "It healed me, and it also brought his sanity back. Hence the reason he's here. When I first saw him, they had him on a leash, and he couldn't talk. Apparently, I'd broken his mind, but my blood made him sane again. I don't know how dependant he is on my company yet, so I'm keeping him around for a bit."

"Jesus Raven. You've got a pet wolf now?"

"He's not a pet, Hammer, he's a person."

"Sorry. It's just that, even for you, this is weird."

"I know. Anyway, needless to say I killed the bitch. Apparently though, I also died for half an hour. I woke up after the fight when dirt hit my face. I was in a grave. I never, ever want to wake up there again. Selma wasn't all that popular with the clan, so there was no kind of retribution; I think her second's replaced her for the moment at least." I paused. "I wanted to call you before, but you don't get great signal when you're chained to a wall."

There was a soft, tense, silence.

"Jesus," Hammer said softly. "If I hadn't been so proud, I'd have called. Maybe I'd have worried, and maybe I'd have sent the cavalry to find you."

I smiled, but it was sad. "Don't worry Hammer, there's not way you could have known. I guess that's the last time I'll ever be in a mood with you and not phone you, though."

"That would be nice. It was odd to not hear from you for a week. The world seemed out of joint."

There was an exchange of smiles, and companionship seemed to float through the very air. Hammer wasn't the kind of guy you hugged, but I was damn near tempted.

"So," I began, getting back to our more usual topic of conversation, "Any jobs for me?"

"There's always work for you. Stacks and stacks of it.

People reckon The Raven is the only one who can sort out their problems."

"You know, I might start taking jobs and getting one of the other Sharks to do it and giving them the money at the end. It'd save a lot of hassle, and the clients would be none the wiser."

Hammer chuckled, but then he turned serious. "There is one job that needs fairly urgent attention. The Lord of Thurudīn has phoned every night to ask if you are able to sort out what he would only refer to as 'the first job'. Do you know what he means?"

I had a second to remember the revenant vamp. "Oh *shit*," I said with feeling. "I completely forgot about that. Shit, shit, shit that does need doing urgently. Gabriel, I can't bring you with me. If I give you blood and let one of the Sharks look after you do you think you'll be okay?"

"Honestly, I don't know. But I'll try. You can always chain me to be on the safe side. I would if I were you."

"Why isn't everyone in my life as understanding and honest as you?" I turned back to Hammer. "Can you get one of them to look after him? Not Shammy, not Predator, not Tin Man. Torturella would, Belle maybe."

"Belle and Torturella are working."

"Shit. Is Ace in?" Ace was big and burly and badass. He'd be able to handle Gabriel if things got bad.

"Yeah. He's in the firing range. I'll go and get him."

Hammer breezed out of his office with contained urgency. I turned to Gabriel. "Sorry I have to leave you like this." I offered him the bend of my elbow. "For the sake of ease I'm going to use a knife, then you can take your blood, okay?" He just nodded. I made a relatively shallow cut, and he only took a little. Even after that small amount, he mellowed, and sunk into the sofa with a content smile on his face. Ace and Hammer chose that moment to walk in.

"Christ, Raven. What's your blood taste like to make a Were euphoric?" Ace said.

"No idea. You happy to look after him?"

"Yeah, babe, I'm cool." I didn't mind Ace calling me babe. I think he and Asher were the only two people that got away with it. Everyone else lived in fear of what I'd do to them.

"Thanks. I owe you one."

"Really?"

"Yes. You got yourself a favour debt. Now I really have to go." I turned to Gabriel and, acting on instinct, kissed him on the cheek. "You behave and take care. Try not to go mad without me." It would have been funny at any other moment, but though Gabriel smiled and gave a lazy salute, I didn't find it amusing. In mild panic, I ran off to where I'd parked the bike.

17

An hour and a half later I was driving across the outskirts of No Man's Land. I'd phoned Bastien and told him what had happened. He was shocked, and insisted I find the revenant another time, but I refused. I'd left it too long already. My arm was bandaged up, and didn't hurt enough to be a hindrance, but I ached from the fight with Selma. Although the flesh was healed, the skin over my chest hurt. It was probably psychological, but it was still a bit of a bitch. I was a little weary of getting beaten up all the time.

On the phone, I had asked Bastien if he wanted any souvenirs. I meant the kind of souvenirs Nero had in his Hall of Horrors. Bastien didn't want anything that would be too messy to bring to him, he just asked for the spine and the fangs.

The last sighting of the revenant vamp was right at the edge of No Man's Land. He had apparently disappeared into the trees and they'd lost him in the undergrowth not very far in. It was perfect. It was easy.

It is a fact of life that motorbikes make noise and that

vampires have good hearing. Well, that's two facts. Usually, revenants don't really pay any attention to a bike, unless there's something bleeding on it. I parked my beauty at the edge of forest where he had last been seen. The dead land of cracked and barren earth stretched out behind me. The closest tarmac path to the Sunken City was a way away, and glowed dully in the stark moonlight. The Sunken City itself was lighting up the sky in the distance, glowing like hell was spilling up out of the ground.

Somehow, I didn't think wandering into the woods and calling out 'come out come out wherever you are' was going to be much good, so I had a better method of vampire luring arranged. I was wearing thick knee high boots over my leathers that were gappy enough to fit in extra weapons down the side. From my right boot I pulled a long silver blade out of its inner sheath. It glinted almost wickedly in the light. Sometimes, I thought my blades had a mind of their own. Other times, I rebated myself for how stupid that was.

I didn't want to remove my jacket and gloves, but I was intending to re-open the wound I'd made for Gabriel. In the end, laziness won out, and I cut through the leathers and the bandage. In the grand scheme of things, I could afford two new leather jackets, considering I had to replace the one Selma tore. From trying to cut through the leather and gauze, I actually cut my arm too deeply. I knew, because it didn't hurt, but it was bleeding quite happily.

Seeing as I wanted the vampire to find me, I didn't need to be quiet as I walked into the the forest that seemed to shrink back from No Man's Land in fear. I trailed the blood about twenty metres in and then ran back the other way. Vampires were fast, and I wanted him out in the open where I could see him. He'd be able to find me in the trees, I was bleeding and he'd smell me out, but I wouldn't be able to see him. I didn't like disadvantages much.

I stood in the moonlight, my silhouette stark against the landscape behind me and faced the trees. Knowing how revenant's brains worked (or rather didn't) I knew he would emerge exactly where I had, following the blood in a straight line. Surely enough, I heard crashing noises through the trees, the sound of sniffing, and a garbled gurgling sound that may have been the vampire salivating.

He was a blur, but he was a blur exactly where I expected him to be. Butcher, Pierce, and I had created the gun/crossbow hybrid that fired mini wooden or silver stakes. I say mini, but they were an inch in diameter and six inches long. My first shot caught the slobbering vampire on the shoulder. There was a crack and a pop as the bone came out of the joint and the stake went through the shoulder blade beyond. He gave a primitive roar, and came at me again, but slower this time. It never even crosses a revenant's mind that if they pull the stake out, they'll heal.

He was a mess. To have been on Master Death's guard he'd have been a vampire with dignity, but it was all gone now. His hair had fallen out, leaving the greying skin on his skull bare to the moonlight, showing it had a sheen of something akin to fever-sweat, and dark veins running over it. His teeth were long, but caked in old blood, as were his chest and fingers. His eyes were wild, but they focused on me all too quickly.

I backed up to give myself a running start, and launched both my feet at his chest, knocking him onto the floor. It was then just a case of firing more mini-stakes into him to pin him down. I fired into every joint; some pinned and some just hurt. Lots more things cracked and popped. I unzipped my jacket and reached over my shoulder to pull a stake out of my custom back sheath. The stakes I used were fairly narrow so I could wear them on me. On a vamp job, unless I thought I needed a gun more, I carried one wood and one silver stake crossed over on my back. For revenants I always used wood.

He was attempting to thrash, but a long piece of wood wedged into your body and in the ground underneath does make escape considerably more difficult. He heaved up as I came close as if straining to bite me, which helped me drive the stake all the way through in one blow. I felt an otherworldy energy swirl around me as I killed him. It always happened when I did something I shouldn't physically be able to do – like driving a stake through in one go. If you've ever tried to stake someone, you'll know it's incredibly hard.

The thrashing stopped. I pulled pliers out of my left boot and yanked out his fangs. I pulled the mini-stakes out and turned him over to get at the spine. I left the big stake in, just in case. I concentrated on the swirling energy and thrust my hand towards his neck. It was always a surprise when it went *through* and I grabbed the top of the spine. Using more of that energy, I yanked his spine out. He flopped sickeningly to the ground, face down, with the stake protruding out his back.

I pulled out my gun, and blasted his head away to mush. Blowback was a bitch, and I got bits of skull and brain on my clothes and in my hair, but at least that was the head and heart taken care of.

My bike was close by, but I wanted to be back on it before my arm started to hurt. The adrenalin was keeping any pain at bay for the moment, but I still rushed. I started the engine, and it growled as I moved off into the night.

The smell hit me first. It was the smell of dead flesh, but I wasn't next to the site where I'd killed Master Death's ex-minion.

A headless vampire, decaying around the stake through its heart, jumped me. The bastard was a rotter – a vampire that rots when it goes to ground for the day and re-forms at full dark. They didn't die if you took out the head and heart, and they still moved, as I just found out, if you took out the spine. It was further proof that whatever powers a vampire when it's 'alive' at night wasn't natural.

Grey gobbets of flesh fell onto my leathers as it slid off the bones of a tightly gripping hand. Fortunately for me, I was very good at battling the impulse to throw up by now. The smell was almost unbearable. I was lucky, though, that this was no average civilian bike. I had a flamethrower attached to one side, and a heavy-duty machine gun attached to the other to balance it. I yanked the flamethrower off, fire being the only thing that can kill a rotter, but realised too late that I wasn't meant to be actually riding the bike when I removed it. It was too unbalanced, and the weight of the gun on the other side tipped the bike over. I'd had to lean to compensate for the vampire, but he was on the same side as the gun, and I had no chance.

My right leg was pinned between the rotting vampire and the bike. I couldn't feel it, which was not a good sign. The vamp gripped harder on my arm and it was going to break, so I torched the fucker where my stake was sticking out. It ignited beautifully, and the vampire flopped, boneless, in its futile attempts to escape the fire. It even pushed the bike off it, thus pushing me back upright, sitting on the bike, with the engine running. I leant on my left leg and well and truly burned him before sticking the flamethrower back on the side and driving off towards Thurudīn.

By the time I arrived at Bastien's castle. I could feel everything. I wished I were still numb. There was blinding agonising pain all the way along my right leg, and my left arm was covered in my congealing blood. My upper right arm had the ache of a deep, deep bruise.

I'd never gone through the main entrance at the castle before, but in my slightly grey spotted vision, the beacon of light that was the main doorway was the only clear thing I could head to. The entrance was a long gravel drive with a paved circle at the end, and a glorious fountain in it. It was like a less menacing version of the one at the British Court. The front door looked like it was glowing. It was under a colonnaded porch, and the doors were thrown wide open. There were limousines and shiny black cars galore pulling up in the circular glorified drive. I skidded a little on the gravel, swore loudly, and slid in between two of the cars. The bike hit the bottom step and I toppled over and onto the hard stone of the stairs. It hurt, but I had an irrational moment of worrying about how my weapons bike was holding up after all the damage she'd taken today.

A woman screamed, that high pitched squeal that only a woman can make. It felt like it was splitting my skull in half. Armed guards came running. I recognised Thurudīn's weretigers when I saw them. One of them roughly pulled my bike off me.

"Who are you?" another demanded.

"I'm the fucking Raven!" I practically shrieked through the pain. Screams, more of them this time, louder, shriller. Some of the men were screaming too, but most were trying to stay calm and be macho in front of their female counterparts.

I saw a face I recognized, then I passed out.

When I woke up, there was a soft twilight feel to the room I was in. The ceiling was dark blue in the light, and the walls were the same hue. I was guessing white paint. Why I was analysing the ceiling I had no idea, but it occurred to me then that I was lying down. I tried to sit up, and felt the familiar tug of tubes in my arm. It was a hospital bed, but not in a hospital, of that I was fairly certain. I raised my head up, and the room swam, I hated it when they pumped me full of drugs. I didn't like being out of it.

"You'll feel better if you lie still, they tell me." The voice was deep, and not one I recognised. It made me want to settle down on the bed and sleep, permanently. I was looking forward, in that moment, to the feel of the earth welcoming me back.

I tried to shake the vivid image and turned my head in the direction of where I thought the sound had come from. I had guessed right. There was a man sitting there, but I couldn't easily discern his features in the twilit room. He was very broad shouldered, and seemed to be hunched over, like the chair was too small for him and he was trying not to dwarf it so much. If his hair hadn't been short, I'd have said it was Edouard. Of course, Edouard didn't normally make me think of how lovely it would be to be in my grave.

The man sat forward so that a sliver of moonlight fell across his face. His skin was chocolate brown, the colour leeched a little by the dark, but with a soft gold sheen to it. He had jet black hair, that wasn't short, but tied back. He also had yellow-gold eyes.

It was Bastien's face, but not Bastien.

As I focused on the stranger, I realised I could feel his heartbeat as if it were my own. I felt wonderment, puzzlement, and sorrow. He must have been the clearest broadcaster I'd ever met. Intrigued, I concentrated harder. He was old, so very old. In fact, the more I focused, the harder it became to breathe, because the weight of the years was crushing down on me like some leviathan pressing me to the bottom of the sea. I couldn't bear it and, with a shuddering gasp, pulled back into my own head. I didn't even know vampires that old existed, and I knew, with certainty, that I hadn't reached his full age in that short meander through his mind.

The stranger watched me silently. I sat up and pulled the

tubes out of my arm. Other than discomfort, there was no sensation, no pain. I looked down at my leg. Either I couldn't feel it, or it felt fine, I wasn't sure. What I saw, however, did not look fine. It was absolutely covered in vampire bites, littered with them like some macabre pattern on a cloth transferred onto my skin. Around the bites disgusting bruises, each the size of a CD, were blossoming in shades of purple yellow and green. They covered my entire leg.

I was only after realising I could see my entire leg that I became aware that I was in my underwear, and unarmed. I wasn't embarrassed, at least I had nice matching underwear on, but I was cold. With some difficulty, I pulled the sheet out from under me, and wrapped it around myself. The stranger made no attempt to help me, which I was pleased about. The day I needed help to get a sheet out from under me was the day I had to stop doing what I did. I looked at the stranger.

"Could you tell me what time it is?" I felt a wave of mild surprise and increased curiosity that were not my own.

"It is ten to three, two nights after you collapsed," he said without consulting a watch or moving his eyes from my face. His voice was warm and deep, again reminding me of the deep rich earth. I could almost feel it pulling around me like a thick blanket, to rest evermore. I really had to concentrate better than this.

"Damn. Do you have any idea where they put my phone?" After the recent werewolf incident, I wasn't taking any chances; I needed to phone Hammer.

"No. Sorry." It was a little easier this time to not think of a nice cosy grave. After a brief pause he said, "You don't react like a normal person." He said it softly, as if afraid to offend.

"In what ways?" I asked. I wasn't trying to make conversation; I was genuinely interested. People's random observations of me were always intriguing.

"You didn't demand to know my name, or what I'm doing here. No questions about where you are, or where Bastien is, or what happened to your clothes. It's very odd."

"I don't see why I have any right to demand your name from you when no-one knows mine. As for where I am, I figured Bastien has put me somewhere to recover, seeing as I recognised one of his weretigers and I got injured doing a job for him. So, by that theory, I'm safe and Bastien isn't far away. You don't want to hurt me, I can tell, and I've woken up more exposed than this before. That was in a hospital room. I know the removal of clothing is sometimes necessary for speed when trying to stop someone from dying or suffering permanent injury so I appreciate the attempt at decency."

"Astonishing," he said. "I had heard from Bastien that you were different."

"I'm sorry if I unsettle you, but I can't help it."

He studied me for a few moments, sitting back in his chair so the moonlight fell in front of him and he was once more obscured by shadow. At length, he said something very startling.

"I am Kyvernaw, the Queen's Death, and Bastien's maker, member of the Council."

The first response that came to my head had too many expletives to be voiced, so I settled for, "It is an honour to meet you Master Death. I apologise for former rudeness and incivility due to my ignorance."

I looked back at him, to see he had leant forward again and was shaking with silent laughter. His eyes, I noticed, had a gradient to them, pale yellow, to butter yellow, to gold. They were very beautiful, but looked less like Bastien's citrine eyes on closer inspection.

"I thought you were no good at sticking to the rules, Raven, but you are smarter than you are given credit for. No need to apologise to me. I prefer to go without the pomp and ceremony."

I had a thought then. "Were you at Nero's Ball?" He nodded, one slow movement of the head. "So, that was why two Council Members were said to be there, but I only ever met one." My respect for Master Death rocketed in that moment. Mort was all, and perhaps only, pomp and ceremony; too in love with himself to allow people to treat him as anonymous at a public event like that.

We both lapsed into thoughtful silence. After a few moments of deep contemplation, I registered that he had said he was Bastien's Maker. I looked back at him, but he was so deep in thought that I didn't want to disturb him; it was too much like waking a sleeper. He reminded me of stone angels, weeping over the graves of the deceased, he was that silent. I resolved to talk to Bastien later. I slid off the bed tentatively, expecting everything to hurt. I ached, but it wasn't that bad. Some of it may even have been left over from my fight with Selma. I really needed to stop getting myself badly hurt in quick succession.

I felt very vulnerable without my personal arsenal secured about my person. I turned back into the room to see if any of my weaponry was lying about. It wasn't, but Kyvernaw was standing behind me. I hadn't heard or felt him move, he was just there, standing about a foot away.

In bare feet, I was five foot eight. He was, at a guess, six foot four. He had a wide chest, covered by a high neck top that clung very tightly to reveal the planes of his torso through the cloth. Black trousers and boots completed the look, finished off with a knee length black matte leather coat. Everything he wore complimented his body perfectly, but it was oddly utilitarian. My kind of guy; monochrome, practical, and badass. He offered me the coat, but it was far too wide in the shoulders to be comfortable, so I gave it back.

"You would go out in your underwear, rather than have an ill fitting coat?"

"An 'ill fitting coat' could hamper my movement and get me killed. My underwear can't."

"Practical and unemotional, forgive me for the sweeping generalisation but I often don't see that in beautiful modern women. They're more interested in appearance and dignity than practicality."

"Beautiful modern women, eh?" I said, arching an eyebrow. He gave me a sweeping gaze, from feet to head.

"I would be considered blind if I didn't think so Raven."

I chuckled. "As for the dignity, you don't need to worry about that getting in the way of me doing something, because I never had any."

"Raven, even in just purple silk underwear you have dignity."

"That's just about the nicest thing anyone's ever said to me, Master Death." I smiled, and gave him a low bow.

"I do mean it that you don't have to bow, or curtsey, or anything Raven. You may dispense with titles too. I am Kyvernaw, and you may call me such." He shifted his weight to one foot, and drew a gun from behind his back. It was black, and it was mine. He silently handed it to me. "It is fully loaded."

"Thank you Kyvernaw." My gratitude was genuine. If he'd given me clothes, I'd have been less grateful; in my line of work I'd take a gun over clothes any day. He just kept going up and up in my estimations.

We must have been quite a sight emerging from that dark room. The corridor we stepped out into was well lit, too well lit, so we stood out starkly against the white. I winced at the change in light; if it bothered Kyvernaw, it didn't show.

My distinct lack of clothing meant all my wounds, bruises, bites, scars, and tattoos were on show. No wonder people's eyes flashed white and wide. Most of the vamps and Weres we encountered were civilians, with only a smattering of guards, but guard and civilian alike parted a way for us as we stalked those corridors. Kyvernaw was leading the way. I didn't know where to, but I trusted him to not get me killed.

We emerged into the main entrance hall, with all its marble pillars and black candelabra. The floor was very cold underfoot. I glanced over at the stairs that swept up and then parted into two to form the gallery above, like the sweep of birds' wings in flight. I'd never had that thought before. I gave Kyvernaw a sly sidelong glance. He looked at me and nodded; I was getting his thoughts. Surely he of all people should be able to shield better than this.

Like a stone thrown on the still waters of a lake, hush spread out through the room in ripples, and Kyvernaw and I were the epicentre. We'd reached the centre of the hall by the time complete silence reigned supreme.

I heard heavy bootsteps, which got louder as they got closer. Their owner had been hunkering down significantly to be hidden behind the crowd, but as he reached us, he unfolded to his full seven foot four height. Cannibal stood there for a moment, then swept me up in another surprising hug.

"You need to stop getting yourself almost killed. We'd lose a bunch of money without you around," he said, jokingly, but there was an underlying seriousness and worry to him that I didn't often see.

"I'm fine. Two near-death experiences in quick succession

are nothing." Then something terrible occurred to me. "How's Gabriel?"

Cannibal's eyes hardened, those red pupils somehow managing to be cold, but fiery. He gave a slight shake of the head, then murmured as low as he could. "He went mad without you around. Torturella managed to get your blood somehow, and he was fine after that, normal again. You sure fucked him up Raven."

"I know." We had a moment of silent understanding, then Cannibal's eyes flicked to Kyvernaw.

"Who's this?" he asked me without looking away from the taller man.

I didn't manage to reply, because someone was coming down the stairs.

Bastien had appeared with two of his weretigers. They were in half and half form, and looked decidedly unhappy. Behind this trio, was Jean-Pierre, wearing the gold, cream and black of Bastien's House. I think I'd only ever seen him wear black or green; or silver glitter. The four moved down the stairs silently. Behind them, a slightly louder group descended. Hammer was in the middle, flanked by Predator, Belle, and Jade. Jade wouldn't look at me. The hush of the room became oppressive, almost difficult to breath past.

I got the distinct impression that this was not the first time Hammer had been seen at Thurudīn with its Lord. But this was the first time I'd been here.

"Hammer?" I asked in disbelief. His head snapped up and found me in the crowd.

"Raven?" he glanced at my leg once, then moved his eyes back up to my face. There was tiredness and tension around his eyes. I crossed the marble floor as quickly as was decent, but stopped when I got to the foot of the stairs. Kyvernaw had followed me like a warm, breathing shadow. Cannibal was only a little behind him. Hammer moved past Bastien's entourage, breaking formation, and came to the bottom of the steps as if he needed to see me more closely to know it was actually me.

"Before you freak out, I'm fine Hammer."

"Evidently," he rumbled, the beginnings of a fine anger seeping into his voice. He stared pointedly at my leg as he said it; I couldn't blame him, it was hideous.

"Raven," Bastien said coolly. I got the distinct impression that he didn't much like Hammer. "Would you care to join us for a more private discussion?"

"Of course, Lord Bastien," I said, inclining my head out of courtesy.

"May everyone be present for this discussion?" Hammer rumbled, and I could tell this was a point on which much argument had been had. I turned to see Ace standing with Gabriel, Butcher, and Spider.

"It would be better if they were, yes," Bastien said. Ace stopped propping up the wall and glared at Bastien. He moved towards us and the rest of the Sharks followed. Gabriel looked relieved to see me. When he got to me, he instinctively took hold of my hand, like a lost child clings to their mother once they've been found. He relaxed visibly once he was touching me.

"Nice to see you, Rave," Ace said quietly as Bastien headed off and we followed. He led us off to the right of the hall. Kyvernaw followed at the back of the group, so when we got to the narrower corridors, we were penned in by two vampires of the Death bloodline, one the original and one a first generation. Despite our greater numbers, my money was on Kyvernaw and Bastien if things got ugly.

Jean-Pierre wouldn't look at me. He made it very clear that he was with Bastien. In fact, he put the two half tigers between himself and the group of mercs, staying by Bastien as if he were his shadow.

We emerged from the narrow corridor into a hallway of doors. The light was dim, and everything had a muted feel to it, as if there were carpet on the walls absorbing light and sound. It had a very W Hotel corridor kind of feel to it, but the décor wasn't quite as modern, and the W didn't seem like it would eat you alive.

The room we finally entered was wide and low ceilinged. Cannibal had to stoop to avoid the chandeliers. It was an old fashioned drawing room, complete with velvet armchairs, and a lot of heavy looking mahogany furniture. The desk near the window had an inkpot and quill on it, along with some leather bound books. In the far corner, there was even an old fashioned drinks' cabinet with doors made from a diamond pattern of lead and glass. Everything looked like it was an antique.

Bastien settled into a chair, and indicated that we should follow suit. Kyvernaw remained standing near the door, as if he were here to unwillingly supervise a group of unruly children. Everyone was uneasy as they gingerly lowered themselves into the green chairs. I flopped into mine, suddenly tired. There was a lot of velvet rubbing along my bare skin, and I half wished I had Kyvernaw's coat.

"So," Bastien began, "as you are aware we are all here due to The Raven."

"What we want to know," Hammer said a little testily, cutting in before Bastien could continue, "is what the hell you've done to her."

"I'm afraid I cannot answer that." Bastien's voice was reasonable, but it was cold with dislike. No wonder Hammer was pissed off.

"Bullshit," Jade said before she could stop herself. Hammer glared, but didn't say anything as he seemed to agree.

"He is speaking the truth," Kyvernaw said. He had

silently stolen up to stand behind Basiten's high backed chair. With them placed like that, you could very obviously see the resemblance. I wondered if all first generation vamps took on the appearance of their maker.

Evidently not realising who he was, Predator spoke up. "I presume, then, that we are to get that information from you."

Kyvernaw just stared him down until he looked away. Predator seldom averted his eyes, even from horrific sights that made normal people throw up, but he had to look away from Kyvernaw. I could understand; it must be difficult to look into the eyes of Death.

At length, Kyvernaw spoke. "Do you wish me to tell everyone what occurred during your recovery, Raven?"

"You ask me like I know what happened," I said before I could regulate my mouth. I really needed to work on that, especially in front of big Council hotshots.

"I was including you in the everyone." I nodded, and Kyvernaw took a deep, unnecessary breath to begin. He wisely turned most of his attention to Hammer.

"She had passed out on the steps of the castle. One of the weretigers brought her in, and Bastien gave orders for her to be tended to. I happened to be with him at the time, and I offered my services. She had sustained many wounds; a knife wound to the elbow, bruising and fracturing of some of her ribs, bruising to the upper arm, and a fractured thighbone. She had also shattered all the bones in her calf of the same leg. My blood healed most of the wounds, but the leg bones needed more severe treatment. I had to bite and inject a little of my blood into multiple points over her leg to get it to heal. I could have given her more, but we can never be too sure of the potency of our blood. She then slept, and I watched over her. Now, she is well, as you see her."

There was silence, but Hammer eventually rumbled, "Who are you?"

"I am Kyvernaw of the Council."

There was an intake of breath from a couple of the Sharks, and from Gabriel who was sitting at my feet in an effort to maintain his hold on my hand. I thought then was as good a time as any to speak.

"He's no threat, and has treated me well. The leg may look bad, but it doesn't feel bad. It sounds like I owe you my life, Kyvernaw. I thank you for that."

"It was my pleasure Raven. I felt I owed it to you. Luke was a good and devoted servant in life, it is a shame that he fell afoul of a curse, and an even greater shame that you were injured by him."

Jade let out a breath she'd been holding. "I'm with Rave on this one. She tends to know best, even better than you sometimes Hammer." The look our boss gave her was less than friendly.

"Don't be angry at her Hammer, just because she's right. Do we really need to have the 'you're-not-my-father' discussion again?" I said. He had the decency to look down.

"Well. Now that's settled, you are all free to leave," Bastien said, emotional weariness seeping into his voice. "I would like a few moments with Raven. You can wait outside if you do not trust me." He looked at Hammer when he said the last.

Hammer looked at me, silently asking the question. "I'd rather you left Hammer. I'll report back in tomorrow, start working again."

"Fine," he rumbled. All the Sharks left, trailing behind Hammer. Jade gave me a look that clearly told me I would be discussing this with her later.

"You too," Bastien said to the two half-men weretigers. They obediently left.

Jean-Pierre spoke. I'd forgotten he was there. "Bastien, may I leave and report to King Nero?"

"Of course, Jean-Pierre, you need not ask. As long as he doesn't come here, I'm happy with him knowing."

"Why would he come here?"

Jean-Pierre turned to me. "He's been going half-crazy thinking you're dead, even though I assured him I'd seen you. None of us like how many times your life has been in danger and how close together these incidences have been, but he seems to be taking it badly."

"He's got no right to. I don't want to see him."

"You'd better not tell him that."

"I'll tell him what I like Jean-Pierre."

He sighed. "Yeah, I know you will Phoebe." He looked at me, defiant, daring me to pull him up for using my name. The two other men in the room outranked him, and me, and would probably find out my name sooner or later. He must have been really annoyed for him to have done that.

Kyvernaw broke the tension in the room. "Would this Nero be Mort's pet?"

Bastien nodded. "It would, my lord." Kyvernaw waved his hand as if to dispense with formalities. "We might need to have words."

That sounded somewhat ominous.

"As you wish, Kyver." That was the first time I'd ever heard the shortened version of his name. It was pronounced K-eye-ver. I liked it. It also showed that Bastien and Kyvernaw were much closer than it may have seemed. Master Death didn't strike me as one for outward emotion, but a name has power in the old societies of the world. It was something I operated by. The fact that Jean-Pierre knew my name showed my trust in him. I was a little peeved he'd used it without permission though.

"As Jean-Pierre was kind enough to tell you my first

name," I said, letting him know I was irritated by that, "you might as well know my full name. I'm Phoebe Nix. In telling you this, I trust you not to tell another soul."

"You have my word," Bastien said.

"And mine," said Kyvernaw, "but I must ask, are you named after anyone?"

I was a little surprised by the question, and took a few moments to answer. "Not as far as I'm aware. I was abandoned at birth, so I don't know who my parents are, or where my name came from."

"Interesting," was all he said, before he fell silent.

Confused, I turned back to Bastien. "What did you need to talk to me about?"

"The other job. I will understand if you wish to turn it down in light of recent events."

"I'm happy to do it, if you'll keep Mort away from me. I know I said the whole Council before, but really, as long as Mort's nowhere near me, I'm happy." Truth was, I liked him too much, and I didn't trust him because of it.

"Granted. It's in just under two weeks' time. I'll phone and arrange to meet to discuss it further before the event, if that is okay with you."

"Of course. You know where to reach me."

I gave a bow to both of the men in the room. "Thank you for healing me Master Death, and thank you for housing me, Lord Bastien." I stood up straight and gave them a lazy salute with my gun. "Be seein' ya."

When I got outside the room, Edouard was leaning against the other wall. He was hunched in on himself to make him look smaller than he actually was, but he was only just shorter than Cannibal. Not being a drow, it was even more unusual that he was that tall.

"I've been given instructions to take you to a room where

your clothes and weaponry are, and then escort you to your bike." His voice was low, and gravelly, almost hoarse. It was nowhere near as smooth as it had been before. He wasn't looking at me, but staring pointedly at the floor. I suddenly felt the need to cover up.

"Are you…?" I stopped myself, as his head snapped up, and hostility radiated through his eyes. Eye. Cornflower blue. But not solid cornflower blue, I noticed. It seemed to get darker towards the centre, but as if there was a solid ring of electric blue around the pupil, and lightning bolt shaped lines streaking through the lighter blue. I'd never noticed that before.

"Am I what, Raven?"

"It seems a stupid question now. Never mind."

He pushed himself off the wall and crossed the muted hall to stand in front of me, grabbing the tops of my arms. It was the first time he'd ever touched me, the first time I'd felt the power in those hands. "No. Ask me." He was very, very angry, and I had no idea why.

"I was going to ask if you're alright."

He dropped his hands from my arms, and took a small step backwards. His one eye went wide, and the ridge of shiny silver scar tissue that served as his other eyebrow arched, making furrows in the triple scars that disappeared into his hairline.

"He's in a bad mood," a new voice said, cultivated and British. I turned to see a slender man glide round the corner. He was wearing what looked like a tailored silver silk shirt and matching trousers. His skin was honey-tan and smooth. His hair was sandy golden brown, streaked with darker shades and lighter, blonde ones. It fell over his face in a silken, perfectly straight, waterfall, so I could only see one eye. It was turquoise, with stripes of teal radiating out from a dark ring around the pupil, like Edouard's but in greener hues.

I felt a surge of instant attraction, and knew why. He was fey.

"A pleasure to meet you at last, Raven." The new man had completely distracted me from Edouard.

"You too, whoever you are, but can I have a moment please?" I turned back to Edouard.

"I asked if you were okay."

"And you expect me to answer?"

"I don't expect anything, but I'd like you to. I don't understand why you're so angry."

"Any member of the fey would never be so direct, I think it unsettles him," the new man said.

"I'm sorry, but I'm trying to talk to Edouard here, and anyone can see he's a vampire."

"He used to be fey."

I paused, half turned back to Edouard. "That's not possible. Something of so much life cannot become something of death like that, it goes against the natural order of things."

"And what do you, a killer, know of the natural order of things, when you are so intent on disrupting it?" the new man demanded with a smile on his face.

"I'm sorry, who the hell are you?"

"How rude of me. My name is Serge, member of the Unseelie Court, brother of Edouard." His smile was smug, but oh-so-attractive, with those perfectly balanced Cupid's bow lips, a soft kissable pink in all that honey-tan. He drew his hair away from his face, and with a practiced move secured both halves back away from his face with two clips that looked like they were made from bone.

He had an identical scar gracing his softer shaped face, a gentle line running over his nose to intrude ever so slightly onto his left cheek. The same melding of the triple scar wound was evident on his face as it was on Edouard's, three lines disappearing under the hair but melding together in the middle to form one slick, shiny, scar.

"Bloody hell. You're not just fey you're *sidhe*," I turned to Edouard, "and you are too? Or were. Well, isn't life just one mind-fuck after another."

There was a moment of silence. Serge had mild amusement twinkling in the teal depths of his eye, and Edouard had hostility for his brother hunkering down there in the multi-hued blue of that iris.

"I'm not going to get in between a brotherly spat, so please, Edouard, just take me to where my clothes are." I was tired now, tired of all the near-death experiences and tired of all the surprises. I just wanted to go home.

"I was sent here to escort you. It was felt my brother might lose his temper," Serge said.

Edouard growled, a truly feral sound, and you could tell he ripped people's throats out and drained them dry in his spare time.

"Easy." I put my hand on Edouard's chest, which was about level with my face. He felt different to normal vampires, there was an energy thrumming through him that you didn't normally feel with a vamp, normally you felt coldness and stillness. I looked at Edouard until he looked back at me. He relaxed a tad, making no attempt to move my hand from his chest. When I thought he was calm enough to not punch a hole in the wall, I looked back at Serge.

"Edouard is going to take me to my things, and you are going to crawl back to wherever you came from, and stop annoying me, because no matter how pretty you are, it's not going to help if you really piss me off, and pissing Edouard off is going to piss me off."

I glared at him, and he actually took an involuntary step backwards, which made me smile, and made his pretty little face scowl.

But damn he was beautiful.

Cannibal was, technically, fey, but he was a drow, he wasn't sidhe. There's no type of fey quite as beautiful, or attractive in the truest sense of the word, as the sidhe, be they Seelie or Unseelie.

Serge just stared at me while I gave him a thorough looking over. All that mockery left his face and he was just staring back, passive under my gaze.

After a few moments, I stopped staring at him, and dropped my hand from Edouard's chest. "Well, at least I know you can shut the hell up. Now please, I've almost been killed twice in the past week or so. I haven't slept in my own bed for at least that long, and I am getting tired of standing in this corridor in my underwear. Just let Edouard take me to my stuff."

He stood a little straighter, but was still pitifully short next to his brother. Pretty much everyone was. "Fine, Raven. I'll leave. A pleasure to have met you." He gave a courtly bow, then vanished around the corner as quickly as he had come.

"Thank you," Edouard rumbled. His one good eye gazed at the corner round which Serge had disappeared.

"No problem. Care to take me to my things?"

"Of course, sorry. He just... makes me angry."

"I know it's not polite, especially by fey rules, for me to ask, but what's he done to piss you off so much?"

"He's an oath-breaker." He clenched his jaw, and a vein stood out in his face. I gasped. I may kill things, but at least I research what I kill, because if I get captured, or end up in a fight, I don't want to get myself killed because I don't know the rules. I had gasped, because I knew that to be an oath-breaker, to be foresworn, amongst the fey was worthy of banishment from faerie, exile, to wither and die without the touch and magic of the fey of either Court, or to be hunted down by the Sluagh, the dark host. Daytime nightmares.

"That bad? But surely if he's still of the Unseelie Court he hasn't paid the price."

"He broke an oath to me that the nobles of the Court do not wish to acknowledge, though he had been cast from Seelie to Unseelie, which most of the Seelie nobles would think punishment enough. The Dark Court is not thought well of by our family, so in a sense he was banished. But the oath he broke to me was one of brotherhood, of a promise to protect. As twins, it bound us so closely that he received the scar on his face when I received mine. He resented me for that, so did nothing to help me when the vampires took me. Of course, I don't think he'd have been so spiteful if he'd realised what would happen to him. He lost his magic, the touch of the earth, and he can't call upon Gaea as he used to be able to. It serves him right."

It was the longest and most heart-breaking speech I had ever heard from Edouard. His voice was hoarse, I realised, from emotion. Be it anger or sorrow, it had worn away at his very vocal chords until it was a gravelly echo of the smooth, deep sound he had before. I pitied him terribly, but I also knew he wouldn't like my pity.

"Believe me, I get sibling animosity. I haven't seen my brother properly in…" I counted the years off on my fingers, "eight years. Seems to me though, and you can ignore this observation, that you're as much of an oath-breaker as him." I knew I'd spoken out of line, because Edouard went rigid with instantaneous anger.

We'd reached the room my things were in, as Edouard froze, half way through opening the door.

"What?" he asked, turning to me, voice so low I thought it would make the walls reverberate. There was so much anger in that word. "How dare you presume—"

"No, Edouard," I said over him, stopping him, "How dare *you* presume I'm wrong when you haven't even listened to my argument. If your oath to each other was to not let harm come to the other, then by you receiving your scar and your metaphysical twin bond injuring Serge as well, you broke oath first. His letting you be captured and turned, although a greater crime, was in retaliation. So don't sit on your high horse. Come down from your moral pedestal and face the fact that he should be as angry with you as you are with him. Now kindly leave, I can find my own way out."

He was so angry that he had no retort. Denial sat like burning coals behind his eye, and he began to shake. His eye seemed to be very, very bright, like the colour was brighter than the whites of his eyes. Like the iris glowed.

"Your bike will be waiting for you by the steps. I hope I don't see you soon, Raven." He wasn't even talking anymore, he was growling. He sounded like Weres did when they were in full animal form, but still speaking in human language. Only the powerful ones could do that, but you could tell they were animal not human, when they spoke. Edouard's anger was so primal, so great, that he sounded more animal than human. Of course, he wasn't human, and never had been.

He strode off, anger evident in every line of his body, the tension running like crackling energy along his spine, the stiff, high set of his shoulders, the clenched fists and their fine trembling; he was evidently exerting a lot of effort to stop him from breaking something. I was glad, because I didn't fancy dying today after my two recent escapes.

I moved into the room, but turned my head to look down the corridor, only to see the end of his long blonde hair disappear around the corner. I sighed and shut the door behind me. My things were laid out at perfect parallels and perpendiculars to each other. Wearily, I went over to the table they were placed on. The first thing I did was affix my arsenal of weaponry about myself. Only then, feeling better and safer, did I get dressed and leave.

18

My head was spinning when I finally got home. Gabriel and Ace had been waiting with the guard by my bike on the front drive. If Ace hadn't had the foresight to wait, I'd have forgotten Gabriel completely. I wasn't used to being someone's keeper.

I was trying to muddle through everything that had happened in the last week. I'd gone from werewolf, to mercenary, to vampire, to faery politics in what felt like the blink of an eye. I'd met Master Death of the Council, and I'd met a member of the Unseelie Court, rarely found outside the Courts themselves. Bastien and Hammer had established a nice animosity, so my boss and my client were at loggerheads. I'd acquired another mouth to feed and tend to, one so reliant on me I was temped to kill him in his sleep to put him out of his misery – and me out of mine. I hadn't seen Lucille since the argument with Hammer, and I'd ignored all calls from The Sunken City, which meant Nero was getting possessive again.

Also, I'd nearly died. Twice.

When you look at what happened to you over the last week and it turns out like that, you've got to take a moment to ponder how messed up your life is.

Hammer had given me time off until Bastien's second job, which I had agreed I would still do. He'd told me he didn't want me dead before I brought in the biggest paycheck any Shark had ever seen. It was his way of telling me he cared, without the others suspecting he was a real human being with real emotions. It was actually kind of sweet.

My answerphone light as flashing like crazy when I got home. I had twelve messages. One was from Hammer, one from Jade, and ten were from Asher.

They got progressively more panicked, tired, and angry. If I had been trying to get hold of someone for a week I'd be annoyed, and I didn't blame Asher for being irate on my answerphone. After all, he had no idea what had happened to me in the past week.

Well trained even after such a short time, Gabriel went into the kitchen to make tea, while I phoned Asher from the living room. It was the first time I'd seen my flat in a while, and yet here I was, doing my duty yet again. I sighed as I dialled the number.

It rang three times. Four. Five. When he finally picked up, Asher sounded so very, very, tired.

"Hello?"

"Hey Asher. I've just heard all your messages."

"Jesus, Phoebe," he said, recognising my voice. "Where the hell have you been? Nero's had me up night *and* day just in case you phone. He's a bloody pain in the arse, and thanks to your phone avoidance I've not slept properly in longer than I care to remember. Could you be a little more prompt in returning my calls in future?" He exhaled at the end of his rant.

"I'm really sorry Asher that you've been through that, but I have a very valid reason."

"Do tell. Enlighten me Nix because I cannot fathom something important enough."

I sighed. "I had an argument with Hammer, and I resolved to not answer the phone for a couple of days. After that I got kidnapped by a group of werewolves, the same lot that did my back in, who wanted revenge for the death of the their pack leader. I was held there for four days, the night I got out I realised I'd not done a pretty important job. It was to take out a revenant. The bastard turned out to be a rotter and he hurt me fairly badly. I was being healed for that for the last few days. I got home just this minute."

There was silence on the other end.

"Ah shit, now I feel bad."

"Don't. You couldn't know."

Steely coldness crept into his voice. "Which pack was it that took you?"

"I've dealt with it Asher. I killed the bitch who was the leader. Selma of the East Clearing pack, or whatever they call themselves. I've got a new flatmate though. I'd really like it if you could talk to him actually, see if you know a pack he could go to, and see if you could advise me on how to keep him sane."

He sounded normal again when he said, "I do not envy you your life at all. I think I'd hate to be you."

"Hey, Asher, I hate to be me a lot of the time too." I sounded tired and bitter; and so did he.

"Sorry. I'm just exhausted; the brain isn't functioning too well. I guess it's rude to ask you to come to the Court, but Nero told me to ask you. He said, and I quote 'we have matters to discuss, my seeing her is of the utmost importance' end quote."

"Argh, I really don't want to go. I want to just *sleep*. Would he be amenable to me going tomorrow night do you think?"

"I don't know," Asher replied honestly. "He's the bloody King, he's not known for his patience, and when it comes to you he's like a covetous, jealous, five year old."

"Never let him hear you say that."

"He's sung in his coffin, he has no idea what I say about him during the day."

I knew I didn't have to tell him that there were always people who would overhear him and report to the King. A lot of backstabbing went on at the Court because people think that if they report someone else, they are then in favour. It doesn't quite work like that, unless you save the King's 'life'. But then again, Asher was top dog in the Were world of England. I don't think anyone but Jean-Pierre would have the guts to report him to Nero.

"Tell him that if he has any regard for my health, he'll let me off until tomorrow night, and that if he doesn't have any regard for my health I won't come at all. He'll just have to like it, and you can tell him I said that. I am so not in the mood for Nero's metaphysical bullshit."

"You sound tired, Nix."

"No shit, Sherlock." There was a moment of mutual silence, then I hung up.

I slept all night and all day. Gabriel slept in the bed with me. I'd been trying to get one of my sofa's changed for a sofa bed, but he infinitely preferred being in my room. As much as I didn't want him to be a pet, it was like having a dog. He fetched when you told him to, sat, rolled over, and played dead.

He must have woken some time before me, as when I woke up at about 7pm the following evening, he was sitting on the other side of the bed with a cup of tea for me. It was like having another Lucille in many ways, but this one could do daytime too.

"Thanks Gabriel," I said sleepily. The tea was warm and smelled good. I took a sip that burnt my tongue but it was worth it. He'd even learnt how I took my tea. I knew so little about him that I felt a little like I'd been neglecting him. "Did Ace treat you okay when I was... otherwise preoccupied?"

He nodded. "He's actually really nice. I was fine once your friend managed to get your blood from somewhere."

"She has keys, she took some from the stash. I'll have to top that up soon." I yawned, stretched, sighed. "I have to go and see Nero today." The weariness was evident in my voice, and I made no effort to conceal it. "I've got to go to the Sunken City as soon as possible."

"Anything I can do to help?"

"I wanted Asher to meet you, but I haven't checked if you can come along. Get ready just in case and I'll phone him."

I looked back up at Gabriel, away from my cup of tea. His face was pale and he looked a little ill, his eyes flashing white around the edges.

"Asher?" he asked with visible difficulty. Oh.

"He's not as bad as you think. Actually, he's really funny given half the chance. I promised I'd look after you Gabriel, I won't let him hurt you."

He seemed to relax by increments, relief sneaking in on his face slowly and stealthily.

"Okay." One word, soft, quiet. One word of absolute trust. Jesus Christ what was I letting myself in for?

We arrived at the Sunken City on horseback, swords at our sides. Translated into modern times, we arrived on the bike, and I had a fairly hefty arsenal of weaponry with me. After the revenant, I thought I had every right to be paranoid and carry way more than normal. Asher had said he would see 'the wolf' if I brought him. He was grumpy; I think I'd woken him up. He'd suggested I wear something revealing to appease Nero, distract him from being crazy. That didn't sound too promising.

I didn't go in corset and mini-skirt, but I did put on a scoop neck top and some very skinny jeans. That would have to do.

The announcement of 'The Raven and guest' was made, and we were allowed into the Main Court. I don't think I'd ever been to one of the other Courtrooms. I didn't even know how many there were. My plain black high heels clacked on the floor as I crossed it. Gabriel padded softly beside me in converse, jeans and t-shirt. By human standards, he was invading my personal space. He clung to me like a shadow, eyes nervously darting all around.

I was half way across the floor when Nero was suddenly in front of me. He stared at my chest before he looked at my face and said, "Oh holy Mother Dark, you're okay."

"I take it Asher has reported to you what has happened."

He nodded, and stared at me as if he was seeing a ghost. I pulled Gabriel up so he was standing next to me rather than slightly behind, and hugged him to the side of my body by my arm through his. Nero scowled at that, seeming to wake out of his joyous moment of seeing me alive.

"If you don't mind, King Nero, the trials of the last few days have been wearying, and I would greatly appreciate it if we could discuss matters in private." I deliberately slid my eyes to gaze over Nero's left shoulder at Marianna, an upstart vamp with the wrong attitude, whose eyes were glittering eagerly at me like I provided entertainment on a whole new level. I glared at her, and shifted my weight more solidly onto both feet. The unintentional reaction was that Nero stared at my legs and very, very slowly, let his gaze roam from head to foot.

"Of course Raven, we can speak in private. The Hand will escort you to my private rooms."

"I need Gabriel to stay with me, if that's okay?"

"Gabriel?"

I indicated the Were on my arm. Nero narrowed his eyes, but nodded.

Jean-Pierre, Asher, and Carlos got up from their thrones. They really creeped me out – the thrones, not them. They were giant hands. The palm provided the seat, the wrist provided the base, and the fingers were the back, curving up way beyond their heads, macabre clasping claws in silver, white and black.

They deadly dreaded trio seemed to flow down the stairs, rippling, graceful. They came to the centre of the floor where Nero, Gabriel and I were standing. Nero and I were having some strange staring contest, but, as I felt them draw near, my gaze slid to the Hand. Each of them gave me a small bow from the neck, and I gave a slightly more deferential bow. Gabriel let go of my arm to flatten himself to the floor. I wasn't used to dealing with people who were so subservient, I was going to have to man him up a bit. I frowned, but smoothed it away so Gabriel didn't see it when Jean-Pierre told him to get up.

"If you will follow us," he purred in his silken French voice. I realised it was his Court voice, that sultry purr to turn the heads of admirers within a thousand foot radius. Okay, maybe not quite that far.

We followed the Hand along what was I was beginning to think of as the usual route. We reached the now-familiar door and saw two men I'd never seen before.

They were identical, apart from one had slightly darker brown hair. Everything about them was solid, from their inhumanly wide shoulders, to their remarkably narrow hips, thunderthighs, stocky arms, and blunt ended thick fingers. All of this stocky muscle was clad in leather, the utilitarian kind Edouard wore. They looked like they would have been more comfortable in hides torn from a fresh kill, still dripping. They had a savageness to them, and something that made me think Viking, or older.

The stocky vamps stepped aside for the Hand and let us through without so much as a word.

Everyone was suspiciously quiet. I kicked off my high heels and settled on the sofa. Gabriel sat on the floor by me. I tucked my legs onto the sofa, and he leant his head back on my knees, despite me telling him he could sit on the sofa. Asher sat the other end, Jean-Pierre sat in what I suspected was his armchair, and Carlos remained by the door. None of them spoke.

Until Asher broke the silence, of course. "Did you have to be sewn into those trousers Nix?" His voice was playful, but not what it usually was.

"You sound tired."

"We all are," Jean-Pierre said, slumping further down in his pile of cushions, feet hanging over one of the chair's arms.

"You too Carlos?" I looked over my shoulder at the door, where Carlos had been leaning with his eyes shut. There was a small patch of frost on the wall behind him that he didn't seem to notice. He just looked at me with those silver, silver eyes, and then shut them again. I took that for a yes.

Gabriel wriggled by my feet, pressing himself against the sofa, and edging more towards the corner. He was staring at Asher with fear written plain across his face.

I looked over at the tired Wolf King, and prodded him gently with my foot. He looked over at me. "Yes darls?"

"Seeing as we have a little time on our hands, would you care to meet my ward?"

"Sure thing babe, he the guy cowering at your feet?"

"Be nice. I know you're tired, but please, behave. I've scared him shitless enough without your help."

"Fine Nix, I'll try not to be the big bad wolf." He looked at Gabriel a little too intently for the young wolf's liking.

"Asher, Wolf King of Britain, this is Gabriel, formerly of the Eastern Clearing clan, and now my ward and friend." Gabriel got up on queue, and hesitantly took a step forward. Asher stayed lounging on the sofa.

"Get up you lazy arse," I said, and kicked Asher until he moved. It cheered him up, amusingly.

"Alright, alright Phoebe. I'm sorry, I'm just tired, but I did say you could bring him today, and I apologise for being less courteous than was appropriate."

"No worries." I turned, smiling, to Gabriel. "That was an apology from Asher, I wouldn't get used to it."

Gabriel looked like he had no idea what was going on. "Can you find him a clan Asher? I'm happy for him to keep living with me, but I think he needs to be around other wolves."

Asher stretched and yawned, rubbed his eyes in an oddly childish gesture, and looked tired. I got up and went over to him and wound my arms round his waist. He was warm and smelled good, cologne, and wolf, and something else that was just *him*. "You shouldn't be trying to persuade me by such methods," he said.

"Is it working?" I asked as I snuggled my face against his chest, luxuriating in the sound of his heart beating against my ear.

"Mmm, I think it might be." He held me to him gently, and hunched to rest his head atop mine. I had my eyes shut, and when I opened them, everyone had moved. Gabriel had moved round so he could see my face, Jean-Pierre and Carlos had moved up near us so they were close. All of them looked like they were witnessing something strange.

I pulled back from Asher's arms, reluctant to let go. He opened his eyes, but seemed less surprised than I was that everyone was in a different place.

"He can join my pack, if he wishes."

"Are you serious?" I asked before I could stop myself.

"Of course Nix. I'm always serious." He was smiling again and he looked less tired.

I turned to Gabriel, and took a step away from Asher, closer to him. "Would you want to join the Royal Pack, Gabriel?" I asked it softly, as if it would be less shocking that way. Gabriel just looked at me like he was stunned. "Gabriel?"

"I'm not entirely sure I believe what I'm hearing, or seeing for that matter."

"Seeing?" My eyebrows plunged into a confused frown.

"That golden thing that went from you to the King." He dropped his head at Asher's title, and looked at the ground.

"What?" I looked at Jean-Pierre. He stared back at me, and mouthed 'later'. I shook my head as if to shake the thought away, and looked back at Gabriel. "You would have honour and a home for yourself if you accepted your King's generous offer."

His eyes went wide with panic. "I'd have to leave you?" He grabbed my hand with both of his and held it. "But I'm not sure my mind could take it."

I gently eased one of his hands off so I could hold both of them. "I would see you as much as I could and I would make sure you had a steady supply of my blood. The fact of the matter is I cannot babysit you forever." I gave him a concerned look, and he seemed to take me at my word. "Asher," I said, without looking at him. "You have to promise me that he'll be well looked after, and that you'll toughen him up."

"It's a promise, Phoebe."

It didn't even occur to me that it was odd that he would promise such a thing so readily, because right then Nero walked in with his Vikings behind him. The smile fell off his face instantly.

19

"May I ask, as calmly as I can, what the hell is going on?" Nero glared, but after meeting Serge, his teal eyes were almost plain in that handsome face.

I glanced down at where I was holding Gabriel's hands, and let them go, sighing. Nero overreacted to everything. As soon as I let go of Gabriel, he fell flat to the floor in submission.

"Nero, he's my ward, not my lover. You don't need to act petty and jealous. I'm no more your property than I am your maker's."

"I do not wish you for property, Raven, I wish you for wife."

I almost choked on air. "I'm sorry, what?"

"You heard me."

"Nero, there will always be something undeniably attractive about you, but that is because you rolled me." I stopped and corrected myself. "Because I *let* you roll me, and now I will never trust a single feeling I have for you, so put all romantic thoughts out of your head. I came here to let you know I was fine, because it was asked of me, nothing more."

"How dare you speak to our king like that," one of the Vikings rumbled at me, taking a step forward. Nero barked an unintelligible order, and the two muscular towers went to take up their post on the other side of the door once more.

"It pains me to hear this," Nero said. Gabriel was still on the floor, but Nero ignored him like he didn't exist.

"Then I wish you joy in your suffering." I smiled sweetly.

There was a pause, tension crackling in the air. Then the door opened.

Mort stood there pale and perfect. He was wearing a white billowing shirt tucked into soft white leather trousers, encased up to the thighs in pale, slightly creamy suede boots that laced up the back of his legs with cream ribbon set in silver eyelets. His hair looked dark and rich and warm next to all that paleness. His irises were glittering silver discs.

Everyone bowed as low as fit their position. I was hesitant, but dropped to the floor with Gabriel. If in doubt, go lower than higher.

"Rise, Raven. The assembled Council members wish to speak with you."

My blood ran cold in my veins, but I stayed on the floor, knowing if I raised my face he would see the alarm there.

"Forgive me, Mort, but it is not appropriate for me to rise before my superiors are permitted to do so."

"Oh just get up, the bloody lot of you." He was short of temper this evening. He was even losing his seductive purr. Something was very wrong, and I was guessing it was the presence of The Council. Were they all in England now ready for the banquet? I hoped not. I'm not sure I'd survive a private audience with the entirety of The Dark Queen's Council.

We all rose, but I kept my head bowed and would not look at Mort.

"You are to come with me, Raven, whether you wish to or not. This lover's spat can be held at a later date."

"I assure you there is no lover's spat occurring."

"'Tis but that of unrequited love. I am glad your hearts affections are not so damaged as our fair King's, for you will need all your heart and all your strength with the company you are about to meet. Follow me, Raven, everyone else must remain here."

No-one protested or so much as batted an eyelid at Mort's commands. Everyone knew their place, and it was lower than that of Beautiful Death.

I thought we were going to somewhere in the Court, but instead a car collected us and we were driven, in silence, to Thurudin. Mort took me through secret passageways that were deserted except for the torches flickering in their sconces on the walls. Finally, we reached our destination. The room we entered was more a grand hall than a room. It was Bastien's version of the Hall of Horrors, but his was more refined. Nothing bled down the walls. They were, instead, patterned in various shades of cream, brown, and grey, all relative to the age of the bone hung there. Close to the door through which Mort and I had entered were three very, very old vampires; and one not so old one.

The not-so-old vampire was Bastien. A six foot tall woman with pale skin and knee length, perfectly straight, bright ginger hair had him suspended off the floor by her hand around his throat.

"So if it is not his fault then you are to blame for your own predicament Kyvernaw. Would you go under my tender care in his place?" They were so old they *had* to know we were there, but we were obviously not important right now.

"Yes, Ira, I would rather I be submitted to your attentions than Bastien, but that is only for our Queen to decide."

The redhead sighed and dropped Bastien like a discarded doll. A human would have been gasping for air and possibly writhing on the floor from the burning in his lungs. Bastien just got up and dusted himself off. He didn't look at me.

"I see you have finally brought her Mort. I hope you weren't delaying progress for your chance for a quick fuck in the back of the limo."

I really, really didn't like her. She turned blood red eyes to me. Rimmed in black, it seemed like they flickered with hellfire. I dropped my gaze as soon as I could, and bowed to the floor. I didn't want to give her any reason to hurt me. I was mortal; I would not survive what she did to Bastien.

"Rise, fool. I will not waste time with niceties when what you have been called here for is discussion. Mort, make the necessary introductions so this can be over soon. The tedium already bores me." There wasn't sarcasm or boredom in her voice, but hostility, anger, even rage. She was just so damned angry. And I got the feeling it wasn't personal.

Mort led me over to the powerful trio. "Master Death you already know, but this man is Tartarus." The man in question was over six feet, slim, icy skinned, blond haired, blue eyed, and smiling hellishly. He suited the name. "And this," said Mort, indicating the redhead," Is Iratus Nex, first child of the Queen and founder of The Council. This, Ira, Tartarus, is The Raven."

I bowed to the most frightening members of the Council I had met. Ira gave me a scornful look, and Tartarus just kept on *grinning*. It reminded me a little of skull, it can't help but grin.

"Good." The one word was full of malice. Iratus Nex certainly lived up to her name, as it meant Wrathful Dead. Everyone knew she scorned humanity, and despised all races other than vampire. She was also the very first vampire the Queen had ever made, Wrath turned into immortal flesh. "Now we can commence business. You've been called here, Raven, because you are to be apprehended, and detained either here or in the cells of the British Court until we, the Council, have left to return to our sovereignties. You will have no say in where and how you are kept, and you will not disobey the rule of the Council. Understood?"

"Yes my lady, though I know not the reasons why."

"Pretty words won't help you. You are too much a danger to Master Death and therefore the rest of the Council for us to allow you freedom of movement. A cell is the only place you'll be safe."

"The only way *you'll* be safe you mean."

That was possibly the most stupid thing I had ever said.

I awoke in the same room, on my back, with Kyvernaw cradling my head in his lap and arms. There was blood on the floor, but not much. My neck hurt a lot.

When my eyes could focus properly, the red blur I'd thought was fire turned out to be Iratus pacing a small section of floor. The very air seemed warmer with her anger.

"She broke your neck Raven, I again had to loan you my blood to heal. Apologies."

I tried to sit up, found it hurt, but persevered. "I should learn to keep my mouth shut."

"Yes, you mongrel mortal bitch, you should!" Iratus shrieked. Tartarus laughed, which she didn't appreciate, but I noticed she made no move to hurt him. Even Wrath is no match for The Underworld I guess.

"I would pay good money to see you do that again," Tartarus said, a low bass chuckle, like thunder, underlying his lighter voice. He seemed to have the voice of everyone and no-one.

"I do believe, my lord, that I have learnt my lesson about speaking before I think."

"A terrible shame, often people who speak before they think visit me." I just bet they did, fools had been killed for a slip of the tongue forever. Don't let modern society fool you, it still happened. The vampires were an obvious case, but other systems killed for the tiniest insult too.

"Because I like you," Tartarus continued in a more normal voice, one that didn't echo with the screams of the souls of the ages, "I will tell you why you have been deemed too dangerous to be free. The blood lent to you by master Death has bound you tighter than you realise. He can find you wherever you are through thinking of you, as he proved accidentally earlier when in our presence. Dear Lady Wrath assumed that the same would be of you, so if you were ordered to harm or, as foolish as any attempt may be, fatally wound Master Death during the time his blood has an effect on you, you would be able to find him instantly."

"May I speak relatively freely, Tartarus?" He smiled, bemused, and nodded. "By that notion Master Death would be able to feel me coming, and any attempt I made on him would be thwarted before I could get close."

"You do not protest that you had never dreamed of such a thing?"

"There is no point, I can be innocent and still a threat. Sometimes it is merely who you are that makes you a threat, not your intentions."

"Wise beyond your years Raven. But still, we cannot allow any compromising of *our*," he smirked at Iratus, "safety."

I looked at Bastien, then back at Tartarus. "But my lord, by keeping me locked up until you have left you would be compromising your safety. I am to be head guard at the banquet held for the Council and the Queen. By not having me as your protector and coordinator of all the other guards you put yourselves at risk."

"You have too high an opinion of yourself, human," Iratus practically spat at me, but at least she had stopped pacing. The floor looked like it was cooling from the tread of some pirate who had traded his peg legs for giant red hot pokers.

"No my lady, merely a low opinion of others."

Tartarus laughed again, and it made me feel ill. "She must certainly be our head guard for the night. If there is no danger, she can be entertaining. I vote for her being allowed to keep her freedom."

"You can't, I have—" he cut Ira off short.

"You are not my Queen, Iratus. I answer to only one Dark Lady, and she is not you."

Grinding her teeth in fury she merely said 'fine' and stalked along the length of that bone-covered hall to disappear out the far door.

Tartarus smiled down at me where I was sitting, still half supported by Kyvernaw. "Isn't it fun making new friends?" His icy blue eyes glittered evilly like they were lit by an internal fire. I shuddered, and looked away, which made him laugh again. That laugh haunted my dreams in the following nights, echoing off skulls and spines and fangs, trophies of conquered foes and lost friends.

20

I was so very, very glad to be back at home. Lucille was up and we had a reunion the way only Lucille and I did – with copious amounts of blood and tea. Gabriel couldn't stop smiling. Apparently, Asher had not only offered him a position in the Royal Clan, but had shown him the room in which he could live, and the whole werewolf arrangement at court. He had met some others who lived in The Sunken City and had been overjoyed with being part of such a clan. Asher had even said he could live with me when he wanted, which made Gabriel even happier. His happiness translated into eagerness to please. I don't think Lu or I got up once to refill our drinks.

It was quite fortunate that I had the two weeks off, because it meant I was free to help Gabriel move out. I also gave him a present of a mini-fridge with plastic sacks of my blood in it. As weird as that is, he appreciated the gesture. He was nervous when he was all moved in, the realisation that I would be going home and he would be staying finally settling in. I promised to visit him at the weekend. I went during the day to the Court, and Asher actually helped move Gabriel in. Once he realised that the big bad wolf king had a nice side, Gabe relaxed and he and Asher got along well. It warmed my little black heart.

I worked for Guillaume quite a lot, because I found I didn't know what to do with the time on my hands. I went shopping and bought a motorbike. My weapons bike had been damaged, and taken a lot of repairing after the revenant, so I decided to have a halfway bike. I had a civilian one, a weapons one, and now I had one half armoured and with half the weaponry on it. It took most of the two weeks to fix the bike up, but I was enjoying the job so much I drew it out as long as I could. My normal bike was a Harley, but once I'd got that one, I wanted a Ducati. My weapons bike was made from all sorts of shit, but now, finally, I had my Ducati, and it was the most badass Ducati in the world. I got a bit carried away and, with a little help, it was like something from Mission Impossible. My weapons bike looked a little like the bike from Ghostrider, but this one looked normal, until you pushed the little red button.

One night, I went to Guillaume's on my new shiny red bike (I wasn't known for subtlety) in a very chipper mood, wearing a short dress to please Guillaume and relatively lightly armed for me. I only had one set of throwing knives, one hefty knife, and one gun. The gun was even in my bag, because the dress was more on the body-con side of things than I usually went for, and there was no way I could hide a gun without a jacket.

Bastien was in that night with his entourage. He was also in a very cheerful mood, as he stole a cheeky, but chaste kiss, when he arrived. "Why the joviality?" I asked as his entourage stared. To them I was a random woman, but Bastien, like Nero, could recognise me. Initially, I'd worried about it, then I decided it was too much effort to worry.

Bastien replied, a low murmur in my ear. His accent was delightful. "All the Council have arrived safely and are very pleased with their hospitality. It would make any King proud. One or two of them are meeting me here later, just to warn you."

"Can I tell Guillaume?"

"They would like the surprise, but for the young one's nerves it is probably wise." I smiled at him calling Guillaume 'young one'. Of course, Bastien was stupidly old, but Guillaume was no spring chicken, he'd seen his fair share of centuries. My smile, as Bastien had intended, made it look like he'd been muttering sweet nothings into my ear, merely chatting up a waitress he seemed to know.

A couple of hours passed in a relatively blissful haze. If I was this happy, I should take a break from work more often. I had just served Bastien's table, and gone behind the bar to retrieve my phone from my bag when all hell broke loose.

The first thing I noticed was the trademark knife, longer than my arm and with a wicked curve that clearly said it was used for hacking at things. The second thing was the matte black gun, too high a calibre necessary for a bar environment, but then again, he had always been fond of overdoing it.

Tin Man stood in the doorway, face stranded white and stark in the midst of his black clothing and hair. His eyes were a flat grey, lifeless and glazed. I'd never seen much of a spark in the Tin Man, because he lived up to his name. It was a name we had given him, The Sharks, when we came to the conclusion that he didn't have a heart. He seemed to have no emotions whatsoever, as if he'd gone beyond sociopath into a black empty void of nothingness.

People screamed and were silenced with a look. I hid behind the bar, hoping not to be noticed. You didn't interfere with another merc's business, and as much as I disliked the

Tin Man, I had to adhere to that. He took slow, sure steps across the room. None of the vampires seemed bothered until he made a swift move and pointed the gun at Bastien's head. One of the vamps jumped him, tackled him to the ground, and got a chestful of stake. Never underestimate how much weaponry Tin Man can hide on him.

"Leave him!" I bellowed, grabbing my gun from the back and jumping over the bar, which was not easy in my short dress. I dropped the glamour as I did so, and my tattoos and scars became visible. I was wearing flesh-coloured tights, so you could even see the bullet wound scar in my left knee, the poison in which had bled a starburst around what would otherwise have been a neat round scar. You could see the crow tattoo on the inside of my right ankle, and the four slash marks curving over my calf that I'd received the day my back was marred. Almost all of my war wounds were on show. That was enough to make the vamps hesitate. Bastien seemed calm, all things considered.

Tin Man was up, and had his gun pointed at Bastien's head again, and this time, no-one tried to stop him. I wondered, vaguely, were Edouard was, and cursed Serge on the suspicion that he was the reason Edouard was not with his lord tonight.

"Thank you Raven," Tin Man said, assuming I'd come to aid him. He was very wrong.

I hit his arm out of the way and pressed my gun against his forehead, standing between him and Bastien. "When I said leave him alone, I meant you to leave Bastien alone."

"You don't interfere with another mercenary's business, it is our way."

"You're interfering with mine by trying to hurt the King of Thurudīn," I lied. "Why else would I be here unless on a job? I'm here to protect him." I had to lie, because Tin Man could not know that I was friends with Guillaume. He'd certainly use it against me.

He allowed himself a little frown, which I felt more than saw as my gun was pressed between his eyebrows. "I must admit I am perturbed that you simply will not die."

"Excuse me?"

"I thought identifying you for the wolves would kill you, but they failed to reap their revenge as I had hoped they would."

"Are you telling me that you're the reason I was chained to a wall for four days?"

"You take my jobs and my money. You're just a problem I need to be rid of."

I had had enough. I drew a knife so quickly it was just a flash of silver before it embedded itself in his chest. Unfortunately, I felt the deep bite of his arm length blade in my upper arm, the one that was holding the gun up. It hurt, but I had to keep the gun on his head. It was my only advantage at this point.

There were gasps and a few more screams, but we ignored them. The world had narrowed down to the Tin Man and his weapons. Fury built up in me, warm and comforting like an old friend. I knew he was beyond all psychological help, and I knew that it wasn't personal, but I had suffered for days because he had given my identity away, and I was not having that.

"You are going to leave, and you are not going to attempt to harm Bastien, now, or ever again."

"I'm not sure that's a very profitable business, Raven."

"I don't care. You're still going to do it."

"Why?"

"Because I'm better than you." There was a moment of hesitation, like the calm before the storm. All at once, Tin Man pulled his knife free from my arm and made a bid for my throat, ducking below my gun despite the fact that it meant my knife tore up his right pectoral muscle, and I lowered my gun and fired. I shot him in the stomach, and he screamed. It was the only time he'd ever show any emotion.

"Do you really not have a heart, Tin Man?" I asked. My voice was cold and even, despite the fact that he stabbed his knife through my leg. I didn't even feel it, I was in a place beyond the pain and the damage, which meant it would hurt like a bitch when I came back to myself. As he fell to the floor, I pulled the knife in his chest out, and plunged it in over his heart. I knew I'd missed when he howled but did not seem to die. Screw this.

"Pleasant dreams in Hell, oh heartless man," I said as I sighted down the barrel of my gun and pulled the trigger. His head exploded, brains and blood hitting the vampires nearest, sticking to the chairs. A few humans threw up. Lots of them screamed but, oddly, no-one was fleeing. The vampires all sat calmly at their tables, a few of them carefully removing the bits of skull and brain with a napkin, most not bothering.

My leg buckled, and my knee landed sharply in the soft mush that had been Tin Man's head. A tan hand with a golden sheen was offered to me to help me up, and the yellow eyes I found when I looked up were indeed Bastien's.

"Your assistance is much appreciated, especially since I did not pay you to protect me."

"I never liked him anyway, and seeing as he set me up to be killed by the werewolf clan that tortured me, I think we're even now."

"You think death is suitable recompense for putting you through a few days of pain?" one of Bastien's entourage asked.

I simply said, "Yes."

"She is not a woman to cross, is our Raven," Bastien

said, still staring at me intently, as if I had done something particularly interesting.

"No," Guillaume said, walking over, "She's not." He was frowning at the mess I'd made.

I sighed. "I'll clean up, Guillaume, I'm not just going to leave you with this."

"You bloody better." I grinned, but the pain hit me then and made me catch my breath. Guillaume frowned again, but this time at me. "You really need to stop doing this to yourself."

"Occupational hazard," I said, finally giving up and sitting on Tin Man's bloodied body, his brains squashed all over my knee. Guillaume offered me a freely bleeding wrist, which I took. I drank a little of his blood, and the knife wounds closed. The one on my arm vanished, but the one on my leg was more persistent. At least now it was the dull ache of a mostly healed wound, not a fresh slice that had cut up my calf muscle. I wouldn't have been able to walk if it weren't for Guillaume's blood.

Bastien was now staring from me to Guillaume in fascination. "I saved your life Bastien, I'd appreciate it if you cut down on the staring." I got up from Tin Man's body, using Guillaume's arm to haul myself off the corpse. I asked him to get my bag, and he obliged. Bastien finally spoke.

"Do you love him?"

"Yes, but not how you might think. He and his sister raised me when I killed my parents. They are the only certain things in my life."

"Interesting."

Guillaume returned with my bag. "What is?"

"That I love you."

He smiled, and it was both very male, showing all the vamps that he thought the sex was good, but underneath it was genuinely pleased, happy that I would admit such a thing. I gave him a gentle kiss. "Will you help me shift the body? I'm not sure my leg will like it too much if I carry this much weight after injuring it."

Without a word, the vampire who had asked me if I thought death was a fit punishment for betrayal got up, scooped the body off the floor, and took it outside. I followed him, to find he was frozen just outside the door in an awkward position. I realised after a moment that he was trying to bow and hold the corpse simultaneously.

He was bowing because Tartarus and two female vampires I didn't know were heading towards the Red Fang's entrance. Tartarus laughed when he saw me.

"How delightful. I take it we missed the show and business has eased for the night."

"Unless you're fussy about brains on the floor, I'm sure Guillaume is happy to stay open for you."

"Raven, you are ever full of surprises. I am saddened I did not get to see you kill this one. What had he done?"

"Betrayed me."

"A grievous crime indeed." I didn't answer, but instead bowed low to the Lord of the Underworld.

I left as soon as I could. Guillaume came out, gave me my bag, and greeted the Council members. I didn't find out who the other two were, because Guillaume ushered them inside. Bastien's vamps had cleaned up, so I was free to go. The big vampire who had carried the body for me stayed with me until I had burned it in a skip. I phoned Hammer from the car park to tell him what had happened to Tin Man. He almost sounded relieved that one of his mercenaries was dead. Tired, I got on the bike and rode off. The tall vampire was still in the car park when I looked back over my shoulder.

21

"I've never had to do this before." Hammer sighed as he said it. "I may not have liked the guy, but still."

"I know Hammer, and I'm sorry it came to it, but he betrayed me. Who's to say he wouldn't do it to any of us. None of us really liked him, not if we're honest. Everyone always says you can't speak ill of the dead, but if the dead were bastards then I don't see why not."

"Do you want to call Tin Man's family? I'm sure they'll love to hear that from you," he said, the hints of a chuckle in his voice.

I just looked at him and he didn't find it funny anymore.

He dialled and a man picked up the phone.

"Hello, am I speaking to Mr Cartwright?"

"You are, who's calling please?"

"I'm not a call centre. I'm phoning about your son, Matthew."

There was a pause on the other end.

"What about him?"

"He's dead." There was another pause.

"I know. He died when he was fifteen. If this is your idea of a joke I don't find it funny."

"I assure you sir, it's not. Your son is Matthew Cartwright isn't it? Black hair, pale skin, grey eyes?"

"Yes, but he disappeared when he was fifteen, they found his blood in his room, the police told us he was dead as they never found him alive, or ever found a body." There wasn't any strain in his voice, he could have been telling us what time the next train to London was.

Hammer and I exchanged a glance. Hammer nodded, then asked, "There is someone here who wishes to talk to you, do you mind being put on speakerphone?"

Mr Cartwright sighed. "No." Hammer pressed the button.

"Hello. Can I ask who I'm talking to and what the hell this is about?"

"Of course. I'm the Raven, you have just been speaking to Hammer of the Hammerhead Sharks. We called to let you know your son is dead."

"He's been dead for seventeen years."

"I'm afraid not. Your son was the mercenary known as the Tin Man. He must have run away. I'm sorry to have to be telling you your son has been alive all this time only because he now most certainly isn't."

"I'm afraid I'd have to see a picture of him to believe that." Mr Cartwright sounded tired, but not overly distressed.

"Can we meet you somewhere? It can be somewhere public if you'd feel safer."

"This is bullshit, I shouldn't have to be going through this. He's been dead for seventeen years, there was blood all over his bedroom!" Okay, now he was starting to lose it.

"He had scars on his arms that would account for such

blood loss. It is possible he staged it so you would not think he had run."

There was some swearing on the other end of the phone. "That little bastard. Sounds like something he would do. His mother and I split up after he supposedly died. He'd been wrong in the head all his life, and now he was gone we didn't have anything to keep us together."

"He did have the name the Tin Man for a reason."

"Heartless, no emotion, sociopathic."

"Exactly."

The pause this time was longer, and punctuated with the occasional sigh. "It must be him. If it's convenient I can meet you in the centre of Peterborough."

"We can be there in an hour. Where would you like to meet?"

"Do you know Central Park in Peterborough?"

"Yes."

"Can you meet me at the Buttercross Café?"

"Certainly. In an hour then Mr Cartwright."

He sounded very grim when he agreed and hung up. Hammer and I just looked at each other and sighed. "Do you reckon we should take anyone else with us?" I asked.

"Who was closest to him?"

"None of us were Hammer. Absolutely none of us."

We arrived at the Buttercross Café precisely an hour after our phone call with Mr Cartwright. Butcher came with us because he was bored and fancied getting out of the Concrete Palace for a bit. He couldn't give a shit that Tin Man was dead. Neither could I.

A man got up when we came near. I guess there was no-one we could be mistaken for, especially as Hammer's face was as famous as a film-star's. He was short, but then again, everyone was short in relation to Hammer. He was shorter than me, and I'm five eight. Tin Man had been five nine; I was guessing the height had come from his mother's side of the family. We said our names and shook hands in turn, Hammer, Raven, Butcher. Mr Cartwright was pale. We were probably the three most frightening people he had ever seen.

We sat on a bench looking out over a pedestrianized roundabout with a massive willow tree in the centre, sitting far enough away from the tables outside for no-one to hear. The weather wasn't particularly good, so the park wasn't busy. A little curly haired schnauzer barked at a teenager on a skateboard as he went by.

Butcher went in and got drinks, because I had been complaining I needed a cup of tea. When he returned, and placed a cup into Mr Cartwright's hands, they were shaking. He seemed more frightened of us than he seemed upset about his son's death.

I handed a picture to him, and his eyes went wide. It was a photo of the all of us taken a couple of years earlier, when we reached seventeen mercenaries and decided that that was enough. Hammer and I had a thing about odd numbers. The next photo I gave to him was one of Tin Man when he joined. It was taken four years ago. He was twenty-seven in the picture.

"That definitely Matthew. It's so surreal to see his face grown up when I never thought I would. Can I keep this?"

"Yes, it's a copy, we have the original kept on file for security reasons, you understand."

"Of course. How did he die?"

This was the hard part.

"I'm sorry to have to tell you this, Mr Cartwright, but I killed him. He had me tortured and tried to have me murdered by a werewolf clan because he thought I was taking his money by getting all the highly paid jobs. He told me this while attempting to murder someone I had sworn to protect. The only solution was his death, and I'm sorry it was so." I'd said it as simply and as gently as I could, but really, how do you tell someone that?

There were tears shimmering in his eyes, but he didn't look away from me. He went way up in my estimation for that. "I can well believe my son jeopardised your life for his own gain. He threatened his mother for not giving him his pocket money when he was twelve, he had a knife from the kitchen." He paused, sobbed once, and hung his head. "We did our best for him, but his mind was too damaged. I don't know what we did wrong." The last sentence was said in between broken sobs. His whole body shook, but he was oddly quiet. We let him have his grief, we did not try to comfort him, and we did not tell him it was going to be okay. We were hard as nails mercenaries; we couldn't afford to show we could feel.

Eventually, he stopped crying. His voice was quiet and hoarse when he spoke again, like the tears had cost him more than they appeared to. "I'm sorry that my son has brought such grief to you, and I thank you for telling me."

"Do you have a contact number for his mother?" I asked softly, "Or his brother, we need to let all the family know."

His eyes were dry when he looked back up at me. "His mother committed suicide a few years after we split. Jack's moved to America. He doesn't talk to me anymore."

"I'm very sorry, Mr Cartwright, to be bringing up such sad memories. But there's one more thing we need to check. Are you happy for us to release his name to the press?"

"The press? Why?"

"He was a Hammerhead Shark. We're world-renowned. If one of us falls, protecting the nation from the threat of malignant supernatural forces, the world needs to know. It's like the name of a fallen soldier being announced on the news."

"I see." His face was grim. "He may have been damaged, but he was still my son. You may tell the world he was loved by his father."

"Thank you."

He sighed and stood. "I'm sorry, but that is all I can take." He produced a scrap of paper and a pen from his coat pocket and scribbled down a number. "That's the last number I had for Jack. Let me know if you find him?"

"Certainly." I got up, and shook his hand. He was a braver man than I thought, because he had just shaken the hand of the one who had killed his son. I had a Priam and Achilles moment, before I just felt like shit.

One of Green's specialties was finding things, and people. Green was an elf, a member of the fey, and he was connected to everything living. Blood makes the crops grow, so his killing people didn't offend Nature, and she still chose to favour him. He had pale green skin, almost iridescent, but nothing that could be mistaken for white. He had green hair that shifted colour as it pleased, falling just enough on either side of his face to cover the pointed ears. People often mistook elves for faeries as they believed the fey had pointed ears, which was just not true. To have pointed ears was a sign of being elven. Cannibal had them too.

By being connected to nature as Green was, he had a link to life like no other in our band of misfits. He could tell you when a flower was going to burst from the ground, when it was going to rain, who was coming round the corner, and he could find you when you didn't want to be found. We gave him the task of finding Tin Man's brother. Being of earth and all that, Green hated planes. Cold iron, man-made metal, electricity, all freaked him out a bit. He could deal with guns, and he could deal with the Concrete Palace, but he absolutely hated planes. I had to fork out a lot to even persuade him to go near one, but I'd given my word that we would find Jack, so find him we would. Spider and Pierce went with him, to keep him calm on the flight, and to help him should he need it.

Spider called when they landed. Green had, apparently, spent the whole flight with his eyes shut and his hands clenched tightly round the seat arms. The thought was almost funny. The last number Mr Cartwright had had was a New York one, so they'd flown there, but Green was so freaked out that he was currently hiding in Central Park to be amongst 'growing things'. She promised to report back in later.

We'd gone back to HQ after meeting Mr Cartwright. I wasn't even meant to be working, but here I was. Butcher, Hammer and I were sitting in his office, in silence, contemplating that no-one mourned the loss of Tin Man, not really. His father loved him but he knew he was a monster, he knew the world was a better place with that little piece of darkness gone.

"Well, as cheerful as this ruminating is, I'm heading home. I'll try not to kill anyone tonight."

"Good luck with that," said Butcher, slight hostility in his voice. I paused, and turned to look at him on the drug dealer sofa.

"Did you like Tin Man?"

"No."

"Then why are you upset?"

"He was the first one of us to die, Raven. That means something."

"I guess it does." My mind was led down a dreadful path. Butcher might not, but Hammer and I knew who was most likely to die next. Coal. She was a mother of three and her husband had left her. She was only twenty-six. But none of these hardships were fatal. What was going to kill her was her cancer. People kept remarking on her bald head, how the shaved-hair look actually worked for her. But I knew it was the chemo.

I sighed. "If I stay here any longer, I'll be depressed until Tuesday."

"Can you come back in tomorrow Raven?" Hammer rumbled at me.

"Why? I'm off for two weeks, remember?" He just gave me a look that clearly said I was testing his patience.

"I need you in to tell all the other Sharks what happened, we need to work out what we're going to tell the press, and you need to write something that one of us can read in your place on television."

"You think it'll be that big news?"

"He's the first Shark to die, and he died in the line of duty. It'll make national television for certain."

"Fair point. Why don't I come back in tonight then, seeing as tomorrow implies day, and that's no good for Vlad, Roo or Leech."

"You can come back tonight if you want, but I've done a full day shift. While you're away we have to do all the work," said Butcher.

"I work harder than you all the time, and you complain about not getting enough jobs."

"Fine, Raven, make me eat my words."

"That's not what I'm trying to do."

"The fact still remains that I'm not coming in tonight."

"This is crucial, Butcher. And it's for Tin Man," Hammer said. "How would you feel if you were the first to fall and someone couldn't be bothered to come in?"

"Trying to emotionally blackmail me isn't going to work. Firstly, I'd be dead so I wouldn't give a shit. Secondly, I actually have friends here, people like me. They'd come."

"You can't argue with that Hammer," I said. It may be harsh, but it was the truth. No-one liked Tin Man.

"Well, at least I know not to appeal to everyone's warm and fluffy side to get them to come in off shift."

My phone rang in my pocket, making me jump. Butcher laughed. I scowled at him as I picked up.

"It's Spider, we've found him."

"Already?"

"Green's very good."

"Evidently. Is he with you now?"

"Yes."

"Does he want to speak to either me or Hammer?" I heard the movement of cloth as she shrugged before she said, "I'm not sure he gives a shit."

"Well, just tell him and come home then. We're going to have a meeting tomorrow night, so the vamps can join."

"Fair enough. We'll see you then." I heard some muffled noises. "Green says he wants a raise." I chuckled, and hung up.

The meeting went well, all things considered. We tend to argue when we're all assembled like that. It's very rare all seventeen of us are around at the same time, and when we are, our personalities tend to clash. Vlad, Roo, and I always argued. We bickered like little children, but in the end it was all friendly. However, when we argued we really argued. What we found to argue about this time was whether I should speak publicly. After all, my image wouldn't be visible on camera, it'd be darkness, or a distortion. The two vamps argued I should, seeing as this was the first time any of us had died, and seeing as I had killed him. I argued I shouldn't, of course. And as was the way of things, I won.

Six of us were chosen. We were going to arrange a press

conference. Someone was going to read a statement written by me. My words read by someone else was all the press were ever going to get.

After we'd decided on the press conference and the funeral, I had a chat with Green.

"I hear you did well in New York."

"Thanks Raven. I'm glad to have been put to use. It felt good to use my magic again."

"Do you miss it?"

"Miss what?" he asked, though I had a sneaking suspicion he knew.

"Faerie, and all that entails."

He gave a laugh that had nothing to do with enjoyment, and everything to do with bitterness. "I was cast out."

"That's not an answer."

"In our culture, it's rude to ask, and I know you know that," he said, narrowing his eyes at me. I hadn't really noticed how remarkable his eyes were. His pupils were all shades of blue-green from lightest turquoise to darkest teal. Around them was a rim of dark blue, like tattooed on eyeliner. And as for his eyelashes… they were nothing like human ones, not fine hairs to frame the eye. Instead, they were curving triangles of… something, green in colour, and translucent. He had nine on the top all the way along, but just two on the bottom at the very outer corner of his eye.

"Why are you staring?" He frowned.

"Your eyes are pretty." He gave an abrupt laugh.

"Thanks, Raven, never thought I'd get a compliment from you. Nice to know someone still thinks I'm pretty." He was grinning from ear to ear, and I could do nothing but grin back.

"Alright you two, break it up." We both turned to Spider, with our grins still on our faces.

"That's kind of creepy," she said.

"Kind of?" said Ace. "If you ask me it's very creepy."

"Ah, I love you guys." I said. I flipped a lazy salute, then left for home.

The press conference went well. We told the world that Tin Man had died on a job, which was technically true. Everyone bought it. In fact, they believed it so much, that they had a day of mourning to mark the death of one of the brave seventeen who devoted their lives to protecting everyone from those 'few supernaturals who saw fit to break our harmony and terrorise us'. Of course, it was a load of bullshit. As we told everyone Tin Man had been on a vampire job, I had the amusement of seeing Lucille on television spouting the bullshit we'd come up with. She was very good at it. I mocked her for it when she came home, which earned me a smile and a thwack on the head with a thin paper version of Jane Eyre from 1938; one owner from new.

I didn't go back to The Red Fang, choosing instead to spend the daytime with Tamara, Jade's girlfriend. Seeing as they lived round the corner, I walked round. Sometimes Jade was there, sometimes she was at work, but Tammy was always around. Being a freelance necromancer, most of her work was at night, as people were superstitious and thought you couldn't raise the dead during the day. For a random, untrained necromancer that might be the case, but Tammy was a member of the Order of Valragoth, she was trained, a necromancer by blood.

Jade was out, working. I was sitting on the floor of Tammy's living room, drinking tea.

"Are you back at work tomorrow?" she asked, lounging all six foot of herself on the sofa.

"Don't remind me."

"Is it the big job? With the Council and the whole shebang?"

"Yeah." I sighed and finished my tea in silence.

My two weeks were finally up.

22

It felt like judgement day, and I wasn't even sure why. I was harbouring a deep and irrational dread. I told Lucille about it, and she said it was natural for me to be worried; I was, after all, meeting the Dark Queen and her Council, anyone would be bricking it. That made me laugh, because hearing Lucille speak in an overly modern fashion was always amusing. She got stuck in her ways in the seventeenth century.

The deal Bastien and I had made was that I would be at Thurudīn with my trusted people several hours before the first guests were due to arrive; or emerge, seeing as a few of the Council were staying there. I'd phoned around, and ended up with five people I knew I could count on. I actually asked if Edouard could be on my team, but Bastien told me he and his brother were to be at the banquet. The mention of Serge made me frown, and wonder vaguely if I could add keeping him away from me into the bargain.

My five chosen people were to join with Bastien's castle guards, head of guard, and a bunch of others from all the Houses of the court who volunteered. My five included, surprisingly, a man who was head of his own House in the British Court.

Lyev Vahko was Russian, 6' 5", slender as a willow branch and one of the meanest fighters I had ever seen. Apparently, they'd had a ceremony last night naming his son, Stepan, the head of house should he die protecting his Queen tonight. He was a noble of the British Court, and I had no right to ask him to be one of the guards, but he was more than happy to when I called. He gave up his chance to be at the Queen's table simply because I'd asked him to. Lyev had been my friend when I was at Court, in the days before I left. He had been the one whose table I had wanted to look at so much when I first came back to Court, just to see if he was there. The navy banner with the scarlet heart; the banner of the House of Vahko. When I was younger, if Nero and his Hand had other business to attend to, Lyev would be sent with me to amuse me, which he was very good at with his dead pan wit, or I would sit at his table in the Court and watch proceedings. I'd missed him when I'd gone.

The second was Conor Callaghan, who liked to be difficult and spell his name the Gaelic way, Concobhar. He was a werewolf, head of a clan who he also insisted had a crazily spelt Gaelic name. Most people knew them as the Highland Wolves. Conor was an Irish-scot, and never let people forget that he had both types of Gaelic blood in him. Hey, at least he was proud of his heritage.

Maurelle was the third. I'd never known if she had a surname, but she was a very good witch indeed. She was the most imposing woman I had ever met, not because of any physical height or a tendency towards violence, but because she had a perpetual sense of barely contained magic, like there was a huge power thrumming just below her skin.

I didn't want to get any other Sharks involved, but being second in command, Cannibal got a whiff of the job from

Hammer, and told me he wanted to help. I'd lay my life in Cannibal's hands any day, and I must admit it made me feel safer to know he'd be around.

The fifth and final addition to those I was bringing in was somewhat unexpected. Nero had insisted that his Hand provide protection. One was for The Queen, one for him, and one for the Guard. Bastien had wanted Jean-Pierre to help guard the Queen anyway, so he was with her personal guard for the night. Asher, seeing as we already had a wolf, was guarding Nero, which meant Carlos was the one I got. I had nothing against Carlos, I just got the feeling he wouldn't like taking orders from me.

We were each to chose a colour and stick to it for the night, so we would be more easily identifiable in a crowded room. Carlos naturally chose grey, Cannibal chose white, Maurelle favoured purple, Conor wore green, Lyev wore his House colours of navy and gold, and as for me, I chose red. Our mostly monochromatic looks helped, because I spotted each of them instantly. I roared up the long gravel drive on my weapons bike, clad entirely in dark red leather, from the jacket, to the corset, to the trousers, to the boots. I could wear things with silver buckles that would catch the light, or lighter colours should I so wish, because we wanted everyone to know we were guards; we didn't have to blend into the darkness tonight.

None of them knew each other, so they had almost awkwardly arranged themselves on the steps of Thurudīn while waiting for me, giving each other suspicious glances. It was comical to say the least. They all moved towards me when I roared in on my bike, and only then did they realise they were all on the same side.

All seven foot four of Cannibal was gleaming in a white fey-style tunic with white trousers, white shoes, and detailed white embroidery, lost unless you got up close. It made his black, truly black, skin look even darker, and his eyes were a surprise of colour in all that black and white.

Maurelle was wearing a floor length purple dress in some gauzy fabric, with the symbol of the triple goddess made out of beaten silver clasping the dress together so it pinched in beneath her bust, the low v of the dress ascending from that silver triple moon.

Conor was in dark green-dyed jeans, but with a bright green t-shirt and pale green hoodie on. He wasn't dressing up because if he had to shift, he didn't want to ruin any good clothes.

Lyev was resplendent in his House finery that I had seen him wear at Court on occasion. He wore navy trousers with gold embroidery around the hem over polished black leather shoes. As was his wont, he also had on a military jacket with gold buttons and more gold embroidery. It even had gold epaulets. The high neck of a round collared shirt peeked out white over the top of the thick navy material.

When Carlos had chosen grey as his colour, he had lied. He was dressed entirely in silver, fabric woven from some metallic thread, for he shimmered in the soft moonlight. His hair was a uniform grey, not of age, but of the storm, not so silver tonight as it had been, which was odd. It was blacker towards his roots, but swept away from his face as always. Nero had obviously demanded he wear eyeliner for the night. He normally didn't, but damn did it make the silver of his eyes burn like they were internally lit. The silver cloth made his skin look like polished alabaster, all high sharp angles and perfect lines. There was no softness to Carlos, just as there is no softness to the winter, but he was still beautiful. He looked just as breath taking as he had the night of the ball, but now I had no Asher or Jean-Pierre to distract me. I never usually paid much attention to Carlos, but now I couldn't help myself. The clothes were much the same as

Cannibal's, but done in a different colour. When he turned round, there was the surprise of a teal and black dragon, covering the entire back of the tunic, embroidered on the silver cloth. Nero wanted him to be branded as his tonight, despite the fact that he wasn't to be with his King for this momentous event.

We marched into a relatively quiet Thurudīn like a multi-coloured storm. Between a witch, a member of the fey, a werewolf, a weather worker, a Head of House and a… whatever I was, we had a lot of magic and power. You could almost feel it buzzing in the air around us.

Bastien actually looked a little startled when we arrived. He had evidently been waiting for us, as he was sitting on the steps in the grand hall. He got up and gave me a wide-eyed look.

"My, my, Raven, you certainly know how to bring in the cavalry. I did not expect such…" he trailed off and waved his hand in front of him as if he had no words.

"It's okay Bastien, I have friends in high places. I would like to introduce to you Cannibal, one of the mercenaries who you may remember." Cannibal grinned at my sarcasm. He was a seven foot four drow; you didn't forget him easily. "Lyev Vahko, Lord of the Fifth House of the British Court, who I'm sure you know."

"Pleased to meet you again Lord Vahko, I did not expect to see you here as a guard."

"It is my honour to protect our Queen, Bastien, and of no less renown than being at Her table."

"I meant no offense," he replied with the utmost civility. I glanced from one to the other.

"Okay, whatever animosity, however mild, there is between you, put it aside for tonight. Now, if I may continue. This is Conor Callaghan, packmaster of the Highland Wolves. Maurelle, a powerful witch and a very good friend, and Carlos of the Master's Hand, who again I am certain you are acquainted with." Bastien surprised me by bowing to me and my entourage.

"A pleasure. Gratitude is owed to you for your services tonight. Now, if I may introduce my guard as well?"

We waited for a moment as a troupe of men filed in, all in black outfits to match their black guns. They had a lot of guns. Despite them having far more places to hide it, I still had more weaponry than them. I had a moment of feeling superior before shock wiped all superiority from me.

"Raven, may I introduce my head of guard—"

I cut Bastien off. "Nathanial Woodroffe. Nate." I was positively beaming as I moved over to him. "You fell of the map a couple of years ago, I thought some big bad nasty had got you."

Nate grinned at me. He was much like Hammer, very tall, very wide, skin a little lighter, more *café au lait* than Hammer, but where he and Hammer differed was that he was like a teddy bear, not a grizzly bear. Not to undermine his ability to kill and maim, but he was just so damn *nice*. He always had been. I'd known Nate as long as I'd known Jade and Tamara, we'd all gone to school together. I thought he was dead.

Nate smiled in disbelief and shook his head, sending his halo of soft brown curls gently swirling round his face. "If I was dead, I'd have come back to haunt you. Come here, you." In one long stride he closed the gap between us and pulled me into a bear hug, which lifted me off the floor. I laughed, a rare and joyous sound. When he put me back on the ground, I turned to a slightly shocked Bastien, still smiling. "I don't think there's going to be any problem with me getting on with your head of guard Bastien."

"Evidently. I admit I was a little worried. I thought Nathanial's optimism might jar with your pessimism to the extent that you wished to hurt him." I gave a surprised burst of laughter. It was so honest, and so accurate, that it couldn't help but be funny.

"Oh you know Raven alright," said Conor, grinning wolfishly.

"Shut it you."

"Sir, yes sir." If I'd had a pen or other harmless object, I'd have thrown it at him. Instead I just shot him a look, which he laughed at.

I should know that an evening that gets off to such a good start can only get worse.

Guests had been filing in for the best part of an hour. I was on front door duty with Lyev. Carlos had disliked me telling him to attend to the doors of the ballroom, or whatever you want to call it, banquet room, main hall. Apparently, he'd started sulking, and had frosted up the wall before Maurelle jolted him with some fire magic. He didn't like it, but he stopped sulking. I don't think he much liked being 'demoted' to guarding a door, when his two companions were guarding The Queen and Britain's vampire King.

Conor and Cannibal had decided, almost instantaneously, that they liked each other. They were in the banquet hall, circulating. I checked in with them every so often via microphone earpieces. We certainly looked like security. The thing about being security is that you require as much attention as a wall. Nero broke this rule when he arrived, pausing to kiss my hand. He also politely turned his attentions to Lyev. Fine if there had been no-one around, but his halting meant everyone behind him was held up too, and for the next few minutes people were showing far too much interest in us. Of course people showed respect for Lyev as was due him as a Lord, but I also got a lot of sidelong glances and whispering, which pissed me off a little. The

Castle guards were doing their best to keep the press at bay, but their best obviously wasn't good enough because someone with a camera got through. After getting me on camera, which I knew wouldn't come out, I'd had enough. I scared him off with vaguely violent actions.

"You are the same in some ways, yet so different," said Lyev, amusement sparkling in his black irised eyes.

"I've always had a temper."

"Aye, that you have."

Just when I thought door duty couldn't get more fun, my favourite person turned up. A coach and four, with horses black as the night, pulled up at the foot of the steps. A figure all too familiar to me got out and glided up the stairs.

"Ah ma chere, the outer guards were most persistent that I arrive by a side door, for my own safety I am to understand. I found out, through the methods available to us vampires, that you had requested I be kept away from you. So, naturally, I am here." Mort grinned at me, flashing his fangs. "I thought we were getting along so well." He was a little more serious as he said this, but I had to admit, I was having a hard time not staring at his outfit. He was resplendent in yet another billowing shirt, this time black, the rounded draped neck fastening at the top with an inch-long ruby set in antique silver, blackened by time. He had on patent leather trousers that clung oh so tightly, what you could see of them, for they disappeared into thigh-high soft leather boots. At first glance, the side of his boots had patent leather patches, but on closer inspection it was actually that the sides of the boots were cut out, and instead there were buckles with silver clasps, fastening the boots from thigh to ankle down the outside of each leg.

I was glad I was propping up the wall, because my legs didn't feel too sturdy. I absolutely *hated* that he had that much of an affect on me. I felt a little better when I looked around and saw both men and women swoon, fall to the floor, and look at him with such adoration it was close to pain. At least I wasn't one of those people.

"Last time I saw you, you did something to me that I can't explain, so naturally I distrust you. This being said, you're going to have to excuse me for telling you to go to hell."

He laughed and it rubbed along my insides in a fashion not entirely unpleasant. His voice was silk to caress the inside of the ear. "Hell doesn't want me, so I stand here before you, Raven."

"Just get inside."

"You cannot avoid me all night," he said with another knee melting smile, suspicious seriousness deep in his eyes.

"Watch me." I was glad my voice sounded sturdy and level.

He merely smiled wider, and glided inside. I was more worried by that than any kind of retort he could have come up with.

After he was sure Mort was out of earshot, Lyev said, "I was afraid you would become acquainted with him."

"Believe me, Lyev, I am not happy that I have." I frowned.

"Do not be like that Ph… Raven. He may be narcissistic and enjoy tormenting you for his own pleasure, but he is, all in all, a good and just man."

"Hah. I'll believe that when I see it."

"Of the ten Council members, I can only think of three nicer than him."

"Really?" I couldn't keep the disbelief out of my voice, but then again, I had met Iratus and Tartarus the other day. I suppressed a shudder. "Fair point. Out of curiosity, who are the nicer ones?"

Lyev smiled. "I shall only answer that question as it

is you who is asking. Chanson de la Sang, Phoebe, and Kyvernaw."

"I can agree with the last." Lyev looked like he was going to reply, when a new arrival said, "How sweet," voice positively dripping with sarcasm.

There were two women ascending the stairs, clutching their full skirts with identical elbow length gloves on, postures matching from rigid corseted bodices that offered up their breasts like ripe fruit. Their skin was flawlessly creamy, and they each bore a perfect imprint of teeth in black on the column of their throat. The only instance in which they differed was that everything the one on the left was wearing was in black, and everything the one on the right was wearing was in white. The one on the left had black hair to match the dress, and it was in the exact same style at the one on the right's, though hers was blonde. Lyev bowed very, very, low, and I followed suit.

I realised then who they were. They were the women I had seen with Tartarus outside The Red Fang when I had killed Tin Man. They were identical twins, but as if one had been painted in white and one in black. They bore the black teeth imprint on their necks, the sign of The Queen's Kiss. Standing before us was The Beautiful Chance, sisters made vampire by the Queen herself, which made them Council. The one in black was Jesabelle Balthazar, beauty, and the one in white was Chanson de la Sang, blood song, known as Chance.

"My lady, I meant no offense," Lyev began.

"None taken, my little lord. We all know my sister has a softer heart than I. Though I cannot begin to compete with Iratus or Moragorth, I take it as a compliment." With that somewhat frightening remark, they swept inside. Chance smiled at me as she went past. I knew immediately which sister I preferred.

"It's going to be one of those nights," I said, letting out a breath I hadn't known I'd been holding, and mentally cursing Bastien for recommending a time for me to rotate off front door duty.

"Agreed," said Lyev, slumping against the carved marble archway of the door.

Seeing as I'd already met a lot of the Council, I thought to hell with it, and stayed there. When it had been quiet out the front for half an hour, Nate's voice came over the earpiece. He sounded cheerful as ever, so maybe he'd avoided all members of the Council thus far.

"Raven, Vahko, all's quiet on the western front so you guys can come inside and some of my lackeys can guard out there instead. You're wanted in the main hall with Conor and Cannibal."

"Yay, just what I wanted, to be *closer* to the Council."

"Hey, I just take orders Nix."

"Raven, you have to remember that."

"Yeah, yeah, sure Raven. See you in here in a minute."

"Wait, you're in the banquet hall?"

"Yeah. And you're missing the show."

That sounded very, very, ominous. Lyev and I exchanged a glance.

"I swear to protect you, Raven."

"I would not have you forsworn, I'm fairly good at getting into trouble."

Grim faced, we headed inside.

23

Carlos did not look happy when we reached the doors. He was scowling for all he was worth.

"You're a winter weather worker, I thought you were better at being as blank and unreadable as fresh snow than this Carlos."

"Not of late," was the only response he would give.

"Go and be with your King if that is what grieves you."

"It is not."

'Then what, Carlos, because you either need to lose the attitude or stop guarding."

He pushed himself up off the wall in a forceful motion. Frost spread underfoot as he strode towards me. With one powerful hand, he grabbed my arm and started to walk me away from the others. "Lyev, take up post with Maurelle on the door and tell Nate we've gone for a walk for a minute," I said over my shoulder. I didn't bother checking if it was okay. They were under my orders tonight.

Carlos' grip on my arm was cold and painful. My breath

came out in a cloud of condensation. "Let go of me before you freeze me to death, Carlos." He let go abruptly.

We had reached a darkened corridor off the main hall, and were far enough down it to be out of earshot, even of Lyev.

"I do not wish thee ill, Raven."

"Why the formality?"

He gave a grunt of frustration. "So many questions, know you not it is rude to ask that which is not willingly given? I would not give you an answer."

"Then why are we here?"

He breathed slowly, a long cloud of condensation appearing before him like he was exhaling cigarette smoke. "I would tell you why I am so out of sorts."

I didn't demand he tell me, I merely leaned against the wall and waited for him to be ready. Eventually, he spoke, very quietly like the hush of a snowstorm.

"My old Queen is here."

I frowned, puzzled. "I know. She sits upon her throne in the banquet hall."

"No," he shook his head continuously from side to side, as if trying to shake some thought out. "No she is my new Queen. My *old* Queen is here."

I waited for him to elaborate, and when he didn't, I had to say, "I don't understand. Are you saying you had a Queen before this one?"

"No, I am saying I was not always vampire. My old Queen is here with her daughters and her guards. I cannot go into that hall without feeling shame."

"You have nothing to be ashamed of."

He turned on me and started shouting. "How would you know?! You know not what I was before! How do you think a vampire, something of so much death gets be in control of something that nature dictates! I am not a worker of wintry winds from my vampire blood, but from my faerie blood! They killed me and they turned me as an experiment, to see how much power I would retain. I was alive once, Phoebe, I was master of the seasons and now I have been reduced to this! My old Queen would see my shame, and her daughters would loathe me. I am already cut off from them, I cannot bear to be despised by my people too!"

He had been shouting in my face, but he collapsed to his knees and buried his face against me, clutching at my arms as if I were his only anchor. He was sobbing silently, the tears wracking his body but not being heard.

A shadow appeared at the end of the hallway. I saw the silhouette of a gun, as someone ran towards us.

"Raven! Are you okay are you hurt!" Nate yelled as he ran towards me, obviously thinking Carlos was making attempts on my life.

"I'm fine. You should go Nate."

"But—"

"Go. Now."

He paused, and half turned, so the light from the hall touched his face. His eyes were wide. "Sometimes you scare me Nix."

"Good. Now leave."

I had been petting Carlos' hair, stroking it to try and calm him down like you would a frightened child. So this was why he was cold and grim faced, this was why he was icy and shut down. He'd lost what he was, and lost a lot.

Eventually, Carlos stilled, and after another minute he stood up again. You would never know this tall, icy man had just had such a display of emotion.

"Thank you Phoebe."

"Any time." I didn't even tell him off for using my name.

He smiled, like sunlight coming through winter clouds, pale, watery and cold. "I do not think it will happen again."

"The offer still stands."

He nodded in affirmation, then sighed. "It used to rain when I cried." His voice was empty, but I knew what it cost him to say that, his internal landscape was deep in snow, each flake a frozen tear of the sky.

"I will go in with you if that is what you need."

"I would prefer to not go in at all."

"You have two Queens in that room. At least one must be attended."

Nate's voice chose that moment to come over the earpiece. "Get in here Nix. Now. They're putting our guards outside, all of your guards inside, and sealing the room. Whatever's happening, it's not going to be pretty."

I looked to Carlos and opened my mouth to tell him but he said, "I heard. Let us go."

He had shut down his emotions again, and as I slid my arm through his to give him comfort, I felt as if I was walking towards that banquet hall on the arm of an exquisitely carved and magically animated ice sculpture.

As Carlos and I entered, Conor and Cannibal appeared but our sides. Maurelle and Lyev followed in behind us, and the doors were shut. Nate came over. The seven of us strode into the room, to much inspection. Everyone was quiet, and their attention was on us. I pretended as if I could not feel it, the piercing of a thousand pairs of eyes, and instead silently touched each guard and pointed to their post. Carlos indicated with a furtive glance where the faerie Queen was placed. She was at a table right at the front of the long hall, by the stairs that led up to the throne. I told Carlos to go on the opposite side of the room to her, near Nero's table, and I walked towards the faerie Queen and her entourage of daughters and guards.

I could feel the magic buzzing around them as I got

nearer, and actually gasped involuntarily as some magic lanced through me in a stab of pain. It faded as quickly as it had come, and I took to leaning against the wall a little further away from the fey than I was intending to stand.

Looking up at the stage that had been made of the throne platform, I saw what show Nate had said I'd been missing. Mort and Nero were on the platform. Mort was down on one knee, Nero was flattened to the floor. Both were facing the Queen. I got the distinct impression that they'd been bowing for a long time.

I tried to look at the Queen herself, but found I couldn't. Every time I looked her way, I found my eyes staring absently at a chair or a piece of wall, not knowing how they got there. It must be some form of glamour or protection, so I tried to look at her out of the corner of my eye. The only thing I could glean from that glance was that she was dressed entirely in white. A man stood next to her throne like a dark shadow, almost blending into the wall, because I couldn't focus on him properly either. I hated playing with the big leagues; I was out of my depth.

A voice as cold and hushed as a cave deep underground dropped into the silence of the room. "Decorus Mortuus, King Nero, stand and step aside." They rose in unison, despite Nero having father to rise, and stood to one side of the Queen, no longer facing her.

"I bid the Raven come forward." I started like I'd been slapped.

A voice like the roll of thunder spoke. "Do not keep the Queen waiting."

I stepped forward in a shocked daze, but was brought to my senses when another lancing pain shot through me. I fell to my knees, which jarred painfully on the marble floor. A hand touched my arm and warm energy, like sunshine, spilled through me.

"Get up." It was one of the fey, female, beautiful, with hair the colour of fresh blood, skin like milk chocolate, and eyes with a ring of lilac round the edge, fuchsia pink in the middle, and dark indigo around the pupil that bled into the other colours like some elaborate flower. It was dizzying.

I stood with the help of her hand, but coughed up blood onto the floor. I thought the pain had been metaphysical, but the cooling pool of red liquid at my feet proved otherwise.

Some of the younger vampires and Weres tensed, but no-one in this room was truly young and without control. This was the elite of the elite, from the vampire world, the Were world, the sidhe, and the drows. It was unthinkable that any of them rise from their seat to lap up the blood from the floor like a cat with cream.

"Iona, deal with her," the Queen said. The woman holding me let go, and shoved me forward. The Queen spoke again. "Sacrifice must be made." My heart missed a beat, then started thundering in my chest. I knew who Iona was. The whole world knew who she was. The Queen had three protectors, her own mercenaries, who killed on her orders: Iona, Isis, and Iris. I took another step forward, almost not of my own will. I had no idea what was happening to me, but I didn't like it. I felt like I'd been set up, as if this was all some elaborate scheme to get The Raven once and for all. I couldn't even blame them, I was, after all, the biggest threat to the supernatural community. I went all over the world killing their kind if they put a foot wrong and got caught. I should have expected something like this. How could I be so stupid?

I took another involuntary step, and as I did so a very real-feeling lancing pain went through my body, through my heart. I tried to draw breath but my lung had a huge hole in it, and blood trickled out of my mouth. Before my eyes, a spear appeared materialising like they did in *Predator*. A hand was attached to that spear, and a woman to that hand. I looked down, and couldn't believe the weapon I was seeing had actually gone through me. And it was a killing blow.

"Thank you, Iona," the Queen said. I looked up, and the last thing I saw was a woman standing in front of a throne, a white floor length dress on, skin white as snow, and hair of the same pale hue, straight and silken hanging to her knees. I had a moment to see slightly pink lips curve in a smile, and to see the Queen's silver eyes, before the spear through my heart bested me, and I passed on to death.

24

The world around me was painted in different shades of grey, but had a sickly light to it, as if, somewhere far beneath me, there was pale green fire burning, and it cast its waxy hue on the stone.

For it was stone I was sitting on, and stone that made the ragged walls, and stone, cold and hard, that stretched out unfeelingly before me.

I shivered and tried to clutch my arms, but felt just how insubstantial I was, like air, or a whisper on the wind.

"You do not normally shiver when you pass this way." I recognised the voice, and turned to look behind me. Tartarus was leaning against a sharp jut of wall, clothed in swirling shadow. The darkness around him writhed, and faces boiled to the surface, screaming faces that made no sound.

"I have never been here before." My voice sounded echoing and hollow.

"You have Enya, many times."

"Enya?"

He sighed. "I thought you would remember by now."

"You speak in riddles."

He smiled, and it wasn't as frightening as it used to be. "You do not know where you are. Think upon my name and you will realise."

Tartarus? Think upon—oh. I remembered the spear through my heart, remembered the Queen's smile. I was in the Underworld, because I was dead.

"I see the realisation in your face. Do you recognise this place yet?" I shook my head. "You pass through here every twenty-one years, my little Enya. You have had many twenty-one years."

"I still don't understand. I am twenty-one, how can I have had many?"

"You are not twenty one."

A figure emerged out of the shadows. "Stop playing with her, Tartarus."

"As you wish, Erebus." Erebus and Tartarus were both names for the Underworld, but as Tartarus was the place itself, the rocks, the walls, Erebus was the essence that filled it. The Dark Silence.

"You were the man by the Queen's side," I said, the chilly knowledge dropping into my brain.

"I am her guard."

"But you two are the very underworld, you cannot be solid beings on earth."

"We became the Queen's Council," said Tartarus, "So we could keep having a solid form, as belief in us was waning and we were fading. We did not want to give ourselves up to our natures. Nyx did not much like the thought of being just the night forever, nor did Phoebe like to think she would just be moonlight, and a rock in space." Phoebe, Titaness of Brilliance and the Moon, Nyx, night itself, mother of the day, Tartarus and Erebus, the underworld; everything clicked into place.

"You are Chaos' children, the titans of long ago. You're older than the earth."

"Only Erebus is older than the earth, for the dark silence came before there was light and an underworld."

I finally looked properly at the tall dark man. He had black skin, truly black, blacker even than Cannibal's. His eyes were without any white, as if his pupil was his whole eye, as they were just black orbs set into that ebony face. When he moved, stars glittered underneath his skin, but his eyes remained a solid wash of darkness. I knew that face, somehow.

"I have been here before," I said a little shakily.

"Many, many times," said Tartarus with amusement in his voice.

"How many?"

"You were born in the years Before Christ, before the years were even counted in that way. If you are good with multiples of twenty one, they you can work it out." Tartarus seemed to be doing all the talking; Erebus was ominously silent, as was his namesake.

"But I'm human." Tartarus laughed then, it felt like it was cleaving my skull in two.

"Far, far from it, little Enya. Your mother and father are waiting on the other side if you would but go to them."

"But I'm dead."

"No you're not, you're immortal." With that, he took hold of my hand. The screaming souls that clothed him flowed up my arm and over my eyes so I could not see. He led me between two rocks. The substance of the underworld felt thin here, less solid, and I passed through.

Then God said let there be light. And there was.

I awoke with my head resting on someone's knees. A

cool hand was petting my hair, gently, almost lovingly. I was very startled at the face that met me when I opened my eyes. Tartarus was gazing down at me, his eyes seeming now to be pale green, like the light in the underworld, and not at all like the definite blue I remembered. There was softness to him that made me want to smile at him. So I did. He smiled back, and helped me sit up. I found that I wasn't wounded at all. I looked down at my chest to see if there was any evidence of the spear wound, but found not only that I was perfectly healed, but that my skin was a different colour. It was a rich, chocolaty brown, and had a slight sheen to it that was a gold-green. It reminded me a little of Bastien's skin, how it looked like it had a gold shimmering coating over the tan.

"What the fuck?" I said slowly, and with feeling.

Tartarus merely smiled, and when I looked at him for answers I realised that he didn't frighten me anymore. I looked away from him when I realised the enigmatic smile was all the answer I was getting from him, and found The Queen next to me, kneeling on the floor. A Queen never kneels.

"Many wondered why I chose to make this trip, Enya, and now their questions can be answered. I came here for you."

Again with the Enya thing. I was freaked out, and so I focused on that rather than think about where I'd just been. "Excuse me your majesty," I said, flattening myself to the floor, "But my name is Phoebe."

"Ah little Enya, I see your memories have not returned." She stood up in a rustle of skirts, and indicated I should follow her. There was an empty throne by the side of hers, and she bade me sit in it. "There are truths that this assemblage of supernaturals needs to know, and so they shall be revealed to you and them at the same time."

I just nodded, bewildered, and hating that I was on show in this glorified chair.

"Phoebe," she called, talking over her right shoulder. "Nyx, could you come here please?"

Two women got up from their thrones on the slightly lower platform and walked to their Queen. Nyx was nearly seven feet tall, ebony skin with patches of blue-grey, like night time clouds. She was wearing a leather catsuit that clung to her like a second skin and shone, patent, in the light. It went from ankles to neck, but there were no sleeves, and the front was just two triangles of material, the v shaped neckline stopping half way down her abdomen. She had long, straight hair, which trailed over the floor behind her as she walked. She also had clawed feet, harpy feet as I thought of them, and taloned nails. Her eyes were glassy black, blue, purple, red, with stars in them, swirling galaxies of stars. Her clawed feet clicked ominously over the marble as she approached.

Behind her, much shorter, more my height, came a women with skin the colour of moonlight, a dusting of silver freckles across her nose like the craters on the moon, marks of beauty. Her hair was a charcoal grey, getting darker towards the tips, and cut so it hung longer in the front, but was almost to her scalp at the back. Her eyes were palest blue, and ringed in black eyeliner. Phoebe was wearing a dress that fastened round the neck, with a sweetheart neckline cut out so the pale skin of her collarbones was visible. It had a full skirt made of gossamer or something equally thin and soft, layered in strips like the petals of some ethereal night-blooming flower.

Both women were stunning, and formidable.

"These, Enya, are the women who have been your namesake in the past twenty one years. At your last death, you shot yourself in the head, obliterating your memories, in order to save the man you loved."

"The man I loved?"

"Yes, Enya, your husband."

I was definitely in shock. Profound shock. I stayed mute and waited for her to continue. When I realised she wasn't going to, I asked the question she had obviously been waiting for me to ask. "Who was my husband?"

"Mort, of the Council. You and he were married for two hundred years, give or take." I felt, more than saw, the Queen smile. What was less subtle was the gasping of the assembled clans, houses, kingdoms, and queendoms.

"She cannot marry him again now she remembers." The woman who spoke was the fey who had helped me up. Her fiery hair seemed to move about her head of its own accord.

"But I don't remember."

The Queen sighed. This was all too much for me to take in. I hardly believed it. I shook my head, and got another shock. My hair was the colour of garnets or dark rubies, a deep red not found anywhere but a hair salon. I froze as the silken waves of my hair fell back into place. I lifted an arm to gaze again at the change in colour of my skin, and if I hadn't seen my scars there, my tattoos, I would not have believed it was me.

"Princess Vita, heir to the Unseelie Throne, do you have your brother with you?"

"Aye, Dark Queen, Ainmire is present."

"Would he be able to give little Enya back her memories?"

A beautiful man stood up. His hair was in a plait down to his ankles, and was of the same blood red as the fey woman's. His skin was the same colour as mine, and his eyes were lime green, though I couldn't be sure of the exact colour from here. "Aye, I can unlock the door that the bullet closed."

"Then please, do so."

He gave a half bow, and I realised that if he was the brother of Princess Vita, then he must be a sidhe prince. He

269

walked gracefully, like he was gliding. The smell of grass in the rain wafted towards me as he approached. He smiled, and I was lost, for a moment, in the beauty of it all. He placed his hands on each of my temples, and bade me close my eyes. I did not want to, for to do so was to lose the sight of this beautiful man. After much persisting, I shut my eyes.

Then I felt it. Magic. It prickled along my skin and danced through the very air I breathed. I swallowed it down into my lungs, and it felt so good. It felt like home. I whimpered, once, at the thought that I should ever be without this touch of magic, but the hands on my temples shooed that thought away, for they felt like sunshine was streaming out of those fingertips and into my brain.

I saw thousands of years pass in moments. I saw Lucille and Guillaume for the first time all over again, for I had not met them this past life, but many, many years before that, in seventeenth century France. The more I remembered, the more I felt the weight of the years on me, seeping into my bones. I was old. I was very old. I was older, perhaps, than Bastien. No, not perhaps. My memories stretched the chasms of a millennia, and another, right back to when Rome ruled the world. I saw memories for the first time in this life, but they were memories I had had for thousands of years. The Roman camp where I had met Mort and Kyvernaw for the first time. The day Iratus Nex had beaten me to death. The first three hundred years of my life spent inside faerie walls. The rest of my life spent mostly on the run, never staying anywhere too long. The day I met Lucille and Guillaume, not sixteen years ago, but in the 1600s. The day I shot myself in the head, twenty-one years ago.

With every memory I regained, I felt a little bit of myself return. When it was finally over, and I opened my eyes, I saw that beautiful sidhe prince smiling at me, and I cried.

25

"Do you now remember?" the Queen asked softly. I nodded for I did not trust my voice. I held onto the sidhe prince's hand, because I wanted the comfort of the touch of something alive. He sat on the floor beside the throne I had been given, silently, still smiling, not complaining that the floor was not a fit place for a prince.

"Enya?" the Queen said. I turned to her, for I now knew that was my name. I had been named after my Aunt, as was tradition. The first born was always named after the first born of the generation before. I also knew that my Aunt spelt her name the Gaelic way, Aithna. The final thing I knew, was that my Aunt Aithna was the woman who had helped me stand, the woman with the blood red hair.

I looked over to her, and found her crying too. In fact, as I looked around, tears spilled over the cheeks of many people. Mort was crying, great wracking sobs that spoke of terrible loss. I did not cry any more. I felt secure, and solid, and real, as if the past twenty-one years as Phoebe Nix, I had been a ghost. A shadow. My anchor to the world was the hand in mine. Prince Ainmire, my uncle.

When I looked back at Mort, my heart broke. I had a sudden flash of nightmarish vision and knew why I could not marry Mort again, just as Aithna had said. The Host had been sent after him, as we were not fated to be married. The Sluagh, a Court of faerie, the seventh point on the star, the Wild Hunt. We had run from them for two centuries, but if the Wild Hunt pursue you, all you can do, in the end, is be caught. I remembered the gun, old compared to current weaponry, that I had shot myself through the head with. If the Sluagh had no couple to hunt, then they would stop hunting Mort too. Mort, whom I loved.

Everything was simultaneously overwhelming, and not at all. Phoebe Nix was overwhelmed, Enya was not. Twenty-one years in a lifetime of thousands was a very short time. I didn't feel like Phoebe Nix anymore. I was not the girl who had wanted vengeance on a vampire king, who had been consumed by it. I was a daughter of the fey, a daughter of… who?

"Dark Queen, I know now who I am, but not who I am from. All that is clear to me in my mind is that Ainmire is my uncle, and Aithna my aunt. I know not my mother or father, not even in my long, long memory."

"Little Enya, your mother and father have been kept from you forever. You have a fate, daughter of the fey, that your goddess wishes you carry out. It was not your fate to know, just as your heart was not to be swayed by Nero as it was by Mort. It would mean the death of a king by Sluagh. That was why I bid he torture Guillaume Delacroix, so he would fall out of your favour."

Too much information. I ignored the bit about Guillaume, because, selfishly, I wanted to know who my parents were.

"You said it *was* not my fate to know who I am descended from. Does that mean that I am to know now?"

"It does," she said with a smile. "Your parents are both in this room. As you must have guessed, your mother is one of the five other daughters of Queen Rhoswen of the Unseelie Court. Your mother knows she bore you, but your father knows not."

"Then who are they?" I was looking over at the table of faerie princesses, waiting for my mother to rise to her feet.

She did.

She had knee-length green hair, the colour of grass in sunlight, with streaks of darker green running through it like ivy hiding in the shadows. Her hair seemed to shimmer with green and slightly blue glitter as she rose. Her skin was the same colour as mine, and upon it were marks of the fey. On her forearms were swirling lines, purple and blue, like someone had dipped a wide, round brush in colourful ink and painted her. Her face bore four thin black lines on each side from cheekbone to jaw in the same swirling style. Her neck had two on each side, in purple again. She was wearing a strapless, pale lime green dress that clung to her breasts and ribcage. It was floor-length, but had slits in it so high on both sides that it was mostly just a strip of material down the middle, baring both of her legs. On her right leg, on her upper thigh, she had matching black swirls that went from inner thigh to outer, fanning out like rays of the sun. She had matching purple swirls climbing up her left leg from her ankle to her knee. Marks of the fey, all of them.

Her eyes were the last thing I looked at, but they captivated me. They were deep crimson, but it was if my eyes could see better than before, as I discerned a similar pattern to them as Aunt Aithna's eyes, but done in four different shades of red. The fact that I could see that clearly from this distance meant my eyesight had improved significantly.

What was most shocking, though, was that my mother wore a circlet of woven gold, with a garnet set in the centre, marking her as heir. My mother, Princess Vita of the Unseelie Court. Last time I had been at the Unseelie Court, in something BC, she had been far away from the line of succession, which is why no-one had minded my Aunt Aithna taking in a stray like me.

I stood, and pulled my uncle with me, not wanting to let go of him. I needed the comfort of the touch of someone I knew and loved. My memories showed me it was Aunt Aithna and Uncle Ainmire who had helped raise me. They told me they were my relations, but, no matter how much I begged, could not tell me who my parents were. I loved them, I had always loved them, but now... now I had a mother. She was beautiful and powerful and wonderful and I loved her, though I didn't know her.

She spoke. "Enya is my daughter, conceived millennia ago. Now I am heir to the throne, I have protection that I did not all those years ago." There were tears shimmering in her eyes. "As The Sluagh hunted you and your husband, my little Enya, so they would have hunted your father. I did not tell my mother of you for fear the Wild Hunt would be sent after him for getting me with child, because your father is not fey. He is a force of nature, but not of faerie. I did not know who would win the fight, he or the Sluagh."

Queen Rhoswen finally seemed to realise what was happening. She looked at her daughter with an interest that hadn't been there moments before. "Who is the father, child of mine?"

The Princesses looked startled, as if their mother hadn't made sense for a very long time.

"She was conceived of me by the Dark Silence. Erebus is your father, my Enya."

She hung her head, as if in shame. The fey that were

around, including the drows, though they were a court unto themselves, and not ruled over by the sidhe, be they seelie or unseelie, went mad. They accused the tall man by the Dark Queen of raping my mother, of coercing her, for no fey would stoop to take the darkness and silence of the void before life into them.

Princess Vita yelled, "Enough! I went willingly to Erebus. My mother has so many daughters because she was blessed by a fertility goddess. The Dark Silence was not supposed to be able to get me with child, as emptiness has no ability to create, but Goddess gave me a child, and that cannot be undone."

I turned, slowly, like I was in a horror movie turning to look at the monster, and faced Erebus. The man I had seen in the Underworld stepped forward to look around the paleness of The Queen to look at me. If I had expected emotion to be plain on his face, I would have been disappointed, but the Dark Silence is empty.

Staring into those glassy black eyes, I knew he felt nothing at this revelation. And yet... I looked more closely and saw fire in those eyes. It was black flame, almost impossible to discern against the black of his eyes. The stars did not glitter under his skin here; it was just black. He blinked, and the fire in his eyes was gone.

This time it was the vampires who went crazy. They felt they had claim to me, claim to something from the fey.

The Dark Queen rose, slowly, from her throne, a column of pale flesh, pale hair, pale clothing. "This child has been raised by both the fey and the vampires. But she is not vampire. She is high court sidhe, and must return to the Unseelie Court, her home. No vampire has any right to ask anything of the sidhe now it has been revealed the Raven is descended from Chaos."

And then, for the first time in the mortal realm, I heard

my father speak. It was a low rumble like the sound of dusk falling if ever you could hear it. "I knew not I had a daughter, but from both myself, and her mother's side she is a child of Chaos. The place I have chosen is by the side of the Vampire Queen, but I would wish it that she return to her mother's home, with her family. But know this, all who are gathered here: any harm to my daughter is a personal challenge against me."

The silence in the wake of that was profound, and left the air thick with fear. At some point in their lives, everyone is afraid of the dark, and here he was.

I looked away from my father, and over to my mother, where one of my aunts was holding her hand. She had long magenta hair, a similar dress to my mother's, and lime green eyes. Where my mother had swirling marks of the fey, she seemed to be dusted with green glitter. She wore a thinner gold circlet on her head. Second in line to the throne.

"Daughter of mine, please come to me," Princess Vita asked. I walked down the steps. Walking felt different. I felt like Ainmire had looked, graceful and flowing. My uncle held my hand firmly, and when we reached the Unseelie royal's table, he put my hand in my mother's. I touched her for the first time, and something in me felt, finally, whole. I fell against her, burying my head in her neck. She was six foot at least. She pressed her hand to my hair, and we embraced. Thousands of years of life and I had been motherless. Now, I was home.

26

It didn't seem real. Lifetimes upon lifetimes of memories and experiences had just been returned to me, that my brief life as Phoebe Nix, a name made up by The Queen from two of her Council, was a ghost. A blip.

I didn't see Marianna, or Conor, or Lyev. I didn't see Carlos. I didn't see Cannibal. I just rode home on my bike as fast as it would take me. I could feel the earth humming underneath my wheels, the magic I knew to be lying there sending me little waves of joy that I returned to myself. The night smelled different, richer, as if sentient. My garnet-and-rubies hair billowed out behind me, with the wind rushing through it in celebration. I could feel in my veins the power to answer the call of the earth, to manipulate it, to change the winds, to reverse the flow of the rivers. I was, after all, two and a half thousand years old, a faerie can gain a lot in that time.

Not, not merely fey: high court sidhe. Of the seven Courts, the Seelie and Unseelie were considered the authorities, no matter how much we were at war with each other. The elves, drows, goblins, and demi-fey all had their allegiance with one or the other. The Sluagh… they were a different thing entirely. I tried not to remember that night so long ago, but I had to. It had been given back to me, and if I was to truly be me again, I had to take the good with the bad.

The most alive thing on this earth is a faerie, and the most dead is a vampire. Opposites attract, but some things are just not meant to be. If the Fates have spun a different thread for you, then that is the path the Sluagh will uphold. I had diverged from mine. I knew with every fibre of my being that I was not meant to be with Mort. He was dead, he was narcissistic, he had a disregard for the balance of life like no other man I had ever met; yet I also knew I loved him. But for a woman fated to bring the fey back to strength, like I had always been told I was, I could not love a dead man. The nightmares of the fey hunted us, and no-one escapes the wild hunt. Black terrors, monsters of unspeakable shapes, raw magic made flesh, filled the sky until the moon and the stars were veiled by their unbending will. The gun felt cool in my hand. I did not fear dying; I did fear the Sluagh. Mort was writhing on the floor, tearing at his beautiful face in madness, mind broken from seeing such a thing. I allowed myself tears, but I would not give them my terror, no matter how badly I wanted to join Mort in his madness. I had seen the Dark Host on a hunt before, I could see this and not go mad. I could see this and not go mad. Maybe if I said it enough times it would be true. I pressed the gun to my head and I prayed. I prayed to the Mother Goddess, the fountainhead of the fey, mother earth, nature, the sun, sea, and sky, I prayed that she would let me forget, that Mort would forget, so he did not have to suffer the memory of our parting.

And who says wishes are never granted.

By the time I'd finished picking over that particularly

sore wound, I had arrived back at the flat. I couldn't think of it as home anymore, because the touch of my mother's hand to my face was home, not this place. It was Enya now. Phoebe Nix was dead.

Lucille was up, still in the dress she'd been wearing that evening. There was blood all over her face from her tears.

"Did you know?" I asked softly. Her face crumpled, but she remained silent, and just nodded. "And Guillaume?" She nodded again.

"We were the only ones allowed to know, bar The Queen, what had happened. Everyone else had their memories taken, and kept for them by someone else. You were wiped from the face of the earth. Of course, we did not have the memories of… your mother, Ainmire, or Aithna taken. You always had myself and Guillaume watching you, and you always had someone from the Unseelie Court watching over you too. Don't think your family did not care for you Enya."

My name sounded bizarre coming from her mouth, but she had known me longer as Enya than as Phoebe.

"I know the memories of my long past are true, but I also know I have the memories of a child from the past lifetime, which is not possible, so whose memories are in my head, whose memories have given me my recent childhood?"

"They are your own."

"Impossible, Lucille."

"I assure you they are. It is something to do with your glamour. Did you know your Phoebe appearance was of your own devising? Your glamour and your defence mechanisms were so strong, you projected into everyone's minds the body of a child, then a teenager, then an adult. When you finally reached twenty-one, your familiar face was staring back at me, just coloured in differently. Your glamour was so good, you even tricked your damaged mind into believing it. You would never have been scarred by any of the injuries you sustained, but because you believed you were mostly human, you reacted like someone mostly human."

"I don't understand, no fey can trick *themselves* with glamour."

"Maybe it was your aunt," she said softly, like she was waiting for a penny to drop.

"My Aunt?"

"Your father is Erebus, lord of the Underworld, The Dark Silence before the earth. Who else was born from chaos? Who do you think his sisters are?"

"The Night, The Moon… The Earth." I breathed the last one softly.

"If Erebus is your father, then the creator of the fey, your Goddess, is your Aunt, Enya. Maybe she made you a child, to truly be born again, and live again, as you wished deep in your heart."

"So I did grow up with Tamara, and Jade, and Nate. I was adopted by those awful people, and I did kill them."

"There is no word of a lie in your memories."

We looked at each other for a long time. Somewhere around the five minute mark, I knew this was goodbye. I had to get back to my real life, as if my Phoebe life was a sham, an immaculate lie. But there was something I had to know.

"You and Guillaume argued over me knowing The Queen had ordered his torture at Nero's hands. I never did get an explanation."

"What happened with Mort was devastating. You don't remember, because you were in between at this point, but when the Sluagh no longer had a couple to hunt, they left a deadly wake. The Hunters to do not like to be cheated of their catch. Plague fell, like something biblical, in the French town in which you had been living. The people were so ill; they rotted upon themselves but remained alive. It took necromancers to put them in the earth, to rest. Wards had been set up around the town as soon as the Sluagh made their return journey so no-one visited or traded with the town, so once all the townspeople had been put in graves there were no mortals left alive to speak of it. Mort remembered nothing of you, and only those with the strongest connections to you had any idea. What do you think would have happened if you had fallen in love with Nero, as you had with Mort, and the Sluagh had come to The Sunken City? They have not lost any of their powers of old, and age only increases their strength. It would have been a cataclysmic disaster."

"All that just for wanting to be with a man my parents disapproved of, so to speak?"

"That is Phoebe talking. Enya understands that Fate and the Goddess are the ultimate authority. If Fate had wound you a thread, you walk along the line that thread follows. You are so instrumental to the power of the fey world, its monsters were the price for diverging from the path."

"So, I'm fucked then."

We kept on talking through the night and even the next day. Lucille was as surprised as I was that she did not need to go to her coffin, but I thanked the Mother Goddess for that. It felt like she was giving us the time we needed for me to get my answers. Lucille explained that the many attempts on my life recently were due to the fact that, since leaving the Unseelie Court for the first time when I was roughly three hundred years old, I was fated to die every twenty-one years. As I believed I was mortal, I had resisted death when he came knocking, rather than accepting it like I had done. She told me it was suspected that, because I was fey, twenty-one years was the longest I could go without being on faerie land, but as I was truly immortal, every time I died, I came back. The Queen had had to resort to getting her assassin, Iona, to kill me. Her sisters Iris and Isis had killed me before in the past too, to save me from a more horrible death. Just because I came back, didn't mean it didn't hurt.

"You now have to go home Enya. Go back to your family, and be the woman you were born to be, not the one you've been masquerading as. You belong in the Unseelie Court."

"I do." I paused, stared at my newly dark-skinned hands, then looked back up at Lucille. "I will miss you," I said softly.

"I hear a but." She smiled, and it was not sad, which warmed my heart. "But you will be home Enya. You have wanted that your whole life."

I nodded. "Yes, I have. But I will miss you all the same."

Guillaume came over that night. He cried when he saw me with ruby hair again; he had not been at the banquet. He hugged me as if he knew this was goodbye forever.

I didn't cry, because I knew he was young still, so much younger than me, and he could not possibly know the world as I did. Not all goodbyes are forever.

I hadn't slept since the banquet, but I no longer felt the need. It was as if, now I wasn't expending so much energy on intricate glamour, I had a lot more of it to keep me going.

There was one goodbye I did not want to make, but had to. No matter how brief the absence was, I wasn't going to be going to work for a while. I pulled my old Phoebe glamour back around me like a comfortable cloak, and knew I would look exactly as the Sharks expected me to. It would freak them out less if I turned up looking normal to them.

The Concrete Palace's firing range was empty, which was unusual. When I opened the outer door to Hammer's office, I found almost all of the mercenaries in there. For obvious reasons, Leech, Vlad and Roo were not there. Coal was also missing.

Everyone turned to look at me as I came in, as if they expected me to be dead or something.

Cannibal looked up, and paled.

"He won't tell us what happened at The Queen's banquet. He says you can be the only bearer of that news." Hammer's voice was almost a growl.

"Thank you Cannibal for your discretion. What have you told them?" I asked calmly.

"Nothing. Nothing at all."

"Raven," Hammer said, "Can you please tell me what the hell is going on."

"Let's get the hard bit over with. I'm leaving—" Hammer looked like he was about to yell, so I put my hands up to stop him, "but hopefully only for a while."

"Why Raven? What have you got to do that's so important?"

I sighed. Young and fiery. Wait, wasn't I like that? I just didn't know anymore.

"I have a confession. You all know me as The Raven. Only two of you know my name as Phoebe Nix." There were a few gasps, as I had just broken a serious merc taboo. "That is not my name, Hammer. My name is Enya. I was named after the first born daughter in my mother's family, my aunt Aithna."

"But… Phoebe," Hammer said, "you don't know who your parents are."

"It turns out, the banquet was a way of getting the supernatural community together to witness… oh I don't know what the hell to call it. They were gathered to see me be given back my memories, my old face, my life. These past twenty-one years have been a blip, Hammer."

"What are you saying?" he asked through gritted teeth.

"I'm saying that I know who my parents are. My mother is Princess Vita of the Unseelie Court, and my father is Erebus, the Dark Silence."

"You have got to be kidding me," Shammy said. He looked pale beneath his freckles.

I had to tell them everything, even if it was information overload; I owed them that much. "I am fey, Hammer, and truly immortal. I was born in 478BC in the Unseelie sithen. I was raised for three hundred years by my Aunt Aithna and my Uncle Ainmire. I left the Unseelie Court and lived the rest of my life wherever I could. The real mind-fuck is why I was Phoebe Nix for the last twenty-one years. It's a borrowed name, Hammer, given to me by The Queen, made up from the names of two of her Council. I shot myself in the head and prayed for memory loss to avoid a horrible fate, and wound up with exactly that – total amnesia."

"What?" Jade said, trying not to screech. I smiled sadly at her, and continued.

"I grew up with you, that wasn't a lie. Apparently I produced this glamour to protect myself, subconsciously. I even aged accordingly, but I was not born twenty-one years ago."

"I've known you all my life," she said, "And here I find out you've known me for a blink of an eye."

"The years I have known you mean no less to me now that I remember what came before."

She hung her head, and would not look at me.

"I don't believe you," Ace said flatly. He was leaning against the wall, and looked a little ill in the harsh light.

"Why?"

"You told me about the fey after my little run in with that Seelie bitch. You told me royal Unseelie sidhe generally have a colour palette of brown, green, red and gold. You look too human to he royal."

"The glamour didn't just age me. I don't look like this at all, not really."

Hammer ground his teeth. "Let me see what you really are, Raven."

I could understand his anger, but I did not feel the need to respond to it. Phoebe Nix would have been at his throat. I was older and wiser.

I dropped the glamour slowly, so as to not freak any of them out. I started with the hair, and could feel the golden brown drop away to show the ruby glittering tresses underneath. Next, I dropped the glamour on my skin, feeling it darken, feeling the sheen run across it as if it were fresh magic. Lastly, I dropped the glamour on my eyes. I hadn't seen my eyes the first night I had been returned to my true form. When I had looked in the mirror, I had been startled.

My irises had five bands in them. The outermost circle was magenta, like my mother's. Next was a band of gold, which left lightning streak lines in the magenta. The middle ring was deep grass green, lighting streaked too from the next band of gold. The final band around the pupil was lime green. My mother, when I had got up close, had eyes like Green's. They had those translucent triangular eyelashes. Hers were lime green, and so were mine. On the bottom, she had two eyelashes, but unlike Green they were not triangular. They were shaped like a rounded spear tip, the straight shaft, then the softly curved bottom corners, reaching towards that final point. My mother's were dark blue, but mine were dark purple. Also like my mother, I had a mark of the fey around my eye. It looked to all the world like a band of eyeliner, but was in fact part of my skin, like a tattoo, which I'd had from birth. It was such a dark purple it was black, but when it caught the light right, it was purple. It tapered to a point near my temple on both eyes.

Someone wept, another moaned, a few reached out to touch me, as if I could not possibly be real.

I think Hammer spoke for everyone when he said, "Holy fucking hell."

I smiled. I was different, but the world had not changed.

"You really are high court Unseelie then, Raven?" said Ace, bewildered.

I nodded. "Yes, Ace. I am. And I am also leaving," I said, returning to my original point. "I finally have a family and a home. I'm moving to the Unseelie Court; I came to say goodbye."

Jade got up then, and hugged me tight. "You're going to have to come and tell Tammy." She unwrapped her arms from my shoulders, and took my hand in hers. When she did, she fell to her knees. "Jesus Phoebe. You feel like an electric shock made of sunshine."

"Nice way to put it." She grinned and got to her feet, wiping tears away.

"At least at your height you didn't have far to fall," I said smiling.

"Glad to know your still in there." She grinned at me, and the rest of the mercs smiled. To them I would always be The Raven. I think, even to me, I would still be that woman, just a faerie version.

"We'll miss you, babe," said Ace.

"But at least you won't take all our work now," The Scarlet Belle smiled, but looking around the room there was a sheen of tears to everyone's eyes. I was touched that they would waste tears on me, even if they didn't fall down their cheeks.

Hammer strode over and gave me the biggest hug of my life. If I hadn't been immortal, I might have worried about dying, because I most certainly couldn't breathe properly. It was the only time Hammer had ever hugged me. I bade everyone goodbye, and though a small part of me was sad that I wouldn't see them for a long time, I knew I would see them eventually.

I was almost to the outer door when Cannibal caught up with me. He grabbed my arm, but when I turned around he immediately dropped to one knee. I may have been looked after by one of the now royal Unseelie as a child, but never before had I been a princess, and I wasn't used to people bowing to me.

"Please, Cannibal, don't." He got up.

"It's Brom." He smiled at me with watery eyes.

"Brom, meaning raven." I couldn't help it, I laughed. All these years I'd been stealing his name. "Well, Brom, it's been an honour to work with you. You of all people I will miss when I leave here."

"Do you mean it, Enya? Do you?"

I nodded. There was an intensity to him that I didn't quite comprehend.

He smiled, then leant in so quickly I almost didn't see him move, and gave me a fierce, crushing kiss. He bruised his lips against mine, cradling the back of my head with his powerful hands. He drew back, the fierceness still in his eyes.

"I think I have loved you since we first met. Now I know why."

"Love me? Cannibal, you cannot possibly love me."

"I can and I do, and it breaks my heart that you are going where I cannot follow."

"The sidhe are not such great things that we can inspire love in the heart of a drow, Cannibal," I said, avoiding this uniquely painful subject.

"I was exiled from my court long ago, Raven. I fear I will never see you again."

"You may not, time will tell, but I am certain you will find someone to love." I stroked the side of his face, really took in the beauty of his full lips, his square jaw, his straight nose, his big eyes. I let him see in my eyes that I found him beautiful. My hand lay against the curve of his cheekbone, and I mourned, mourned that he had loved me and said nothing, mourned that I did not love him back. I wanted to chase away that look of loss in his eyes, so I kissed him, softly. When I drew back, he was smiling. It was worth it to see that smile on his face.

"I have to go now, Brom."

"I know, but you should know something. Coal's in hospital."

That warm, fuzzy feeling? Gone.

27

I hate hospitals, all the waiting around, all the rushing about. Nothing ever seems to go at a normal pace: it's either too fast, or too slow.

Today was a too slow day. I had been sitting in the seated area of the cancer ward for and hour and a half, waiting to be let in to see Coal. Or should I say Sophia. It seemed wrong keeping her anonymity on her deathbed, because that is what I was finally led through to see. The selfish part of me wished I'd been kept there in the lounge until visiting hours were over. Hanging around in a depressing environment I could deal with. Seeing my friend with that many tubes coming out of her, I might not be able to get over.

Coal was by no means tall, 5' 4", and she'd always been slim, but this... she was shrunken. Her eye sockets were deep and black, like bruised caves. Her cheeks were hollow and sunken, her arms sticks. The sheet over her legs somehow made her skeletal thinness worse, not better, almost as if it was so horrible, it had to be covered up.

She was on so much morphine, she didn't know who I

was, and quickly fell asleep. I stared down at my friend and felt like I could see her dying. I let the tears flow down my cheeks in silent waves.

I sat by her bed for an hour. Eventually, she woke up. It had been longer since her last dose of morphine, so she was much more herself. "Raven?" she whispered uncertainly.

"I'm here." She smiled and took hold of my hand.

"You feel so warm."

"Benefit of a good circulation." She gave another weak smile, and shut her eyes. We just sat there, her hand in mine, in companionable silence. Eventually she spoke again.

"Make sure my kids go to a good home. Don't let their father have them." I tried not to cry. That she would ask me to take care of her children was the highest compliment she could have paid me, because it meant I had her absolute trust.

"I will Sophia. I promise."

Her face split into a slow grin. "I've only ever heard you use my real name once, Rave."

"It's Enya, my name is Enya."

"Enya?"

"I'm fey."

She tried to laugh, but coughed, which hurt. "Holy shit, you kept that one under wraps. No wonder you never die."

I laughed. "Yeah, I'm really lucky."

She paused. "I love you, you know. You're wonderful."

"I love you too darling."

The next few days were spent saying my goodbyes. I didn't know how long I would be at the Unseelie Court before I returned, so I said my goodbyes as if they were forever, just in case. Bastien paid me handsomely for the two jobs I did. I left the money for the Hammerhead Sharks, saying they could divide it up between them. In the envelope with the money, I left three black feathers.

I went to the British Court and said goodbye to Nero. He did not try to kiss me, for which I was grateful. It was more painful to say goodbye to his Hand than it was to say goodbye to him. Harsh, but true. Carlos would not touch me, for to feel sidhe flesh again was too painful for him. It saddened me, but I let him have his way, as much as I wanted to hug him to me, properly, just once. Jean-Pierre and Asher both bestowed light kisses on my lips before I left, and both reacted much as Jade had when she held my hand, but less violently and with no falling to the floor.

The most painful part of leaving the British Court was Mort.

I had loved him. Loved him so deeply I had been married to him for over two centuries. A love like that didn't just fade, but it was locked away in a part of my heart I knew I could never crawl into again. I saw before me, as if it were happening right now, the roiling black clouds above, the high-pitched screams, that were the Sluagh's winged creatures. I could hear the shuffling and scuttling and slithering and sliding of the Sluagh's earthbound beasties. I could feel again the unmentionable terror. There are only two ways for a true immortal to die; you choose to fade, or you are killed by the Sluagh. I felt in my hand the weight of the gun.

We both cried when I said goodbye. I kissed him over and over, hoping to never have to leave, never have to end the kiss, but of course I did. A few days ago, the part of me that was Phoebe Nix had hated him, and now I loved him so deeply that to part was painful; Shakespeare was wrong about sweet sorrow, it just hurt. I could never see him again if I wanted him to live, and I did. So I left the British Court, left my husband, and returned to the flat.

Lucille brought more tears to my eyes. She and Guillaume had made me tea as if it were any other night. We had a casual chat around my small kitchen table. Eventually, I had to tell them that I was leaving the flat to Lucille. I was leaving the car to Guillaume, but I was taking all my bikes.

Everything was packed up. Aunt Aithna came to the flat to help me with my things. She brought with her Aevum, the one who looked like my mother, but with the green and the red swapped over, with the dusting of green glitter to her skin, who was second in line to the throne. She insisted I call her Auntie Aevum. My things were transported by truck, and dumped at a lakeside, where my other aunts and my uncle were waiting for me. My mother embraced me again, and looked perplexed at the motorbikes, which made me laugh.

"You will not need those in the Unseelie sithen, daughter mine." She was frowning, which made me laugh more.

"I think it would startle a few of the sidhe to see me roaring down a hallway on a motorbike, it might be worth it to see the look on their faces."

"You are too much like Caoimhe," my mother said, but smiling. Caoimhe was yet another aunt, wearing a tutu and point shoes, with lilac hair that fell in loose curls to her hips. She was standing next to my blind aunt, Raelin, who had the same sugared lilac hair, but straight and falling almost her knees. The youngest of my mother's sisters was Edana, with curly dark purple hair and gold eyes. I looked around at my newfound family, and tried not to cry. Then, with very little warning, Caoimhe said "Here we go," and there we went. I felt we were at a Thin Place, an in between spot where reality was thinner. The fey used Thin Places to travel great distances. I felt us move through space and then we landed outside a hollow hill, the Unseelie sithen.

The ground shook beneath us, and a tree sprung up where I had been standing, its branches waving as if in an invisible wind. My mother smiled.

"The land welcomes you home, Enya. Home at last."

L. G. Hale is a young author from the east of England, who started writing at the age of eleven. She has an A Level in English Literature, and would have studied it at university had she not gone on to study Animation at the Arts University College Bournemouth, where she is currently living.

Lightning Source UK Ltd.
Milton Keynes UK
UKOW051434120312

188825UK00001B/16/P